THE
OF TH S

★ "Stork offers yet another story with complex characters, rich and powerful themes, and a vivid setting. . . . Stork's latest marks him as one of the most promising young adult authors of the new decade; it features unforgettable characters confronting the big philosophical questions in life that will resonate with readers long after book's end."

The Horn Book Magazine, starred review

★ "Characters that are just as fully formed and memorable as in Stork's *Marcelo in the Real World* embody this openhearted, sapient novel about finding authentic faith and choosing higher love."

— *Publishers Weekly*, starred review

★ "This novel, in the way of the best literary fiction, is an invitation to careful reading that rewards serious analysis and discussion. Thoughtful readers will be delighted by both the challenge and Stork's respect for their abilities."

— *Booklist*, starred review

"Stork's greatest gift, however, is for capturing Pancho's inner conflicts and the psyche of an adolescent suffering an anguish he feels he cannot reveal to anyone, even the people he is coming to love."

— *The New York Times Book Review*

"The strong characters center the novel and guide this ultimately engaging and affecting read. Readers will relish the powerful friendship between the two teens and perhaps will even find lessons for their own lives in the rules of the Death Warrior."

— *The Bulletin of the Center for Children's Books*

"It will be a hard-hearted reader indeed who fails to root for the tentative unfurling of this unusual friendship or closes the book without a renewed appreciation for life's ephemeral beauty."

— *Kirkus Reviews*

Also by Francisco Stork

Marcelo in the Real World

Irises

THE LAST SUMMER OF THE DEATH WARRIORS

Francisco X. Stork

SCHOLASTIC INC.
New York Toronto London Auckland
Sydney Mexico City New Delhi Hong Kong

ISBN 978-0-545-15134-4

Arthur A. Levine Books hardcover edition designed by Christopher Stengel, published by Arthur A. Levine Books, an imprint of Scholastic Inc., March 2010.

12 11 10 9 8 7 6 5 4 3 2 1   12 13 14 15 16 17/0

Printed in the U.S.A.   40
First Scholastic paperback printing, January 2012

For Charlie Stork, my father

CHAPTER 1

The ride to St. Anthony's took longer than he expected. He always figured you could get from one place to any other place in Las Cruces in twenty minutes or less. Maybe it was a short drive that seemed long because Mrs. Olivares would not stop talking. Mostly she told him how lucky he was to be going to St. Anthony's rather than a juvenile detention center.

St. Anthony's was an orphanage. It was not a place for kids with problems. Mrs. Olivares had worked very hard and called in a lot of favors to get him admitted. She pointed out the high school he would attend in the fall. It was within walking distance of St. Anthony's. He had been given a choice between going to summer school and entering as a senior or redoing his junior year. He chose to redo his junior year. He had other plans for the summer.

There was a white sign on the front lawn with the words ST. ANTHONY'S HOME painted in black letters. Behind it stood a one-story brick building in the shape of a lopsided cross. Next to the building was a basketball court. Kids dressed in gray shorts and blue T-shirts were playing a full-court game. They stopped and turned to look at Mrs. Olivares's car as it drove by. The kids on the basketball court were his age or older, but he could see younger kids on the grass fields. He noticed that there was no fence of any kind around the property.

Mrs. Olivares parked the car in front of the main entrance and popped open the trunk. "Well, here we are," she said. She seemed like she wanted to say one more thing. Pancho stared straight ahead and waited for her to speak.

"I can't tell you how important it is for you to get along with everyone here. I understand you're still hurting, but why make matters worse for yourself?"

He rolled down the window. It was June and it was hot. If she was going to give him another lecture, the least she could do was keep the air conditioner on.

"You need to get over the anger. The police determined that there was no foul play in Rosa's death. It was no one's fault. Not yours, not anyone's. She just died. It happens."

"What did she die of?" He dared her to answer.

"Not that again. How many times have we gone over that? The coroner's report lists the cause of death as undetermined. That just means they don't know the exact reason. It happens sometimes. People die and no one knows why. Even apparently healthy young people like your sister."

"Why was she in a motel room? Who was she with?"

"She was twenty years old. It was not illegal for her to be in a motel room with someone."

"How can they say it was no one's fault if they don't even look for the guy she was with?"

"You talked to the detective. What did he tell you?"

Pancho remembered the detective. He remembered how shocked he was when the detective told him his sister had sex with someone before she died and there was no evidence of rape. He tried his best to explain that Rosa had the mind of a child. She wouldn't go in a motel room with someone unless she was deceived or taken advantage of somehow. "You can't just give up on this," he told the detective.

But the detective wasn't interested. He took notes and grinned as if he had heard it all before. "There's no evidence that a crime was committed, so it's a waste of time to look for him. What are we going to charge the guy with? Not calling 9-1-1?"

Pancho looked out the window. Mrs. Olivares continued, "I know it's frustrating not to have someone to blame. I know you feel helpless. But you can't take your frustrations out on people. I know you're a good boy inside. I know it. I told Father Concha that you were. Are you listening to me?"

"Yeah," he said. But he said it in a way meant to make her stop talking.

"Look." She sounded annoyed. "As of last week, the State of New Mexico, that would be me, is your legal guardian and you are my charge." What a strange word that was, "charge." He was Mrs. Olivares's charge. "There are worse places than this. What you did at Mrs. Duggan's could have landed you in prison. I'm taking a chance here. There's a lot of people back in the office who think I'm making a mistake bringing you here. Am I making a mistake?"

Yeah, you're making a mistake, he thought.

"Pancho, I'm talking to you."

3

He turned toward her and saw beads of sweat on her dark brown forehead. Mrs. Olivares was a heavy woman and for a moment she reminded him of his sister. He blinked to make the memory disappear.

"I'll be all right," he said. Then he asked, "What's going to happen to the trailer and the truck?"

She rolled down her window. "The State's going to auction the mobile home and all the other things. The money will be used to cover the cost of your sister's funeral. Any money left over will be held in trust for you. I doubt the truck is worth anything. Even the trailer won't sell for much."

He shook his head.

"I'm sorry," she said. She looked as if she understood the unfairness of it all. "I wish I could just let you be until you turn eighteen next year, but I can't. My boss feels there's too much liability there. I'll come get you this weekend and take you to the trailer, and we can pick out a few things for you to save. We'll find a place to store them."

He opened the door of the car and stepped out. It was six in the afternoon and the sun was still white, the heat oppressive. He looked around the grounds and saw the trees — pecan trees, the kind his father planted behind the trailer. The grass around the trees was littered with pecans. That was a good sign. At home he enjoyed sitting under the trees, cracking nuts with his teeth. Mrs. Olivares opened the trunk and waited for him to grab the nylon suitcase with his belongings. "Come on," she said. "Father Concha is waiting for us."

Mrs. Olivares led the way to the front entrance. When she got there, she opened the glass door and waited for him. He stopped before entering. He had the sensation that someone was staring at him. He turned slowly toward the basketball court. There were several kids on the sideline, but the stare he felt on his back had not come from any of them. He shifted his gaze toward the trees. There under a pecan tree, a boy in a wheelchair had his eyes fixed on him. The boy wore khaki pants, a black sweatshirt, and a blue baseball cap. His body had a frozen, slumped look, like he had died sitting and someone forgot to bury him.

Pancho stepped into the dark hallway and let the door close behind him. When his eyes adjusted, he saw a glass case full of basketball trophies. On the other side, a cream-colored wall was lined with pictures of boys grouped in different formations. Mrs. Olivares stopped in front of a glass door and knocked. She waited, knocked again, and tried to open the door, but it was locked. She looked at her watch and pointed at one of the two plastic chairs next to the door. "Wait here. I'll check out back where the Brothers live."

He sat down on the chair, the suitcase next to him. She went down the hallway and turned left, the tapping of her heels filling the silence. He stood up and walked over to the trophy case. There on the bottom shelf was a small, dusty trophy of a boy about to throw a right hook. He knelt down and read the engraving. Luis Rivera — Golden Gloves — 1998.

Mrs. Olivares had left her briefcase by the glass door. The sound of her heels had faded away. He crossed over to the briefcase and took out a folder the color of a grocery store bag. The words "Coroner's Report" were stamped on front in purple ink. He opened it and read. He read slowly because slowly was the only way he could read. When he heard her heels in the distance, he closed the folder, placed it back in the briefcase, and sat down in the chair again.

He stood up when he heard Mrs. Olivares's voice. Then he saw her and a tall man walk toward him. The man wore black pants and a black short-sleeve shirt. He did not have the white collar Pancho had come to identify with a priest. His hair was gray and short and his skin was white except for dark circles around his eyes.

Mrs. Olivares said, "Father Concha, I want to introduce you to Pancho Sanchez." Father Concha nodded. Pancho kept his hands in his pockets.

"Pancho. Is that short for Francisco?" Father Concha's voice was deep. There was nothing friendly about it.

"No."

"Is that what you want to be called?"

For a moment, he thought about making up another name. Since he became involved with the authorities, he had stopped liking his name. It sounded childish in the mouths of policemen and judges and social workers. Now someone was offering him the opportunity to call himself something more formal, more grown up. But the only other name he could think of was Vicente, and he didn't think he should take his father's name.

"Pancho it is, then." Father Concha turned toward Mrs. Olivares and said without smiling, "I'll take it from here."

"Oh. Sure." She seemed surprised by his directness. "Well. You have everything you need? All the paperwork?"

"You sent it last week."

"That's right." She turned to Pancho and said, "Well, I guess I'll be seeing you." She stretched out her hand, but when Pancho made no move to take it, pulled it back. She began to walk away and then stopped. "Oh, I told Pancho I would pick him up Saturday and take him home to get some things."

Father Concha looked at the suitcase. "He doesn't need anything else."

"No, we won't bring them here," she said quickly. "We'll find a place to store them. Someplace else."

"I don't want anything. You can get rid of all of it," Pancho said. What was there to keep? An old TV, hammers, saws, drills, Rosa's dolls? He had his father's army medals in his suitcase. He had his mother's and father's wedding rings. He had Rosa's family album. That was enough.

"You sure?"

"Yeah."

"You don't want me to pick you up on Saturday, then?"

"No."

Mrs. Olivares looked hurt. She lowered her eyes. "I'm going to go anyway. If I see anything worth saving, I'll get it for you."

Pancho shrugged. She could do whatever she wanted. He didn't care.

CHAPTER 2

Father Concha opened the door and held it long enough for Pancho to step in with his suitcase. Then he walked to the desk and sat down. He picked up the receiver and punched the buttons on the phone. Across the room, Pancho heard a busy signal. Father Concha hung up. "Sit down," he said. It was more a command than a request.

Pancho sat on a wooden chair that looked like it came out of someone's kitchen. He prepared himself to hear a speech. When he first got to the foster home, Mrs. Duggan had sat him down and listed all the things he could not do.

Father Concha asked, "You like to fight?"

Pancho sat straight up. "What?"

"You got into a fight with another boy at the foster home. You must like to fight." Father Concha looked at the scarred knuckles on Pancho's right hand.

Pancho covered his hand. What surprised him about the question was the word "like." He remembered his fist striking

Reynolds's cheekbone, the pain of the impact traveling up his arm, the way Reynolds clutched his face. Yes, he had liked it. It felt good to hit someone. But he was not about to admit that to a priest. He looked up and saw Father Concha waiting for an answer to his question. "I was defending myself," he said.

The smallest of smiles appeared on Father Concha's face. Pancho sensed that every one of his thoughts was being read. Father Concha picked up a manila folder and flipped through the pages, deep in thought. What did those pages say? Pancho had never read his file, but he could imagine. *The mother dies when the boy is five years old. The father raises the boy and the older sister. The father dies in a freak work-related accident. Then the sister dies from undetermined natural causes three months later.* The list of losses that made up his life was so unbelievable, it was embarrassing. It was like he made the whole thing up just so people would feel sorry for him.

Pancho glared at Father Concha. He did not want pity. Pity turned his stomach. The priest put the folder down and met Pancho's eyes. There was no pity there. "You need a job for the summer," he said after a few moments. "Your father was a carpenter. Did you ever work with him?"

"Some."

Father Concha picked up the telephone and entered a number. Pancho heard a man's voice on the other end of the line. "Mr. Lawrence," Father Concha said, and swiveled his chair away from Pancho. "This is Father Concha at St. Anthony's. . . . Fine, thank you. I have a new student. I'm wondering if you'd be able to put him to work in your construction crew?" There was a pause. "I see. No, I understand. Yes, call me if you need someone."

Father Concha put the receiver down and exhaled all at the same time. Then he stood up. "Come with me," he said. "Leave the suitcase."

Pancho followed Father Concha down the hallway in the direction that Mrs. Olivares had first gone, only instead of turning left where she did, they turned right. At the end of that hallway, a side door opened, and the kids who had been playing basketball streamed inside. They were jostling each other but stopped when they saw Father Concha. Pancho sized them up as he walked by. A few were taller and a few were older, but he didn't see anyone he wouldn't be able to take down.

Father Concha stopped before the exit. He pulled out a ring of keys and opened an unpainted wooden door. He entered and waited for Pancho. The room was stacked full of cardboard boxes, rusty filing cabinets, aluminum bats, dusty baseball bases, old hoses, burlap sacks, and bed frames. Father Concha swept the room with his arm. "Starting tomorrow morning, I want you to clean up and paint this room. Someone will help you sort through the boxes. The stuff that is useless, take to the Dumpster. I'll get you some paint." He pointed to a door at the end of the room. "There's a bathroom through there. We'll get new fixtures for it."

The room had two windows. Pancho saw two kids outside on the basketball court playing one-on-one. Father Concha saw them as well. He stepped out of the room and stuck his head out the exit door. "Mass in twenty minutes," he said.

"Aww," Pancho heard one of the kids say, "just when I was about to win me five bucks." There was a moment of silence. Then he heard the same kid say, "Just kiddin', Father. He don't even have five bucks."

Father Concha walked past Pancho. "Let's get your suitcase and take it to your room," he said.

Father Concha led him to a dormitory that looked like a converted gym, where all twenty-five, now twenty-six, students slept. What he called "your room" was a space shaped like a stall. Each space contained a bed, a desk, a chair, a nightstand, a bureau, and two lamps, one on the desk and one on the nightstand beside the bed. The three walls that formed the enclosure were chest high and made out of plywood. If you were sitting at your desk or lying down in bed, you'd have privacy on three sides. Otherwise, you were out in the open.

As he and Father Concha walked down the aisle, they passed by kids changing out of their gym clothes. He was glad that Father Concha did not introduce him to anyone and glad that once he was in his stall, no one came up to him. Maybe the kids had been warned to stay away from him. Maybe they'd been told what he had done to Reynolds.

Father Concha told him he could either unpack or attend Mass at the chapel. He chose to unpack. He wasn't big on church. His father used to take him and Rosa to church on the anniversary of their mother's death. That was about the extent of it. He hoped Mass was not a daily requirement, but he would deal with it if it was. He had plenty to think about while the priest did his thing up at the altar.

The bureau had a cupboard for hanging clothes next to four drawers. Pancho put all his clothes in the drawers. He had nothing to hang. The desk drawer had a key attached to it. He sat down, opened the drawer, and put his sister's album, the wedding rings, and the medals inside. He took out the wallet with the twenty-dollar bill that Mrs. Olivares had given him and threw that in there as well. He locked the drawer and looked for a place to hide the key, but there was no place to hide anything.

"Hey!"

He looked up, thinking that someone from the next stall was speaking to him. Then he turned sideways and saw the boy in the wheelchair. He was still wearing the blue cap and black sweatshirt, even though it was hotter inside than it was outdoors. Up close, the boy seemed older than he was, but it was hard to tell by how much.

"No one ever steals anything around here," the boy in the wheelchair said.

Pancho put the key inside his pants pocket. "Yeah, sure."

"If it'll make you feel better, you can get a chain from Lupita and hang the key around your neck."

"Who?"

"Lupita. She works in the front office."

Pancho stared at the wall behind the desk. He found it hard to look at the boy directly: the dark eyes sunk in their sockets, the yellowish skin, the cracked lips, the long, thin strands of blond hair poking from underneath the cap. Looking at the boy made him feel ill. He pushed his chair back and stood up. The mattress had a dark stain where someone had once wetted it. Two white sheets, a pillowcase, and a gray blanket lay at the foot of the bed. He put the pile of bedding on the chair and then extended one sheet over the bed. He hoped his silent movements would make the boy roll back to wherever he came from.

He had to walk around the wheelchair to get to the other side of the bed. He was stuffing the pillow into the case when the boy spoke again. The voice had a raspy, exhausted quality to it, like there was a limited quantity of sound in there and it would soon run out. "The Panda asked me to help you sort out the papers in the storage room."

The flat, skinny pillow filled only half the pillowcase. He threw it on the bed and sat down next to it. *The Panda?* It took him a few seconds to see the resemblance: Father Concha's white face, the dark circles around his eyes. He almost smiled, then he caught himself. "What's wrong with you anyway?" He stared at the kid's ankles. They were the width of broomsticks.

"I'm training for the Olympics." The boy tried to laugh but began to cough instead. When the coughing fit ended, he said, "My name is Daniel Quentin, but everyone calls me D.Q. You're Pancho."

"That's my name. So is everyone here like an orphan?"

"In one way or another."

"What?"

"Technically, an orphan is someone whose parents have died. Some kids have parents who are still alive but who might as well be dead. You see?"

He saw. "I always figured orphanages were for little kids."

"If the little kids don't get adopted, they have to end up someplace."

It crossed Pancho's mind that these were the kids no one

wanted. He looked around. People were entering the dormitory in twos and threes. One of the walls held a white clock. It was too early to go to sleep, but he wished he could just lie down and close his eyes.

"You want me to show you around?" D.Q. asked.

"What's there to see?"

"Bathrooms and showers are at the other end, where that orange light is. There's a TV room, a game room, a library, computers. . . ."

"Can we go outside?" He looked at the door marked EXIT.

A strange look came over D.Q.'s face. "This isn't a jail," he said. "It's supposed to be a home. There are procedures for telling people where you are, but pretty much anyone can leave at any time."

Pancho could not imagine why anyone would not leave for good if that were the case. He felt himself being studied. "Good," he said.

"I take it you have a place you'd rather be?"

He pictured his trailer out in the desert. He remembered the screen porch his father had built, where he slept during the summer. He saw in his mind the flagpole out front and the tattered flag his father had brought back from Vietnam. "Yeah," he answered.

"This place isn't so bad. The best thing is that, if you want, people let you be. I got a feeling that's what you'd like, isn't it?"

Pancho forced himself to look steadily into D.Q.'s eyes. "Yeah, that suits me just fine," he answered.

"That's all right. We all felt the same way when we first got here. Unfortunately for you, you're stuck with me for the summer." D.Q. paused, waiting for the words to sink in. "I'm your summer job. You're going to be my aide. You'll come with me to my treatments. You'll be my companion."

"I thought I was supposed to clean up the storage room."

"That'll only take a day or two."

"This 'companion' job pay anything?"

"You get to be around me." D.Q. grinned.

"I need to make me some money," Pancho said.

"What do you need money for?"

"I just do. The kids here that have summer jobs working in construction and all — they earn any money?"

"Sure, they get paid. Minimum wage, at least."

"Well, what happens to that money?"

"One-third they give to St. Tony's to help out. The other two-thirds they get to keep for school supplies, clothes, etcetera."

"Etcetera," Pancho said, mimicking D.Q. Mrs. Olivares had told him he would have a summer job. He was counting on the money.

"Oh, relax. It won't be so bad. I'm the best thing that ever happened to you. You'll see." D.Q. made an effort to smile, but the smile turned into a grimace. "Oooo. That was a good one," he said, grabbing his stomach. "Hey, can you wheel me over to my room? Talking to you has pooped me out, literally."

"Where is it?" He did not get up from the bed.

"It's at the other end."

"That's no room. That's one of these — I don't know what you call it."

"We call them rooms. The name helps. Wheel me over

there. The other kids will show you respect if they see you pushing me."

Pancho stood up and walked behind the wheelchair. He turned it around and began to push it. "I can get my own respect," he muttered.

CHAPTER 3

Take care of your sister. Those were the words his father said as he left for work that last morning, and those were the words that circled in his head whenever he allowed silence to enter. Then there were the questions. How was it possible that he didn't know Rosa was dating someone — probably seeing him after work, getting rides home with him? He remembered the sound of a motor idling outside the trailer. How was it possible that he didn't get up to see who was driving her home? How could he not notice the sound of that engine was different from the sound of Julieta's four-cylinder Toyota?

Then he remembered Rosa coming in. "Hi, Pancho," she said loudly, beaming as she closed the door. He was lying on the sofa. "Whatcha watching?"

"Nothing much. Some show."

"Hey, guess what?"

He didn't look away from the set when he answered. "What."

"I got a ten-dollar tip today. Wanna see it?"

"Put it in the grocery jar."

"Okay."

She sat down in the upholstered brown chair and began to take off her blue sneakers. Her legs were thick and she had trouble lifting one on top of the other. "I'm getting fat," she said, rubbing her feet. He looked at her briefly. He had never heard her say anything good or bad about her appearance before. "I wish I was thin and pretty like the other waitresses. Julieta says I should use some makeup."

"Julieta's no expert on pretty," he remarked.

She giggled. "Oh, Pancho." She leaned back, slumped in the chair, yawned. "I'm sleepy," she said.

"Don't fall asleep in the chair," he told her.

"Oh, Pancho." She pushed herself slowly up. She was halfway to her room when he saw her turn around. She took the ten-dollar bill from her purse and waved it and grinned at him all at the same time. Then she pried open the lid of the can marked SUGAR and dropped the bill in there.

It felt as if he had been asleep all of ten minutes when someone poked his ribs. He willed his eyelids to open. Slowly, the gaunt face of D.Q. came into focus. *I don't need to see that first thing,* he thought.

"Wake up, Mr. Pancho. It's time to greet the new day."

"Shit." He fished around for the sheet, but there was no sheet to be found. "What time is it?"

"It's eight thirty. You got to sleep late today. Everyone is already up and about doing God's work."

This can't be happening to me, he said to himself. He shook his head the way a wet dog dries himself, and then, in one forceful movement, he sat bolt upright on the bed. He blinked three times and then tried to swing his legs off the bed, but the wheelchair was in the way. "You mind moving?" he asked.

D.Q. wheeled himself backward. "Hey, look. I got you a pair of regulation St. Tony's shorts and two T-shirts. It's going to be hot working in that room." D.Q. was holding up a pair of gray shorts. On one of the legs, a silver circle with the words "St. Anthony's" curved around a man in a robe, holding a shepherd's staff. "I also found you a toothbrush and a bar of soap. Not that I'm trying to tell you anything."

Pancho stood up and quickly slipped into the shorts. Then he grabbed one of the blue T-shirts and put that on as well.

"Come on," said D.Q., "I'll show you where the dining room is."

"I have to take a leak first," he said.

"It's on the way."

"You gonna watch me do that too?"

D.Q. was moving on ahead. "Nah, you can handle that on your own."

The dining room had five round tables with eight plastic chairs each. A skinny white vase with a fake carnation sat in the middle of each table. There was a serving counter in one wall through which you could see the kitchen. The counter held eight boxes of different cereals as well as two one-gallon jugs of milk, a tin bowl with bananas, oranges, and green apples, and a glass pitcher half filled with powdery orange juice.

Three boys sat at one of the middle tables, talking loudly. They looked up when D.Q. and Pancho entered the room but then went back to their conversation. "You never even came close to making it, you liar," Pancho heard one of them say.

"There's breakfast," D.Q. said, pointing at the cereal. "I already ate, but I'll keep you company."

Pancho grabbed a white bowl and filled it with the first box of cereal. He poured milk into the bowl, grabbed a banana and a spoon, and went to sit down at the table where D.Q. had stationed himself. He put a spoonful of the cereal in his mouth and chewed slowly, not lifting his eyes from the bowl. He wished he had a cereal box in front of him so he could fix his eyes somewhere.

"Want me to introduce you to people?" D.Q. motioned with his head to the table with the boys.

"Nope," he said.

"That's all right. There's no pressure here to be social." D.Q. was wearing a long-sleeve cowboy shirt. It was brown with white designs around the pockets and those pearl-lacquered buttons. His blue jeans looked three sizes too big for him.

"You and me gonna tag along all day?" Pancho asked. He wiped off the milk that was running down the side of his mouth.

"Not all day. I usually take a nap, sometimes two. You'll be on your own then."

After Pancho finished the cereal, he peeled the banana and ate it in two bites. He dropped the peel in the cereal bowl. "You never said what's wrong with you," he said, still chewing.

"I have diffuse pontine glioma," D.Q. said, smiling.

"What's that?"

"An illness."

"Is it in your legs, is that why you can't walk?"

"I can walk all right. There's nothing wrong with the legs." D.Q. slapped both his thighs. The sound reminded Pancho of his father's flag snapping in the wind. "It's a question of power. There's not enough power to move the legs, or if there is, I need to save it for more important things, like answering your questions." He grinned.

"And I'm supposed to push you around." Pancho slumped in his chair. He looked around to see if there was any coffee. There was no coffee. He needed caffeine in the worst way.

"I have some good news on that front," D.Q. said. "I talked to the Panda this morning, and he thinks he can scrounge up some money to pay you for helping me out."

Pancho thought it over. "How much?"

"Thirty bucks a day."

"Pssh." He could never do math in his head, but he knew right off that thirty dollars a day wasn't going to get him where he wanted to be. "Do I got a choice?"

"Sure. I told you, this isn't a jail. If a job comes up and you want it, you can take it. But you won't want to."

"Why's that?"

"You're going to like hanging out with me."

"Yeah." Pancho sat up and looked at the three boys at the next table. "Where do they work?"

"Every day, three different kids stay back to work at St. Tony's. They help Margarita in the kitchen or Brother Javier out in the yard or Lupita in the office. The rest of the time, they sweep and mop and wipe. See that?" D.Q. pointed to a white sheet of paper taped on the wall. "That's the new list that just came out this morning. That last name on the list, that's your name. You'll be up next Friday."

"I thought you said this wasn't a jail."

"Mmm."

"'Mmm' what?"

"Are you done? 'Cause we got work to do."

Pancho lifted himself up from the chair reluctantly.

"You need to put your dishes over in that tub with the dishwater. The peel goes in the garbage."

Pancho stared hard at D.Q. He took a deep breath, picked up the bowl, and plopped it in a pink tub filled with suds. He walked back and stood in front of D.Q. "What now?"

"Can you wheel me over to that storage room, the one the Panda showed you yesterday?"

Pancho got behind the wheelchair. One of the boys at the other table smiled at him. It could have been a friendly smile, or maybe the boy was making fun of his "companion" job. Pancho flipped him the middle finger, just in case.

CHAPTER 4

They sorted documents in the storage room. Pancho opened a box and took out a file. D.Q. read it and instructed Pancho to put it in the garbage or another box. There were bank statements and telephone bills and pictures of boys, all with the same crew cut. Pancho saw no rhyme or reason to what D.Q. decided to keep.

After some time sifting through documents, they started on the sports equipment. There was no thinking involved here. Everything needed to be lugged to the room next door. They organized the equipment by the different sports. In one bin, they put the aluminum bats and the baseball gloves; in another, they put the shin guards and soccer balls.

"What about these?" Pancho pointed at a box.

"What is it?"

He lifted out a pair of fourteen-ounce boxing gloves. The red leather was peeling in places. The box contained another pair of gloves, three jump ropes, and two sets of protective headgear.

"I haven't seen those in years." D.Q. stretched out his hands, and Pancho threw him the gloves. They landed in his lap. He tried to put one on, but the effort required to push his hand through the opening was too great. "Used to be when two kids got angry, they could request the gloves. One of the Brothers would referee. The kids would put on the helmets and whack each other for a couple of three-minute rounds."

Pancho slipped on one of the gloves and smacked his open hand. A puff of dust appeared in the air. "Guess no one gets angry anymore," he said. He remembered the boxing trophy at the bottom of the case. He took the glove off and threw it back in the box. "How long have you been here?" he asked.

"Since forever. They left me out front in a basket when I was no bigger than that football."

Pancho scrutinized him. "Since before you were ill?" He didn't mean to sound like he cared one way or another.

"Yeah. You know that one time when I was about thirteen, I beat the crap out of this kid, Rudy, with those very gloves?"

"You?"

"I know. It's hard to believe, isn't it? Oh, well. Being strong and good-looking isn't everything. It's what's up here that counts." He lowered his head and tapped his skull with his index finger.

Pancho bent down to pick up a baseball that had rolled to his feet. He thought, *What else is someone in a wheelchair going to say?* He tossed the ball up in the air with his right hand and caught it with his left. "How long have you been in the wheelchair?" he asked without looking at D.Q.

"Just recently."

"But you can walk."

"Sure."

"You don't have the strength."

"Correct. They zapped all the strength out of me."

"Who did?"

"The doctors."

"How?"

"Radiation."

Pancho was silent. It occurred to him that this was a good time to stop asking questions. He didn't want to know any more than he already did. Nevertheless, he heard himself say, "You're dying."

D.Q. smiled. "You could say that we all are. You are too. I'm just doing it faster."

"How fast?"

"No one knows for sure. It could be any day. It helps me to look at each day that way. Statistically speaking, people with the type of brain cancer I have usually live twelve months from the time they're diagnosed. I was diagnosed about six months ago."

Pancho laughed. It lasted a second or two at most, but it was still a laugh, and Pancho did not know where it came from or what to say next. "Life sucks," he finally said.

D.Q. considered that. "I know what you mean, but no, fundamentally it doesn't." He paused. "You know what we're doing here?"

There was a tin bucket nearby. Pancho turned it over and sat on it. He hadn't done any heavy lifting to speak of, but he was tired. Just looking at D.Q. made him tired. "Here? Like on this earth?"

D.Q.'s face lit up. "That is *the* question, isn't it? Actually I was referring to this room. Do you know why we're here, in this room, cleaning it up?"

"The Panda said so."

"Yes, the Panda has agreed to let me have this room. After we get all the junk out and paint it and put in some curtains and a new toilet, I'll move in here. . . . Look out that window. What do you see?"

Pancho looked. "The basketball court."

"The head of my bed is going to be right there where you're sitting. I'll be able to lie there and watch the basketball games. I'll hear the kids argue about calls and complain about fouls. At first they'll be aware of me and maybe try to keep it down or something, but after a while they'll forget I'm here and they'll just play. That's why we're fixing up this room. Do you get it?"

"What's not to get?"

"I'll spell it out for you just to make sure, since you're my appointed helper. The Panda and I have reached an understanding. At the point that it's evident that more treatment is not going to do anything besides weaken my body and mind, at that point, I'm coming home. We'll get one of those hospital beds that crank up and down and a nice soft chair and this is where I'll be. The Panda wanted to give me a room at the other end, closer to where he and the Brothers live. He thought it would be too noisy here, next to the door with the kids coming in and out. But I want it to be noisy."

Pancho looked around the room. If you placed a chair beside the second window, you could look at the pecan trees. "You got it all worked out."

"It's all falling into place. Now that you're here, we can pro-ceed with the plan."

"I have my own plans," Pancho protested.

D.Q. ignored him. "Right now, this body plans to take a nap," he said.

CHAPTER 5

He wheeled D.Q. to his "room" and watched him lift himself up from the chair in slow motion and stretch out on the bed. It was a quarter past twelve. "Margarita puts out some bread and cold cuts for lunch," D.Q. said, his eyes already closed.

Pancho walked past the room they'd been working in and out the side door. On one of his trips to the Dumpster, he had noticed some bikes on a stand. They weren't locked. He took one out, the worst-looking one, the one he figured no one would even miss. It was small and bright green, but the paint had begun to peel in places.

He went down some side streets and got on North Valley Drive heading south. He biked in the direction of the traffic, cars whizzing by on his left. It took him an hour to get to the Green Café. He went to the back door, the entrance to the kitchen, and leaned the bike against the wall. He asked one of the cooks if Julieta was there.

"Hi, Pancho," she shrieked when she saw him. She headed toward him as if ready to envelop him in a hug, but the serious look on his face stopped her a few feet away.

"Can we talk someplace?"

"Come on. No one's in the bar right now."

He followed her through the kitchen and past the eating area into a room that smelled like spilled beer. The room had red stools against the oak bar and four green Formica-top tables against a wall. She pulled out two chairs, sat on one, and waited for him to sit.

"You're looking good," she said. "Are you still living with that lady?"

He wondered how she knew about Mrs. Duggan, and then he remembered that he saw Julieta at his sister's burial after he'd been placed in the foster home. "I'm at an orphanage now. A place called St. Anthony's."

Julieta was twenty-one years old, one year older than Rosa. He knew because one time Julieta came home with Rosa after work and, after Rosa fell asleep, he and Julieta ended up alone. They were watching a movie when she asked if she could stretch out on the sofa and put her head in his lap. It turned out to be the first time he had physical relations with a girl. It was also an event he regretted the next day. She wasn't the kind of girl he wanted to get involved with. He made it a point to avoid being alone with her after that. But she was kind to Rosa and so he tried to be friendly. She and Mrs. Ruiz, the owner of the Green Café, alternated bringing Rosa home after work.

"Oh. They treating you okay?"

"It's okay."

"Good." She crossed her legs and tugged at her skirt. Pancho waited. "Oh, before I forget. Manuel, Mrs. Ruiz, all the people at work, we got together and wanted to give you something." She went behind the bar and came back with a large white purse. She opened it and took out an envelope. He could tell there was money in it.

"I don't want any money."

"It's not much. It's just that people wanted to give you something." She held it toward him, but he didn't reach for it. She put it on the table. "I'll leave it here, okay?" She took a pack of Salems out of the purse and then searched around the room for an ashtray. "You mind?"

"No," he said.

She stretched out her arm until she could grab the ashtray on the next table. "This orphanage place you're at, you got an air conditioner in your room or anything?"

"We got fans."

"Oh."

"It's all right."

"Not like home, huh?"

"No."

She uncrossed her right leg and then crossed her left. This time she didn't tug at her skirt. Her legs were smooth and her scent had begun to affect him slightly. She had shoulder-length black hair that swung when she moved her head. Pancho thought that if you erased the green eye shadow, washed the rose cheeks, and wiped off the orange lipstick, she could almost make it to pretty.

"What will happen to the trailer?" she asked, blowing out a stream of smoke.

"They're going to sell it."

"You get to keep the money?"

"Someday, maybe. I need to ask you something."

"What is it?" She looked alarmed. She shifted in her chair, placed the purse on the table, and then grabbed it again. "Want to go outside? It stinks in here."

"I gotta go back," he said. He fixed his eyes on her. "Was Rosa seeing someone?"

He could see her swallow. She licked her lips. Her teeth were smudged with lipstick. She spoke without looking at him. "Why do you ask?"

"She was found in a motel room. Someone was with her. Whoever was with her, killed her."

"How do you know?"

"I know." He didn't want to tell her how he knew.

"I know in many ways she was a child, you know, mentally, but she was an adult too. A woman. She had a right to her private life."

"I need to know who she was with that night. Did you ever see her with anyone?"

"I thought the police said there was no crime committed."

"Rosa's not important to the police. Did the police ever ask you anything? Did they even come talk to you or anyone here where she worked? Did they even try to find out who she was with?"

"No."

"I'm asking now."

She put both feet on the ground and leaned forward. "I asked her. One day she came up to me and said she didn't need a ride. Someone was taking her home. I said, 'Who's taking you home, Rosa?' and she said, 'My boyfriend.' I asked her who it was, but she didn't say. She used to walk out at eleven and meet him down the block. I mean, I don't know, you have to respect a girl's privacy . . . if that's what she wants."

"You never saw him?"

"Not really saw him. One time I was going home and I saw her getting into a red truck with a man. I never saw his face because he was leaning to open the door for her. He didn't have much hair, just some around the sides. He looked like an older guy. An Anglo — I could tell by the top of his head. That's all I saw, Rosa getting into a red truck with some old guy." She thought about it for a minute. "There was something written on the door of the truck — something or other 'and Sons.' Oh, and the truck had a silver toolbox. It looked like he worked in construction or something."

"'And Sons'?"

"Yeah. I wish I could remember the first part, but I know it ended with 'and Sons.'"

"Did Rosa ever mention a name?"

"A couple of times she started to tell me. She seemed happy and you could tell she wanted to girl-talk about him, but then she'd hold back, like all of a sudden she'd remember she wasn't supposed to say anything."

"She must have met him here. Where else would she meet him? Did you ever see her talking to anyone?"

"She talked to everyone. Everyone loved Rosa." She reached over and touched his knee. He pulled his leg away from her. "She was special, delicate, you know. It was like she didn't belong in this world, like any day she'd leave us and go back to heaven."

Pancho chuckled. Julieta's words reminded him of what his father used to say about Rosa. *Es una angelita que nos presto Dios. She's a little angel on loan to us from God.*

"Want some ice tea?"

"I got to go back," he said. Then he thought of something else he wanted to ask. He deliberated for a moment. "There was a boy in the foster home where I got kicked out. His name was Reynolds." He paused. "He said some things about Rosa. At first I thought he was just saying them to piss me off. But he knew who she was and where she worked."

"Ohh." She covered her mouth with her hand.

"You know a kid called Reynolds?"

"No. It's just that . . . I'm afraid of what you're going to say."

"Is it true then? What he said about Rosa?" He could feel the blood rush to his face.

"I don't know."

He took a deep breath. "He said she did things for money. What did he mean?"

She covered her eyes with the palms of her hands and then brought her hands together as if she were praying. "Pancho, there's no need to go into this."

"Tell me. I want to know."

She squirmed in her chair. "This was a while back, when she first started working here. She'd go outside during her breaks. Boys, you know, high school kids, would sometimes wait for her out back, by the kitchen. It was just kid stuff. She didn't know any better. It wasn't like it was dirty to her or that it meant anything.

She was getting some attention. It was just touching, you know, necking, petting."

He remembered what Reynolds had told him, just before he broke his jaw. *I knew your sister. She's one of them ten-dollar sluts at the Green Café.*

"Jesus Christ," he said. "You didn't do anything?"

"I'm sorry," she said. He had his elbows on his legs and was resting his head on his hands. She touched his head as if to bless him. "I'm sorry," she said again. "I really am."

"Yeah, me too." He stood up and headed for the door.

"Pancho, wait. Take the money."

"Keep it," he told her.

CHAPTER 6

He left the bike outside of St. Anthony's where he had found it, drank from a faucet sticking out of the ground, and went into the building. D.Q. was in the storage room, holding a thin black book in his lap. "There you are," he said without looking up. Pancho waited to be asked where he had been, but D.Q. was absorbed in the book. He grinned and shook his head. "Look at this." He handed the book to Pancho. "That little kid in the bottom picture. That's me the first year I got here." The picture showed a smiling, wide-eyed boy in a white shirt and skinny black tie. Pancho looked from the picture to D.Q.'s face. It took some effort to see the resemblance. "St. Tony's has a rule that you have to be at least fourteen to live here. I was the first exception. That's because even at ten, I was old and wise beyond my years."

Pancho ignored D.Q.'s wink and gave the book back to him. His T-shirt was sticking against his skin and his head was still burning from the bike ride. He sat on the upturned bucket. "What now?" he asked.

"We move these boxes to Lupita's office and let her go through them. She's the ultimate arbiter of what is kept and what is tossed. You never did see the library, did you? After we move the boxes, I'll take you there and show you what we got."

"I don't read."

"Not even comic books? We have the best collection of comics anywhere. Imagine kids saving all their comic books since this place opened in the 1950s."

"I don't read comic books either."

"But you can read, right?"

"I can read."

"Good, because later, when we become friends, I want to show you something I've been writing."

D.Q. kept flipping through the pages of the yearbook, apparently unaware of what he had said. Pancho stared at him. He had never heard anyone speak the way D.Q. spoke. And what made this Anglo kid think the two of them would ever be friends? D.Q. closed the book and laid it on his lap. He went on, "This book I'm writing, I call it the Death Warrior Manifesto. You know what a manifesto is, right?"

"No."

"It's a declaration of intention. In the case of the Death Warrior, it is a public declaration of how the Death Warrior is going to live his life."

Pancho took a deep breath. He thought about the thirty bucks a day he was going to be paid and knew it was way too little if you took into account the effort of trying to understand D.Q. On the other hand, he had been fortunate in getting those clues about Rosa's boyfriend, and nothing could lessen his sense of good luck. He decided to let D.Q. speak. It was possible that he would speak himself out.

"I'm not crazy about the name 'Death Warrior,' because it has all kinds of negative implications. 'Life Warrior' is probably more accurate because the manifesto is about life, but 'Death Warrior' is more mysterious-sounding."

An older man. An Anglo. A red truck. A silver toolbox. A company name that ended in "and Sons." He repeated the words to himself so he wouldn't forget.

"Do you want to know the first rule of the Death Warrior Manifesto?"

"No."

"Okay, I'll tell you, but only because I know you to be the kind of person who would understand. The first rule is: No whining. No whining of any kind under any circumstances."

"I don't whine." For a moment he thought D.Q. was criticizing him.

"Yeah, you do. You're a whiner. You just don't hear yourself whine. It takes training to hear one's internal whine."

"I'm no whiner!" Pancho felt a rush of anger.

"You know what whining is? Whining is that little voice inside of us that always complains about whatever happens. The voice doesn't have to be heard by others for it to be whining."

Pancho turned sideways and looked out the window. Kids were beginning to assemble on the basketball court. He faced D.Q. "Are *you* a whiner?" he asked.

"Yes. Like you, I don't whine out loud all that much, and I'm getting better about the inner whining, but I still whine. It's the hardest thing, not to whine. It means you accept whatever is happening to you. I'm not quite there yet. That's why I'm writing the manifesto, as a reminder. 'Rule number one: A Death Warrior does not whine aloud or in silence under any circumstances.' You want to know rule number two?"

"No."

"All right, one rule per day. If you ever hear me whine, feel free to whack me in the head."

Pancho stared at D.Q.'s head.

"Okay, maybe not on the head." D.Q. lifted his cap for a second and rubbed the top of his skull. Underneath the soft thin hair, the skin was fragile and shiny like an eggshell. Pancho looked away. D.Q. placed the cap back on his head, and the cap sank down to his ears. "There's something I need to ask you." D.Q.'s voice was serious.

Pancho stood up. "I'll take these boxes out," he said.

"The boxes can wait. Sit down. I need to ask you something."

Pancho was about to walk out, but he stopped, put the box down, and said, "Look. I'm not much of a talker. I'll push you around and clean rooms until the Panda gets me another job, but that's as far as it's going to go." He pointed at the open window. "Why don't you get one of those kids out there to talk to you?"

"I'll answer your question in a moment. Sit down. This is important." D.Q. motioned to a stool by the door.

Pancho deliberated for a few moments and then sat down. He did it in a way that conveyed he was doing it voluntarily and not in obedience to a command.

"Thank you," D.Q. said. His voice was soft. He rolled the

wheelchair closer to Pancho and fixed his bloodshot eyes on him. "You have to understand that if I seem pushy, it's because I'm living in a different time zone than you are. You perceive time as open-ended. I don't. It makes me want to get to the point."

Pancho nodded. Somewhere in what D.Q. said, there was some kind of an apology being offered. He glanced at D.Q.'s face. It was hard to imagine that the person speaking was his same age. The words, the voice, they all seemed to come from someone not just older, but ageless, if such a thing were possible.

D.Q. continued, "Your question is a good one. Why don't I ask one of the other kids to help me out? There are kids at St. Tony's I've known for years. We're a close-knit group here, a family. Something happens to a kid when he comes here. Maybe it's the fact that we're pretty much on our own. The rules we follow are the ones we all agree on. Or maybe it's the fact that we know the Panda will send us back to where we came from the first time we mess up, and there's no one here who hasn't been a lot worse off. It's an unusual place, you'll see. I hope you stick around long enough to find out."

D.Q. paused, narrowed his eyebrows, and licked the thin, cracked lips. He reached into something like a diaper bag hanging from the side of the wheelchair and took out a plastic bottle with a built-in straw. He squirted water into his mouth. It took a few seconds for the water to make it down his throat. Then he went on, "So, why you, Mr. Pancho? Mmm. Let me see. What's the best way to phrase this so you don't get scared?"

"Scared of what? You?"

"No. Not scared of me. Of what I say."

"What people say doesn't scare me."

"If I told you I was waiting for you to come, does that scare you?"

"I told you words don't scare me."

"Well, that's good, because I don't have energy or time to pussyfoot around the truth. I like the phrase 'pussyfoot around,' don't you?"

"Go ahead then. Say what you have to say."

"Okay. The answer to the question 'Why you?' has no answer at this time. I don't know exactly why you. We'll find out soon, I'm sure. But I do know that you're the one. I knew you were the one when I saw you drive in yesterday. The hard part to explain is how I knew. Let's just say that one of the benefits of this illness is the increased power to recognize a gut feeling and take it seriously. I knew someone would come to help me. It had to be the right person. You are it."

"Help you do what?" Pancho leaned backward and the stool wobbled. He grabbed on to the wall.

"Help me with . . . the preparations. Help me and I will help you."

"I don't need help with anything."

"I can read it in your eyes. There's something you want to do. No, I'd say it's more like there's something you feel you need to do. It's eating you."

"How do you know that?" He sounded more alarmed than he wanted to.

D.Q. closed his eyes and put his hands on his temples like a fortune-teller. "I see D.Q. and Pancho taking a trip together in the very near future."

"There's no way I'm taking a trip with you." What he needed to do was start to look for companies with names that ended in "and Sons," and then find out which of them used red trucks. He needed time to do that.

"I have to go to Albuquerque for some treatments. I want you to come with me. Once the treatments are over, you can do what you have to do."

Pancho was silent. He was thinking about how he would kill the man with the red truck once he found him.

"If you run away from this place, the lady who drove you here yesterday will have the state troopers on you an hour after you're reported missing. What I need to do will take a few weeks or so. Then after that, you can do your thing. You can leave and go wherever and I'll stay there a little longer. People here will think you're with me, and we'll tell the people there you came back to St. Anthony's. I'll help you."

Pancho thought about it. Then he snickered. "You don't even know what you're saying. You can't help me."

"I'll help you if I can."

"What kind of preparations?" Pancho asked, remembering the particular word that D.Q. had used.

D.Q. smiled a knowing smile. "Preparations like these," he said, waving his hand over the room. "And . . . there's something I need to do while we're in Albuquerque, a different kind of preparation. I'll let you know when the time is right. What exactly do you need to do?"

Pancho heard the slap of a basketball outside, then the twang of the ball hitting the backboard. He stood up and went to the window. He felt a strong impulse to speak, to tell D.Q. about his plans, but he stopped himself. "No way," he whispered. But it was loud enough for D.Q. to hear.

D.Q. said, as if lost in thought, "Your purpose and mine are joined somehow. You'll see. We'll figure it out in time. You mind wheeling me up to the basketball court? I'm refereeing this afternoon's game. You play basketball?"

"No."

"I didn't think so. We'll finish this up tomorrow."

"I'll come back and take out the rest of the boxes."

"Sooner or later, you'll have to meet some of the other kids."

"Later is okay with me." Pancho got behind the wheelchair. Before he started pushing, he asked, "Who all is going to Albuquerque?"

"The Panda will probably drive us, but then it'll be just you and me. In Albuquerque, we'll stay at this place called Casa Esperanza. It's kind of a motel for out-of-town people who come to the hospital for treatment. Then, I don't know, we may have to go stay someplace else. I haven't worked that part out completely. First things first. First, I had to wait for the other Death Warrior to arrive."

CHAPTER 7

The next day, Father Concha said he wanted all the sports equipment moved to a different room. Pancho said he would do it while D.Q. and Brother Javier went to get some paint. D.Q. had not taken his usual nap that day, and Pancho needed a break. If it were up to him, rule number two of the Death Warrior Manifesto would be: No talking for more than three minutes straight at any one time.

He was walking out of the dormitory when he felt someone close behind him. He stopped and turned around. There in front of him was a boy younger than any of the kids he had seen at St. Anthony's so far. He looked like the picture of D.Q. in the year-book, only this boy's skin and hair were darker. "Howdy," the boy said. He was grinning, it seemed, from ear to ear.

Pancho stared at him briefly and kept walking. The boy caught up with him. "My real name is Guillermo, but people call me Memo." Pancho glanced sideways. The boy came up to his elbow. "You're Pancho, I know."

"How do you know?" Pancho asked without slowing down. The boy had to skip a few times to keep up with him.

"Know what?"

"My name. How does everyone know my name?"

"I don't know. Everyone just does. I think the Panda first mentioned you were coming during Mass."

"Mass?"

"We have Mass every night, but you don't have to go if you don't want to. That's when the Panda makes announcements."

"What else did the Panda say about me at Mass?"

"That's all. That a new kid was coming and his name was Pancho Sanchez. He didn't say anything else, like about your past and all, if that's what you're worried about."

"I'm not worried."

"Kids come and go all the time. Sometimes they come for a few days. Others come to stay. D.Q. says you're here to stay."

"Is that right?"

"Yup."

They stopped in front of the room where the sports equipment had been stored. Pancho expected the boy to keep walking, but he remained by his side. He stepped inside the room and gathered five aluminum baseball bats in his arms. The boy picked up the catcher's gear. "What are you doing?"

"I'm helping you," Memo said.

"I don't need your help."

Memo didn't answer. "I usually play catcher," he said. "Maybe because it doesn't hurt me to squat. No one else likes to do it." He blew into the catcher's mitt and then proceeded to have a coughing fit. When he stopped, he said to Pancho, "D.Q.'s room is going to be nice when we get done with it. I'm really good at painting."

The room where Pancho had first stored the sports equipment was just like D.Q.'s, except it didn't have a bathroom and it had only one window. Pancho wondered why the Panda had told them to store the equipment there in the first place. Maybe he was making up work for them, which was okay with Pancho. A whistle blew outside. He stooped to look out the window.

"How can it be a foul if he's the one who knocked me down?" one of the kids asked, his arms opened wide and palms turned outward.

"Because your feet were still moving when he bumped into you," a very tall pimply-faced boy explained with complete authority. The boy who was fouled grabbed his head in disbelief. It was the closest thing Pancho had seen to any kind of discord since he arrived at St. Anthony's, and it gave him hope that maybe the kids were not totally brainwashed zombies.

Memo grabbed a green canvas bag on the floor. He was about to put the catcher's gear in it when Pancho reached out and took it from him. "I'm going to use that," Pancho said.

"For what?"

"You know where I can find a shovel?"

"Yeaaah," Memo answered as if he was afraid of what Pancho might do with the information. "In the toolshed out back. Why?"

"I'll need some rope."

Now Memo seemed really interested. "There's a nylon rope out there too. We used it to hang our clothes outside before someone donated us a couple of dryers."

They walked out the side door, past the bicycle that Pancho had borrowed the day before, and past the Dumpster where he had thrown the trash from the storage room. The toolshed was made of unpainted galvanized steel. It wasn't locked. Memo pulled at a string that only he could see and a lightbulb flicked on. They found a shovel hanging against the wall, and a nylon rope neatly curled in a corner with a variety of extension cords. Then they walked outside, Pancho leading the way with the shovel and the green canvas bag and Memo following with the rope.

Pancho found a place by the pecan trees where the ground was soft and he began to fill the bag with dirt. The dirt stayed soft only a couple of inches down and then it became rocky. When he hit rocks, he began another hole. All this time he worked in silence, ignoring Memo's questions. He stopped when the bag was three-quarters full. He took the rope and threaded it through the grommets on top of the bag. Then he walked around, sizing up the pecan trees, until he found one with a strong branch about ten feet from the ground.

"It's a punching bag!" Memo exclaimed.

"Go get the stepladder in the shed," Pancho ordered. In the meantime, he lifted the bag, hugging it with both arms against his chest, and carried it to the tree.

"We're going to need some help hoisting it up there," Memo said when he returned. He set the aluminum ladder under the branch. Before Pancho could say anything, Memo stretched his lips with thumb and index finger and let out the shrillest, loudest whistle Pancho had ever heard. Kids standing by the court watching the basketball game turned around to look. Memo waved them over. Two of them started toward the tree.

"Just hold the ladder," Pancho told Memo. He lifted the bag

again and tried to support it on one of the middle rungs, but the bag slipped and landed on his foot. He tightened his jaw and swore silently.

"Hold on a second. Marcos and Coop are coming," Memo said, clearly trying not to laugh. Pancho failed to see how the pain in his foot was in any way funny.

Marcos and Coop looked at the bag full of dirt with no surprise on their faces. Apparently, filling a canvas bag with dirt and stringing it up a tree was perfectly normal around here. "I'll climb up to the branch and tie the bag. You guys lift it," Memo said. Before anyone could object, he had gone up the ladder and straddled the branch.

Pancho got under the bag and lifted it up to his chest. Marcos and Coop grabbed the bottom on either side of him. Pancho kicked the ladder out of the way and it went clanging down. With one hand, he tossed the ends of the rope to Memo. "Twist the rope around the branch as many times as you can and then I'll come tie a knot in it," Pancho yelled up at him. Then the three of them heaved the bag, and Memo began winding the rope around the branch. When the rope was almost totally gone, they let go of the bag. The middle of the bag dangled level with Pancho's eyes. It was exactly the right height. Pancho got the ladder and Memo climbed down. Then Pancho climbed up and tied a series of knots with the remaining rope. He came down, moved the ladder to one side, and socked the bag with his closed fist.

"Let me try it," said Memo. He punched it as hard as he could. "Ouch! It's hard."

Marcos took a shot. "Maybe the dirt will loosen up after a while."

"You have to jab at it like this. Move around and then jab, jab," Coop said, demonstrating.

"You know boxing?" Pancho asked.

"I've done a little here and there." Coop bobbed left and right and hit the bag with a flurry of combinations.

"What kind of name is Coop? Like chicken coop?"

"The actual name is Cooper," Coop answered calmly. He stopped punching the bag and began to rub his knuckles. Coop was taller than Pancho by a head. He had a bulky body, and it was hard for Pancho to tell whether the bulk was muscle or fat. His biceps looked solid. He was probably a year older than Pancho.

"You have any money, Coop?" Pancho asked.

"Why?"

"Since you've done a little boxing, I thought you might want to go a couple of rounds with me. I found some gloves in the storage room. I have twenty dollars I can put up."

Coop looked at Marcos and then at Memo. Memo shrugged his shoulders as if to say, *Don't look at me.* "I don't know," Coop said. He looked down at the ground and shuffled his feet.

"The gloves are fourteen ounces, padded. There's headgear too. No one will get hurt," Pancho said.

"Who'll decide who wins?" Memo asked. "I could be the umpire."

Marcos slapped Memo on the back of the head. "It's not an umpire, it's a referee," he said.

"I can be the referee," Memo said.

"Usually there's three," Marcos said. "I'll be the second one."

"It's not how hard you hit, it's how many times you land punches," Memo informed everyone.

"What do you know about boxing, you little *pingüino*?" Marcos began to jab at Memo. Memo flicked Marcos's hands away.

"What do you say, Chicken Coop?" Pancho asked. There was no taunt in his voice.

"Oooh," Marcos exclaimed. "Them are fighting words."

"Shut up, Marcos!" Memo said.

"Okay, but we're going to get in trouble," Coop said.

"Why?" Marcos asked.

"It's gambling," Coop answered. "It's against house rules."

"It's not gambling. It's a twenty-dollar prize to whoever wins," Memo argued.

"It's the same as playing hoops for money. We decided not to do that." Coop waited for Memo to respond, but Memo was still thinking about the comparison. "Okay," Coop said after a few moments of silence. "I'll do it."

Pancho was tempted to tell Coop to forget about the twenty dollars, but he needed the money even more than he needed to hit someone. With any luck, those twenty dollars would be the first of many more to come. All he had to do was get kids pissed off enough to want to punch him out. From what he had seen, getting the kids at St. Anthony's riled up was not going to be easy. "I'll get the gear," Pancho said.

"You want to do this now?" Coop asked.

"Yeah, why not?"

"I think the Panda is in his office," Marcos said.

"No," Memo said, "I saw him go out a while ago. He took Larry to the dentist. He won't be back for an hour."

"We need one ref and two judges," Marcos said.

"How 'bout we get D.Q.? He's the fairest ref we got," Memo

said. "I saw him pull in with Brother Javier a little while ago. I'll go ask him." He ran past Pancho toward the front entrance.

Pancho, who had taken a few steps toward the building, stopped. He was about to object, but then he would have to explain why D.Q. was not a good choice and he wouldn't know what to say. He kept on walking. He felt a strange feeling, like he was pulling a fast one on a child. It reminded him of the times he would cheat Rosa out of her allowance by some trickery she was incapable of detecting. He started to jog, but the strange feeling remained.

He walked out of the building, carrying a box with the boxing gear, and saw the crowd of kids by the punching bag. He looked for D.Q.'s wheelchair but didn't see it. He was relieved. The thought came to him that he was about to violate one of his own rules: *Keep a low profile*. But it was not possible to back away from the momentum that had gathered. He didn't know whether the energy came from the crowd of buzzing kids or from inside him.

They parted ways for him, and he saw that someone had drawn a large square in the dirt. Coop had already taken his shirt off and was limbering up. His bulk was not fat. Pancho took the headgear and the boxing gloves and offered them to him. "No headgear," Coop said.

"Put it on," Pancho told him.

"No headgear." Coop threw the gear back in the box. *The crowd got to him,* Pancho thought.

"Have it your way," Pancho said. He walked to the opposite corner of the square. *Don't get angry. You just need to make twenty bucks. Make sure you pull your punches.*

"I want to be the ref," Memo said.

"I'm the ref. Albo and Robert will be the two judges," Marcos told him.

"Help me tie the gloves," Pancho said to Memo.

"Then I'll be Pancho's trainer," Memo said, happy to have an official role.

"Where's D.Q.?" Pancho asked him softly so no one else could hear.

"I tried to get him when you went in for the gloves, but he had a phone call from his mom."

"He has a mom?"

"She lives in Albuquerque with D.Q.'s stepfather. They're filthy rich."

"What's he doing here then?"

"She dropped him off here before she remarried. D.Q. doesn't want anything to do with her. How tight should I tie these?"

"As tight as you can."

"Keep an eye out for the Panda," someone said.

"He wouldn't get pissed about this. Kids used to box all the time," someone else responded.

"Who's going to keep time?" Marcos asked. He had finished tying Coop's gloves and now Coop was stretching his neck like a professional. Pancho could not help but smile. The sight reminded him of the first time his father took him to The Aztec, a boxing club on the outskirts of Las Cruces. He was six years old, and when his father sat him on a stool to watch his fight, his legs did not reach the floor. The man in the ring with his father stretched his neck sideways till his ear touched his shoulder, and Pancho could hear the bones crack all the way over where he sat. The man was big, a giant compared to his father, who seemed at that moment fragile. Pancho started to cry. His father must have seen the tears on his face because he suddenly climbed out of the ring and came to him. He grabbed him by the shoulders, looked straight at him, and asked him what the matter was. But he had no words for what he felt and he already knew that the boxing ring was not a place for tears. "*Mijo*," his father said to him, "I'm not going to let him hurt me. It's not how big you are, it's how fast and how determined you are to hit someone. Boom, boom." His father tapped him lightning fast with a left and a right on his cheeks. The hits were just hard enough to stop the tears.

The tall boy, the same one who had refereed the basketball game, blew a whistle, and Coop jumped into the middle of the square, dancing and bobbing. Pancho stepped forward. There was an intense, concentrated look on Coop's face. It was hard to believe he was the same boy who a few minutes before had worried about violating a house rule. Pancho knew what was happening; fighters often made this mistake in boxing competitions. Adrenaline bursts into the bloodstream with the noise of the crowd and the shouts of the fighter's name, and that energy easily turns to a venomous anger. Then the other fighter becomes an enemy and there are no more tactics, only the desire to assert superiority in the eyes of the crowd.

With this transformation, Coop flung punches at Pancho's face as soon as Pancho stepped into his range. Pancho blocked the punches with his forearms. A chant of "Coop, Coop" started from the sidelines, and Coop swung harder and faster. None of the punches jolted Pancho, and seeing that he did not respond, Coop slowed the barrage, confident and playful as he tried to sneak jabs through the protection of Pancho's gloves. The boxing match became a show for him.

There was something refreshing, pleasurable almost, in the feel of Coop's punches against his arms and the occasional blow that landed on his ribs. It was like being in a daze and getting shaken into wakefulness, or like a ghost regaining flesh and bones. He dropped his left hand and allowed Coop to land a solid hook to the jaw. A collective "oooh" went up from the crowd.

"Thirty seconds," the tall boy holding the watch announced.

He had planned to go like that through the whole match — receiving whatever Coop sent his way until he got tired, and then Pancho would bop him a few times — but something happened. Maybe it was Coop's arrogant smile, or maybe it was his blue eyes and the golden skin glistening with sweat, or maybe it was just impossible to contain the rage that fueled him. Gracefully, effortlessly, Pancho dodged a wild right hook from Coop and buried his left hand in Coop's abdomen. He sent the punch the way his father taught him, as if he planned for the arm to go through his opponent's body. Coop dropped his arms, deflated. His upper body bent forward, his head floating in midair, and Pancho exploded with an uppercut that landed fully on Coop's open mouth.

He stepped out of the way and watched the unconscious body tumble forward. There was a stunned silence. Marcos and others rushed forward to Coop's sprawled form. "Turn him on his side so he doesn't choke on his blood," Pancho said. He began to untie his right-hand glove with his teeth. He knew that Coop was not badly hurt. If they had been wearing headgear, he probably wouldn't have gone down.

"Man, where'd you learn to box like that?" Memo took his other glove and began to untie it. "I think you broke his front teeth."

"I told him to put the headgear on," he said. He was filled with a sense of irritation, the lingering aftereffect of the rage that had surged through him momentarily. The irritation was more with himself, but for what? He didn't know. A week ago when Reynolds called his sister a slut, he had busted the kid's jaw with no regrets. Now he felt as if he had broken a promise. "Shit," he muttered.

Up by the basketball court, D.Q. sat in his wheelchair, watching.

CHAPTER 8

The following day, Pancho called Mrs. Olivares from Lupita's office. He asked if she was still planning to go to the trailer, and when she said she was, he told her he wanted to come. D.Q.'s talk of writing made him remember that Rosa had kept a diary. Now and then he would see her scribbling in it. Maybe she wrote something in there about the man she was seeing.

At ten A.M., Pancho was in front of St. Anthony's, waiting for Mrs. Olivares, when D.Q. showed up. He was standing up, no wheelchair in sight.

"You're walking," Pancho said.

"Today I seem to have some strength."

"Where you going?" Pancho asked and looked away. He didn't want D.Q. to inquire about the fight.

"I'm coming with you," D.Q. said.

Pancho was about to object when Mrs. Olivares stopped her green Toyota in front of them. Before Pancho could do or say anything, D.Q. got in the front seat. Pancho resigned himself to

D.Q.'s company and sat in the back. "Hello, my name is Daniel Quentin, but they call me D.Q. I'm Pancho's friend." He shook Mrs. Olivares's hand with an energy Pancho had not seen before. *The kid doesn't get out enough,* Pancho thought.

Mrs. Olivares and D.Q. chatted all the way to Pancho's trailer. D.Q. was interested in a legal process called emancipation. Pancho understood it as a kind of divorce between a minor and his parents. D.Q. wanted to know if Mrs. Olivares had ever participated in that kind of process and what it took for a minor to prove his case. Mrs. Olivares told him that emancipations were only granted when the parent was abusive or neglectful and the minor demonstrated the ability to take care of himself. Emancipations were very rare. It was easier for the court to appoint another family member or the State as the legal guardian for the minor. Mrs. Olivares looked at Pancho in the rearview mirror when she said this.

Mrs. Olivares veered off Picacho Drive onto a dirt road. The trailer park where Pancho lived consisted of thirty quarter-acre lots. Each lot was separated from the adjacent lots by waist-high chain-link fences. The quality of the mobile homes and upkeep of the yards varied from lot to lot. There were eighty-by-twenty homes surrounded by emerald green lawns and crawling rose-bushes, and there were rusty twenty-foot trailers resting on cement blocks in the middle of a patch of dirt.

Mrs. Olivares pulled into the driveway and turned off the car. Pancho's trailer was sad-looking. The grass in the front yard looked like hay that was ready to be harvested. Jackrabbits or prairie dogs had eaten the tulips around the flagpole. The windows were shut and there were yellow notices pasted to the door of the front porch, as if the place had been condemned. The three of them sat in the car, observing, unwilling to move. Then D.Q. opened the door and swung his legs out. Mrs. Olivares was next. Both of them stood next to the car, waiting for Pancho to get out. Maybe it had not been a good idea to call Mrs. Olivares that morning.

Finally he came out of the car. Mrs. Olivares opened the fence gate and stepped onto the first of the flat, round stones that led to the front door. The boys followed her. The energy that had animated D.Q. in the car was gone. He shuffled his feet as if he could barely walk. It was like they had entered a space where all happiness had been sucked out. Mrs. Olivares opened the door to the porch, tearing in half the yellow announcement for the upcoming auction. "I'll wait out here," D.Q. said.

"Come in," Pancho ordered. He held the door open for D.Q., and D.Q. quietly entered.

Everything was the same as he had left it when the sheriff knocked on the door two weeks ago. There was the cup of coffee he placed on the kitchen counter on the way to the door. There was a pair of white socks on one end of the sofa and a rumpled pillow on the other end. Mrs. Olivares flipped the light switch up and down, but the electricity had been cut off. She went around drawing curtains to let the daylight in. "Oh," she said, remembering. "I brought some boxes to put your things in. They're in the trunk of the car. I'll go get them."

When she left, D.Q. said, "I thought you said you didn't read." He had picked up a book that lay open on the brown chair. He read out loud: "*The Soul of a Butterfly: Reflections on Life's Journey*, Muhammad Ali . . ." Pancho snatched the book from his hands.

There was a knowing grin on D.Q.'s face. "You are not who you purport to be," he said.

"I don't POOPORT nothing," Pancho said. He tucked the book under his arm and headed for Rosa's room. He stopped in front of the closed door and took a deep breath, then he slid the door open and entered. Immediately he was overwhelmed with her smell, a mixture of mint leaves and lilacs. He held his breath. If he didn't breathe while he was in her room, he would make it.

He opened the top drawer of the dresser and immediately saw the diary. It was locked with a small lock that opened with a tiny key. He went to the shelves where Rosa kept her dolls. Rosa liked to hide her money behind the dolls or inside the dolls' dresses when she was a child. He figured she hid the key to the diary there as well. There were dolls from all over the world. His favorite was the one from Holland with the wooden shoes. Maybe the only time he ever saw Rosa get angry was when he cut off the long blond braid of the Danish doll. He was seven at the time, old enough in Rosa's mind to know better. He went through the dolls, lifting them up gently.

He found the key under the Mexican doll. *Of course,* he thought. He stuck the diary in the front of his pants and put the key in his pocket. Mrs. Olivares was calling him from the living room. "What should I pack?" she asked.

"Whatever," he told her, looking down the hall. She had four unopened boxes on the floor. D.Q. was not on the living room chair where Pancho had left him.

"Okay," she said. "I'll go through and see what's worth saving. You might want some of these things someday, you know."

"I'll be in prison," he said. He didn't say it loud enough for Mrs. Olivares to hear.

His room was between his sister's room and his father's at the far end of the trailer. D.Q. was sitting in the chair by the small desk, his eyes closed. "It's nice in here," D.Q. said, opening his eyes. "Who's that?" He was looking at a poster of a boxer on the wall in front of him. The boxer was crouching, his hand cocked back as if about to deliver a left hook. Pancho followed D.Q.'s eyes to the poster but did not respond. It suddenly occurred to him that there was something besides Rosa's diary that he should get. He turned around and went to his father's bedroom.

Nothing had been disturbed in his father's room since his death. Neither Rosa nor Pancho ever considered removing their father's things or moving into the larger bedroom. He found what he was looking for in the bottom drawer of his father's bureau, underneath the work shirts. It was a .22 Smith & Wesson revolver his father had bought to shoot the jackrabbits that ate his tulips. Pancho never saw him use it. The worst his father ever did to the jackrabbits was cuss at them in Spanish. The revolver was not loaded. His father kept the bullets hidden on the top shelf of the closet. Pancho had discovered them just before he was taken to Mrs. Duggan's, when he was looking for his father's war medals. He took out seven bullets and put them in the same pocket where he had dropped the key, then he grabbed his father's blue jean jacket from the closet and folded it around the revolver.

He went into his room, where D.Q. still sat, opened the closet, took out a black backpack, and put the jacket and the diary in there. Then he went to Rosa's room, grabbed the book he had left on the bed, and dropped it into the backpack as well. When he walked out, D.Q. was in the hallway holding a wooden parrot the size of a child's hand. "I'd like to have this for my new room, if you don't want it."

"Take it," Pancho said. He had carved and painted a Mexican perico in shop class during his freshman year. It represented the only A-plus he had ever received. There were so many objects with history, so many memories embedded in things around the house. It would be excruciating to choose one over another. What he had was all he could handle.

"Pancho," Mrs. Olivares said to him. She was standing by the kitchen counter, holding what looked like a large cigar box. "I found some silverware in here. It looks like real silver. You'll want to save that."

D.Q., behind him, said, "Let me see."

Pancho walked outside, the backpack on his shoulder. The sunlight made him squint. "Take a box with you. See if there's any of your dad's tools you want to keep," Mrs. Olivares yelled after him. Across the street, Mrs. Romano was pretending to sweep the front steps of her trailer, but Pancho could tell she had come out to investigate. She motioned for him to come over. He waved to her and walked around to the back.

The two pecan trees covered almost all the backyard with shade. In the far corner, there was a swing set that had been converted to a workout area. The swings had been removed, and a heavy punching bag hung from the overhead pole. A pear-shaped speed bag dangled next to it. Pancho went up to the swing set and sat on top of the plastic toy box where he kept the boxing gear.

When Mrs. Olivares told him that there was no way that the State of New Mexico would let him live in the trailer by himself, he thought they were taking the only thing left to him. What else was there to take? Now he thought that even if they had let him be, he would not have been able to stay in the trailer for long. In there, a few moments ago, he had felt as if his brain were suffocating, as if his head were filled with a mental steam that steadily increased in pressure.

D.Q. was limping toward him, the green perico in his hand. He sat next to Pancho. "We should take these with us, add them to the bag you've already hung." He pointed at the boxing bags with his chin.

"Why?"

"You could start a boxing club. St. Tony's used to have one, you know. It was before my time, but one kid actually won the state Golden Gloves for his age group."

"Luis Rivera," Pancho answered without thinking.

"Right. How'd you know?"

"I saw the trophy."

"I got an idea. We get Brother Javier to come over with the truck and pick up the swing set and bags." He touched one of the pipes. "A little paint and it would look great right next to the basketball court. What do you think?"

"Yeah, sure."

"Yeah, I know, you're not planning on sticking around for that long." He took off his cap and combed the fine hair, what little there was of it, with his fingers. He put the cap on. "I'm not planning on sticking around for long either," he said, trying to make Pancho laugh but not succeeding. Time went by without either of them saying anything. Pancho was about to stand up when D.Q. spoke.

"What was it like living here, before people started dying out on you? I mean, did you have any friends? What did you do when you came home from school? On weekends?"

Pancho thought hard. Did he have any friends? What did he do when he came home from school? His father worked at the Sears Auto Center from seven A.M. to three P.M. As soon as he got out of there, he came home and waited for Pancho to get back from school, and then they did carpentry jobs and construction jobs, building porches, cabinets, additions, whatever came up. He hung out with his father most of the time. His father was his friend. They worked together, trained together, laughed together. Rosa was his friend also, in a different way. The people at the gym were friends, or like friends, you could say. Did he have any friends his age? The absence of friends had never come up before. It was a lack he had never noticed. There were kids at school. He talked to them, ate lunch with them, joked around with them. He could give D.Q. some names, but he knew those were not the kind of friends D.Q. was asking about. "I worked out. I helped my father. I always had things to do."

"Yeah," D.Q. said, as if he understood what that meant — that Pancho didn't have any friends.

Then, unexpectedly, Pancho added, "After my father died, it seems like I was always busy with one thing or another. I had use of the truck. I didn't have a license, but I never got caught. People hired me to take stuff to the dump. There was always some place to go, to buy food, to the laundromat, to take my sister to work."

But you never went to pick her up, a voice said. "There's a gym over by Mesilla," he said quickly. "I had a job after school there."

"You boxed there?"

"Mostly I washed the towels, cleaned the locker room. I used to get a few bucks for sparring with people, whenever they needed someone live to hit."

"You probably did some hitting of your own."

"Manny, the guy that owned the gym, he'd let me pop a few heads now and then. Nothing major. He didn't want to lose any paying customers. It was all right, living here. We never lacked anything. I went to sleep tired every night." He stood up. There was something about the way D.Q. asked questions that lulled him into saying more than he wanted. He waited for D.Q. to stand and then he opened the plastic toy box where they had been sitting. "Let's take these," he said.

"Jockstraps?"

"Groin protectors," Pancho corrected him. "In case we have some more matches. I don't want my pecans getting cracked."

CHAPTER 9

He waited until all the lights in the dormitory were out. Then he waited some more. After they got back from the trailer, he and Memo had painted the storage room, so it had been a long day and it was hard to stay awake. When he thought everyone was asleep, he sat up in bed and turned on the lamp. He dug out Rosa's diary from the backpack and held it in front of him. He searched for the tiny key in his wallet pocket and found it. He paused again for a second before he inserted the key in the lock and turned it. He opened the diary to the first page.

He read: "My DAIRY by ROSA SANCHEZ."

He smiled at the misspelling. There were so many times when he had felt like grabbing the diary from Rosa's hands and tossing it outside. He'd be on the sofa trying to watch television, and Rosa would be sitting on a stool at the kitchen counter asking him how to spell this and how to spell that. "If no one's gonna read it, what difference does it make?" he would say to her irritably. "Oh, Pancho," she would say without looking up, waiting for him to give her the right spelling, knowing that he would. Fortunately, the words she asked about were easy words. He wasn't a great speller himself.

Rosa had learned how to write and read at a school for so-called special students. A light blue van with round yellow lights on top would pull up in front of the trailer at seven twenty-five A.M. to pick her up. His father had already left for work, so it was up to him to make sure she got in the van. Mostly, he hurried her along by counting down the minutes until the van arrived. "Five more minutes," he would say to her. "Thirty seconds," he'd yell, as she ran around looking for a shoe. When the van came, he opened the door to the trailer to let the driver know that Rosa was on her way. He'd watch the van pull away and then he'd walk to the entrance of the trailer park, where he would wait for the regular school bus, the one for students who were not "special" like Rosa. He thanked his lucky stars that he and Rosa did not get on the same bus.

The special school that Rosa attended was a fifteen-mile drive from their trailer park. The first time he went there with his father, he was surprised to see that not all the students looked like the ones he saw in the back of the blue van. Rosa's school was a regular elementary school large enough to have special-education classes. The hope was that at some point, the special students would catch up to the regular students and join them in their classes. But that would never be the case with Rosa. According to her teachers, Rosa's mind would remain forever at the level of a not-very-bright ten-year-old. But a ten-year-old mind could read and write and add and subtract and work certain jobs, and so could Rosa.

Below her name, Rosa had written her address and telephone

number. Below that, she had written in pencil in small letters, trying not to waste any available space on the page:

The story of Rosa Sanchez life. My mother died when I was 8. I have a father that takes care of me now and I have one brother his name is Pancho. I am disebeld and go to special ed class every day. My brother Pancho tells me hurry up Rosa here comes the van. At school I like when missus Chavez reads to us. My papa gave me this dairy today. I will write to you and tell you my secrets I have. Well night now.

He thought that it must have taken her an hour to write those few lines. He flipped slowly through the pages. The pages of the diary were lined, and words crowded every line for forty or so pages. There were no dates on any of the pages, but he knew that their father had given her the diary when she was fifteen. Those forty pages accounted for the last five years of her life.

He hesitated for a few seconds and turned slowly to the last pages. Three pages from the end, he saw the name "Bobby" and stopped. He read:

I met a boy his name is Bobby. He's not like the other boys. He says he wants to take me out in his truck.

He continued reading the various entries.

Bobby bought me a turcoise ring. I love Bobby. He told me he loves me also. He says we need to keep it a secret that we love each other on account he's older. But I told him that don't make no diference.

I want tell Julieta about Bobby. I want Bobby and me and Julieta maybe go to the show with her and she can get a date also. But he say no. We needs to be a secret. I ask him if maybe he was embarased to be seen with me cause of my disbelity. He says no he just shy thats all.

I told Bobby today I want to wait before we do everything. He got mad at me. He thinks I do it with other boys and not him. I told him I don't. I was waiting for my true love to come forever. I believe he is the one. My one and only. I want Bobby to feel the same way. I hope he understands why I wait.

I want Bobby to meet Pancho. Bobby says next week. I hope Pancho likes him. I think if I marry Bobby Pancho can work in construkshun with Bobby. After Pancho fineshes high school. Papa I miss you. I wish you were here to meet Bobby also. Can you believe someone loves your Rosa?

Then he read the last entry.

Bobby says his leaving me. He says his goin back to albuqerqe and wont come back. He wants to break up because he says his to old to play games. He says I'm not fun. I don't even drink or nothing. He thought I was a party girl when he first met me cause I was always happy all the time and he heard I like to have fun. I tol him I love him. He told me prove it if I did. I said I would. I say I don't want to lose him. Tomorrow he will take me to a place where we can just have fun and I can show him if I truly love him. After that he will come meet Pancho. If I love him why am I afraid.

In all the years that he lived with his sister, he had never seen anything more than a few words written by her. When he saw her scribbling in her diary, he thought she was putting down gibberish, nothing that would make any sense to anyone else. But here she was, in her own words, surprising him, showing him a side of her he never saw because he never cared enough to see.

He closed the diary and locked it again with the tiny key. He put his right hand on top of it the way he saw people on TV put their hands on Bibles when they swore to tell the truth, the whole truth, and nothing but the truth. This was the truth he swore: That no matter what happened, no matter what anyone said or pleaded, at the right time, he would honor his sister's life by finding the man who hurt her and making him pay for the wrong done to her.

CHAPTER 10

It rained before dawn. The rainstorm pelted the earth furiously for an hour and then stopped. Pancho walked out to the punching bag before anyone else was up. Rainwater had seeped in and tripled the weight of the bag, but the branch from which it hung had not bent. He began to hit the bag slowly. To work properly, a bag should be light enough to swing back and forth so that the boxer must adjust his feet in response to the movement. This bag did not budge. It stolidly absorbed Pancho's hardest punches. *Thud. Thud. Thud-thud. Thud.* Pancho found a rhythm and stayed with it. After a few minutes, he felt sweat roll down his forehead. He increased the tempo. *Thud-thud-thud. Thud-thud-thud.* His feet slid on the wet ground. The scars on his knuckles opened and began to bleed, staining the green canvas. Faster rhythm: *Thud-thud-thud-thud-thud-thud.* Harder now. Hitting not just with the arms but also with the legs and shoulders. He felt the tension inside his arms soften into tiredness and then exhaustion, and at last there was some relief.

"I wish I could do that."

It was D.Q. standing behind him. Pancho stopped. He took off his T-shirt and wiped his face with it. "You're up early," he said.

"I got up as soon as I heard the thunder."

"You came out in the rain?"

"I got to the cocoon before the rain started."

"The what?"

"Come on, I'll show you."

Pancho slipped the wet T-shirt over his head. He noticed D.Q.'s bare feet sticking out of the baggy blue jeans. They walked. D.Q. bent down to pick up a pecan. "Can you crack this for me?" Pancho stuck it in his mouth and bit it gently. He peeled off the shell and gave the intact nut to D.Q. "Nice," D.Q. commented. "I can never get them to come out in one piece."

"What happens to all the nuts?"

"We keep some, we sell some. We make pecan fudge and give it to benefactors. We fill about twenty big sacks the size of your punching bag back there." When they reached the end of the grove, D.Q. pointed at a green hammock. "That's the cocoon," he said.

There were two patio chairs in front of the hammock. D.Q. lowered himself into one. The hammock had U.S. ARMY printed on it in black letters. Pancho lifted a plastic flap that hung from the side.

"It has a net for the mosquitoes, and when it rains, that flap turns into a tent roof."

"How do you breathe?"

"There are openings on the side for ventilation. It's a neat feeling to be inside the cocoon in the middle of a thunderstorm."

Pancho sat in the other patio chair. The sun emerged over the Organ Mountains. A breeze shook the branches above and drops of rainwater fell on them. "You were inside that thing during the storm?"

"I got in there just when it started to pour. It was nice and scary."

Next to their trailer, his father had built a toolshed with a galvanized steel roof. Pancho remembered the sound of rain on the roof, like a bag of marbles spilling from the sky. "The paint in your room should be dry by now," he said.

"I saw it last night. You and Memo did a good job." D.Q. had his eyes fixed on the mountains.

"When are you moving in?"

"After we come back from Albuquerque. How long do you think it would take to walk over to those mountains?"

Pancho looked at D.Q.'s muddy feet. "On those two things?"

D.Q. wiggled his toes. "Hey, is that like the first time you smiled since you got here?" Pancho looked the other way. "Okay, how long do you think it would take a *normal* person to walk over there?"

"Half a day. Less."

"No way."

"I've hiked those mountains. They're not far."

"What was it like, hiking them?"

"Rocky. You have to be careful not to step on a rattlesnake."

D.Q. sighed. "I've been looking at those mountains since I first came here and I've never set foot on them. Someone told me there were caves with Indian paintings made a thousand years ago."

"The only caves I saw were used by people to take a dump."

"Oh, don't tell me that. I need to hold on to all the good images I have."

"It's the truth. Shit, rubbers, and beer cans. That's what I saw in those caves."

"Oh, well. That reminds me. Our trip to Albuquerque has been moved up. We leave tomorrow. The Panda is driving us."

"How long will we be there?"

"You're coming, then," D.Q. said. He didn't act surprised. He already knew what Pancho would decide.

Pancho thought about what he'd read in Rosa's diary. "Yeah," he answered. "I'm coming."

"You've heard about my mother," D.Q. said. It wasn't a question or an accusation.

"Yeah."

"There's not much to the drama, really. After my father died, she went a little nutty and dropped me off at St. Anthony's, God bless her. She married again, to this lawyer named Stu. And seven years later, it's suddenly become very important to her to be a mother, which means getting involved in my medical treatment." D.Q. paused to catch his breath. "This therapy that I'll be undergoing in Albuquerque is intensive chemotherapy. Typically, what I have is treated only with radiation. The tumor is too diffuse to remove with surgery. I picture it like a low-lying fog that won't go away. Chemotherapy so far hasn't been successful for it. Nevertheless, there are always clinical trials that are trying different combinations of chemotherapy and radiation. My mother signed me up for one. It's complicated. She's threatening to get a court order. She and I have different views on what's best for me."

"Maybe she's right."

"No, she's not. I've done the research. It's a trade-off. Maybe I get a couple more months, but at what price? I need to have my strength and wits about me. What strength and wits I still have. There are so many things I need to do. I need to finish the Death Warrior Manifesto. I need to get ready. I'm not ready. I need to train you to be a Death Warrior. I need to use what time there is to get both of us ready."

Pancho was going to ask what exactly *he* needed to get ready for, but he didn't. Some of the things D.Q. said were just crazy. They didn't always sound crazy when you first heard them, but they sure seemed crazy when you thought about them. He could tell that it would be impossible to question or argue with every crazy statement he made.

"How long will we be there?" Pancho repeated.

"The initial phase of the treatment lasts two weeks. We'll stay at this outpatient home called Casa Esperanza while that's going on. Then there's a two-week period to recuperate and wait for some initial results."

"A month?"

"My mother wants me to stay with her during the waiting period, after we leave Casa Esperanza. She lives on the outskirts of the city. It's a very nice place. You'll like it."

"I didn't sign up for family drama."

"No, that's true."

They were both quiet. Then, as if embarrassed by what he was about to say, D.Q. spoke. "There's something else about the trip to Albuquerque that I should tell you." He stopped. "The last time I was there, six months ago, I had to spend a few days at Casa Esperanza."

"And . . ."

D.Q. cleared his throat, then he made a smacking sound, as if his lips had stuck together and needed to be separated by force. "There was this girl that worked there. Her name was Marisol. I'm pretty sure she's still there."

Pancho waited for more. Was this information something that in any way concerned him? D.Q. was lost in some kind of memory, but it didn't look like a happy one. Finally, Pancho interrupted. "So?"

D.Q. bent down to scratch his feet. "I wanted to tell you all the reasons for the trip. She's part of the picture, part of the preparations. The scariest part of the trip in many ways."

Pancho thought about it. Why would seeing that girl be the scariest part of the trip? He seemed to be on the verge of understanding when a pecan fell, hit him on the head, and bounced to the ground.

"Look." D.Q. chuckled and pointed at the pecan. "Someone's trying to tell you something."

"And what would that be?"

"Knock, knock. Let's go, Mr. Pancho. Let's go to Albuquerque.'"

CHAPTER 11

"What are you carrying in here, a ton of bricks?" Memo asked D.Q. He was dragging a red duffel bag to the van parked in front of the school. Behind him, Pancho carried his backpack and a suitcase in each hand, his own and D.Q.'s. D.Q. was in his wheelchair waiting for them.

"Careful, my books are in there," D.Q. said. "Put the bag next to where I'm sitting. I may do some reading on the way."

"You'll be too busy yapping to read," Memo predicted.

"Where's the Panda?" D.Q. asked.

"He stopped by the kitchen to pick up some sandwiches that Margarita made for you."

Pancho placed the suitcases in the van. He kept his backpack on. "We taking the wheelchair?" he asked D.Q.

"I guess we better." D.Q. pulled the brake lever and lifted himself out slowly. D.Q. climbed into the front seat while Pancho folded the chair. Memo was making faces as if he was trying not to cry. "I want that room ready by the time I get back," D.Q. told him. "Oh, shit!"

"What happened?" Memo asked.

"I forgot the perico."

"The what?"

"My parrot. I left it on my desk. I wanted to take it with me."

"I'll get it for you," Memo volunteered. He turned around and went inside the building in a run.

"What do you want that thing for?" Pancho asked, settling himself in the middle row of the van. He placed the backpack next to him.

"I don't know. I like it. It'll bring me good luck."

"Yeah, like it did me," Pancho said.

"Aaahhh." D.Q. made a noise that sounded like the bleat of a baby lamb. "That's a whine. Remember the first rule of the Death Warrior Manifesto."

Pancho was about to tell D.Q. where to stick his Death Warrior Manifesto when Father Concha stepped out of the building. He was carrying a large plastic bag in one hand and a black briefcase in the other. "Ready?" he asked.

"Memo's bringing me something I forgot," D.Q. said.

Father Concha put the plastic bag and his briefcase in the seat behind Pancho. In the seven days that he had been at St. Anthony's, Pancho had yet to catch the priest smiling. Father Concha got into the driver's seat, buckled his seat belt, and started the van. Pancho closed his door just as Memo came running out. He handed the wooden parrot to D.Q. "Okay, little penguin," D.Q. said to him. "Get my room ready. Don't let Margarita put any sissy-looking curtains on the windows. I want manly stuff, you understand."

"Yeah, manly stuff. Nothing sissy." The van was beginning to move and Memo and D.Q. were still doing some kind of funny handshake. Memo was wiping his left eye with his shoulder. Then the van accelerated. "See you, Pancho," Memo called.

They were all quiet until they got to I-25 and then D.Q. asked, "You know any good jokes, Father?"

"No," Father Concha said. He was looking in the rearview mirror, determining whether it was safe to switch lanes.

"Pancho, when we're in Albuquerque, we need to have us some adventures. We should do fun things, maybe go out drinking, pick up some girls, live it up a little. I mean, how often will we get a chance to visit the big city?"

Father Concha cast a sideways glance at D.Q. Pancho didn't think the comment required a response. Ever since D.Q. woke him up that morning, he had been jabbering nonsense.

"Oh, I just thought of a joke," D.Q. was now saying. "This couple gets married and they get into an accident just as they leave the church. So they go to heaven and are waiting for St. Peter, and the guy says to his wife, 'You know honey, eternity is a long time to be married, maybe . . .'"

Pancho saw Father Concha reach over and touch D.Q.'s arm. "It's all right, you don't have to say anything," Father Concha said. "It's all going to be all right."

D.Q. exhaled loudly. "It wasn't a good joke anyway."

"We'll go straight to the hospital. As I understand it, they'll keep you there overnight," Father Concha said.

"Is she going to be there?" D.Q. asked.

"Your mother? I told her it wasn't a good idea. She'll want to see you in a day or two, after the initial tests."

"The deal was that I would stay with her during the waiting period. I'll be megablasted with lomustine, vincristine, prednisone, and I don't know what else, kryptonite, and then I'll stay with her for two weeks and that is it. She said she'd sign the papers if I did that. Do you have the papers? Did you bring them?"

"I have them," Father Concha said. He continued, his voice even calmer than usual, "She'll sign them, but not today. She'll want to meet with her lawyer."

"She's had the papers since March. Her lawyer has read them. You don't know her. She's going to make me go through this and then she won't sign the papers. She'll just keep me in that ranch house of hers, pumping me full of chemicals and herbs. You can't let that happen! She needs to sign guardianship over to you *before* I undergo this treatment. I thought that was the deal." D.Q. was breathing heavily. Pancho could see droplets of his spit land on the windshield. He watched Father Concha carefully for any signs that he was getting rattled. There were none.

"You need to be open-minded about the treatment. Concentrate on being positive about it. Give it a chance."

The next time D.Q. spoke, his voice was subdued. "I'm giving it a chance, Father. But I have to think ahead. I don't want my last few months to be wasted. I have to take control here. You want me to have a positive attitude toward these trials, okay. You want me to believe that a miracle is possible? I believe a miracle is possible. But I'm not going to be a fool about it. You understand? You understand me. Say you understand what I'm trying to do here. Say it, please."

"I understand."

D.Q.'s shoulders relaxed, the tension going out of them.

"Remember the time we were coming back from Albuquerque, after the diagnosis was confirmed?"

"Yes."

Pancho closed his eyes. He was glad that D.Q. and Father Concha seemed to have forgotten he was in the back. He was tired. Sleeping had been hard. He kept hearing his sister's voice. At one point during the night, he got up and opened the exit door next to his stall. "Rosa, you out there?" he called out. It was entirely possible that he was losing his mind.

"You said that even if the prognosis was correct and my time was limited, that didn't excuse me from the obligation to fulfill my duties in life. Remember?"

"I remember."

"I thought it was a harsh thing to say. I mean, at first I thought you were talking about my place in the rotation, you know, helping Margarita every two weeks and all."

"I was."

Pancho opened his eyes, but it was too late. He missed the Panda's smile. He closed them again and leaned his head against the window. He didn't want to sleep. He wanted to think. But every time he started to think, a rush of anger drowned his thoughts.

"What if you finally discovered your duty? Wouldn't your primary obligation be to fulfill it?"

"Our primary duty in life is to live."

"But to live how? Like a vegetable? With your head stuck in a toilet day and night, throwing up, so doped up against the pain that all you do is sleep?"

The .22 and bullets were in a plastic bag in his backpack. He could feel the revolver's hardness with his hand. He heard on a television show that if a victim is shot more than once, that means the killer had something personal against him. He didn't have anything personal against the man who killed his sister, unless you considered hatred personal.

"So what is this duty you have discovered?"

"Here, let me read you something. This is from *Walden* by Henry David Thoreau." Pancho heard D.Q. turn the pages in a book.

"You should rest," Father Concha said. "You'll need all your strength for the blood tests and other procedures you'll be going through."

"Here it is. I'll just read this and then I'll rest. Pancho, are you listening? Listen to this."

"Yeah," Pancho said when he heard his name. He didn't know what he was saying "yeah" to.

D.Q. read: "'I went to the woods because I wished to live deliberately, to front only the essential facts of life, and see if I could not learn what it had to teach, and not, when I came to die, discover that I had not lived. I did not wish to live what was not life, living is so dear; nor did I wish to practice resignation, unless it was quite necessary. I wanted to live deep and suck out all the marrow of life. . . .'"

He closed the book and put it back in the bag. D.Q. turned his head to look out the side window. He watched the same gliding hawk that Pancho watched. When the hawk had disappeared from view, D.Q. spoke. "Pancho, are you awake? Were you listening?"

"Yeah," he answered.

"What did you think of that passage, Pancho?" Father Concha asked, his eyes in the rearview mirror zeroing in on him.

"My father and I used to take out the *meollo* from inside the bones with a knife, and then we would spread it like butter on a hot flour tortilla. We'd put salt on it and hot sauce. It was good. Real good. Then we'd suck out whatever was still in the bone until the bone was clean."

Pancho couldn't see Father Concha's face, but he was almost certain he smiled.

"You see, Father," D.Q. said, "*that's* what I'm talking about."

CHAPTER 12

He woke up when the van stopped. They were in the parking lot of the University of New Mexico Children's Hospital. Pancho pushed D.Q. in the wheelchair, walking behind Father Concha. D.Q. carried the canvas bag of books and his suitcase on his lap. Pancho wished he had been awake when they entered the city. He had been to Albuquerque once before with his father and Rosa when he was thirteen, and he wanted to see if he remembered the buildings and sights his father had pointed out to them.

Father Concha filled out forms while D.Q. and Pancho sat in the lobby. "I hope Helen sent in the paperwork," D.Q. said.

"Who's Helen?"

"Helen Quentin-Morse. That would be my mother."

"Who's paying for all this?" Pancho asked. The place seemed expensive.

"Helen put me on her husband's insurance."

"Mmm."

"What?"

"If you cut her off, who's going to pay for your treatment?" Questioning the cost of things had become a habit.

"St. Tony's has a health insurance policy for the kids. Besides, after these clinical trials are over, the treatment isn't going to be that complicated or that expensive."

"You don't seem to think whatever they're going to do here is going to work."

"That's something that we need to talk about. The balance of hope and acceptance is at the heart of what it means to be a Death Warrior. It's an equilibrium that needs to be maintained. We'll go over it in time. Anyway, I mention it now because here is where your training officially starts."

Pancho shifted in his chair. It made him uncomfortable when D.Q. spoke that way, like the religious ladies who came to his trailer and tried to talk to him about the need to get saved.

"Why are you in a kids' hospital?" he asked. "Is it because you're a minor?"

D.Q. chuckled. "The cancer that I have occurs primarily in children. Brain tumors are the second-leading cause of cancer in children, behind leukemia. I guess I'm here because this is where the clinical trial is held. In fact, the stuff they're going to pump into me is more toxic than what they would give a child."

Father Concha was walking toward them, a bigger frown than usual on his face. "That doesn't look good," D.Q. said.

"They're going to admit you," Father Concha said, "but they can't start any treatments until your mother signs the forms."

"She didn't do it." D.Q. sounded as if he expected it.

"We called her. She's on her way."

D.Q. turned his head away. "I don't want to see her."

"You're whining," Pancho said. When D.Q. pierced him with a killer stare, he grinned.

Father Concha smiled for what could have been the third time that day. "Someone's coming to take you to your room. I'm going to go look for Dr. Melendez."

They sat next to each other, D.Q. sulking and Pancho taking it all in. It occurred to him that the only other time he had been in a hospital was when he had gone to identify Rosa's body. They didn't let him in to see his father because his father's face, after his accident, was in no condition to be seen.

They were both looking in the direction Father Concha had gone when a woman appeared before them. She wore a nurse's uniform of cotton pants and a blue blouse with green and yellow smiley faces. Her long black hair was woven in a braid. "Daniel Quentin?" they heard her say without either of them registering the meaning of her words. She looked first at one and then the other. A smile flickered across her face, as if she knew exactly why they were dumbfounded.

Pancho elbowed D.Q. back to life. "Oh, that would be me." D.Q. raised his hand timidly.

"I'm Rebecca," she said. "I'm supposed to take you to your room. Do you need a wheelchair?"

"Sure. I mean no. No, I don't need one." D.Q. used Pancho's thigh to push himself up from the chair. "Can he come too?"

"Absolutely," she said. Pancho grabbed the suitcase and the bag of books. They all took a few slow steps forward at D.Q.'s pace.

"You want to hold on to my arm?" she offered.

"Okay," D.Q. threaded his arm through hers. He looked back and raised his eyebrows meaningfully at Pancho.

"Is this your first time at Children's?" she asked.

"No, I was here once before. Initially. About six months ago. For a week or so, but I don't remember seeing you."

"I just switched to oncology." They were standing in front of the elevator.

"Great. That's great." Pancho could tell that D.Q. was struggling to come up with something else to say. It was almost fun to watch. They stepped into the elevator and began to ascend. Then she turned and fixed her eyes on him. He swallowed hard and quickly looked away. "Are you his brother?" she asked in a friendly way.

"Me?" he heard himself say. He sounded stupid. And then he thought, *How can she possibly think that we're related?* He wondered whether he should feel insulted.

"He's my spiritual brother," D.Q. said. Pancho didn't know how much time had gone by from the moment she asked her question to when D.Q. answered. He felt like an idiot.

"I'm Rebecca," she said again, stretching out her hand to him. He put down the suitcase and shook her hand.

"He's speechless right now on account of being dazzled, but he actually can speak," D.Q. explained. "His name is Pancho."

There was a *ping* and the doors to the elevator opened.

"Pancho," Rebecca repeated, looking at him again and smiling. "That's a nice name."

D.Q. held on to her arm as they stepped out of the elevator. He turned around and stuck out a whitish tongue at Pancho. Pancho might have whacked him in the back of the head had his hands not been occupied.

They walked down the hall past the nurses' station. They could hear a group of voices singing "Happy Birthday" out of one of the rooms. The walls were painted bright reds and blues, pinks, greens, and oranges. Pancho felt like he was inside a tube of LifeSavers. One little bald boy popped out of one of the rooms, pushing a red fire engine and wailing like a siren. He made a wide U-turn in the hall and went back into the room. "That's the playroom," Rebecca explained. They stopped in front of the open door and saw kids absorbed in different activities. One older boy played a game of Tetris on a TV monitor. Two smaller boys were building a LEGO castle. A woman sat on the floor reading to a girl. The girl lifted her head and waved directly at Pancho. "You're a hit already," Rebecca said to him.

"I taught him everything he knows," D.Q. piped up.

They went a little farther down the hall. Rebecca opened the door to the next room. "This is it," she said. "It's next to the play-room, but once you close the door, it's very quiet."

D.Q. let go of her arm. "No, I like it noisy!" he exclaimed. "And look!" He walked up to the window and drew open the orange curtains. "You can see the mountains from here."

"Those are the Sandia Mountains," Rebecca said. "Aren't they beautiful?"

"This is perfect," D.Q. said.

Pancho put the bags down just as Rebecca asked him, "Are you staying in Albuquerque?"

A blush colored his face. "With him," he managed to mumble.

"We'll be staying at Casa Esperanza. Who's my roommate?" D.Q. asked, pointing at an empty bed.

"No one right now," Rebecca said. "You have a single."

"You think Pancho can stay with me while I'm here?"

"I can check," Rebecca answered before Pancho could object. He didn't want to sleep in a hospital. Despite all their efforts to be cheerful, it was still a place for sick people. "The hospital rules say visiting hours are over at eight P.M., but on this floor, it's really up to the shift supervisor. Usually, it's just immediate family that's allowed to stay."

"He's immediate family," D.Q. confirmed. He sat on a green chair in front of his bed.

"Your spiritual brother, right?" Rebecca asked, winking at Pancho.

"Right," D.Q. answered. Pancho stuck his hands in his pants pockets, then he took them out.

"Okay, I'm going to leave you and your spiritual brother alone for a while. You" — she pointed at D.Q. — "need to undress and put this little nightie on."

"Not one of those things with the open back. They're so humiliating!" D.Q. grinned.

"They're not so bad, they're very cool. The fresh air comes right in." She smiled back. Pancho could tell it was something she had said many times before. "I'll be back in about half an hour. The remote control for the TV is over on your night table. You can hang your clothes right in this closet. Okay? Nice to meet you all."

Pancho stepped out of her way. He did not have the courage to look at her as she went past him.

As soon as she left and the door to the room closed, D.Q. moaned, "Ohhh! Ohhh! Ohhh!"

"What is it?"

"Oh, Lord almighty, creator of heaven and earth, she is sooo beautiful! I did not need to see that kind of beauty. I wanted to go through these procedures with some peace of mind, some semblance of serenity, and then to encounter such raw, awesome, unadulterated glory. How can I be at peace now? How can I not be affected by the fiery wings of desire?"

Pancho scratched his head. "Is that the girl you told me about? She seems a little old for you."

D.Q. turned serious. "Marisol? No, we'll see her when we move to Casa Esperanza. Rebecca is frosting. Marisol's effect is on the eyes *and* the soul."

Pancho opened one of the two doors inside the room. It was a bathroom with a toilet and a sink. He filled a glass with cold water and drank its contents in one gulp. Then he wet a hand towel and applied it to the back of his neck. It occurred to him that he had left his backpack with the revolver and Rosa's diary in the van and he wasn't sure whether Father Concha had locked it. Father Concha had taken out his black briefcase, so maybe he didn't think there was a need to lock the van.

D.Q. yelled at him, "What are you doing in there, playing with yourself?"

The kid was a nervous wreck today. Pancho stepped out, the back of his head still wet. "I need to go get my backpack," he told D.Q.

"No, don't go," D.Q. pleaded. "You need to be here when Helen comes. Please."

Pancho went over to the other green chair. He turned it so that he too could look out the window at the mountains and then sat down. "What luck," D.Q. said. "A mountain view. Human beauty, natural beauty, we're surrounded by beauty on all sides. And then there's Helen."

"You need to put on that gown like the lady asked you," Pancho said.

"I don't want to be bare-assed when she comes."

"When who comes? The nurse?"

"No! Helen. Dearest Mother."

"How do you know she's going to come see you? Maybe she just signs the papers and leaves."

"Why do you think she didn't sign the forms before when she could? She needed an excuse to come over."

"You're her son. She wants to see you."

"What she wants is control. She wants to make sure I get the full treatment. In more ways than one."

Pancho shook his head.

"What? Why are you shaking your head like that?"

"I don't understand family squabbling. Family's family, you know? Isn't there something in your Dead Warrior Festo about that?"

"It's Death, not Dead. And it's MA-NI-FES-TO. Not Festo. Dumbo."

"Whatever."

"But you have a good point. I have to reflect on what you just said. But not now. I'm tired. I had no nap to speak of today. I couldn't get the Panda to stop talking." D.Q. tried to smile, but the smile ended abruptly. "Seriously, though, didn't you find her beautiful?"

"Who?"

"Oh, like you didn't even notice. I could hear your heart beat like a lunatic all the way up in the elevator."

"Yeah, sure. I guess."

"You know, I think she liked you. She kept eyeing you, I noticed."

"That fog in your brain is getting thicker."

"You are right about that, my friend." Then he said, looking at the mountains, "Ah, Pancho. Can you imagine what it would be like to touch every inch of her body with your fingertips?"

They were both silent, each one of them lost in his own imaginings.

CHAPTER 13

There was a knock. Before D.Q. could say anything, the door opened and Father Concha stuck his white head in. "You decent?" D.Q. put his baseball cap back on. Father Concha opened the door wide and a thin, tall, elegant woman entered the room. She looked at Pancho and was disconcerted for the fraction of a second that it took her to find D.Q. She wore gold slacks and a pale yellow blouse, and her shoulder-length hair — blond with blonder streaks — lay perfectly in place. She did not fit the mother that Pancho had imagined. For that matter, she did not resemble any mother that Pancho had ever met.

"Hello, Daniel," she said. "How are you?" Whatever had gone on between D.Q. and her did not come through in her tone, but D.Q. remained seated, and she did not make any move to embrace him.

"Dr. Melendez is on his way," Father Concha said. "Your mother signed the hospital forms."

"What about the other forms?" D.Q. asked, looking at Father Concha.

The woman smiled at Father Concha as if she had predicted that D.Q. would ask that question. She turned and fixed her gaze on Pancho. "You must be Pancho," she said. Her piercing green eyes made him feel like an uninvited guest.

He stood. "That's me," he said.

"I'm Helen, Daniel's mother," she responded. She did not move her hand, so he didn't offer his. She looked at D.Q. again. "Are you comfortable here?" she asked D.Q. "It's close to the playroom. It may be noisy. I can talk to the hospital administrator about moving you."

"I like it noisy," D.Q. said. "The noisier the better."

Pancho saw her tilt her head. She seemed to be surprised by the hostility in D.Q.'s voice. "Well, as long as you're comfortable. I made sure you had a single room."

"It wasn't necessary," D.Q. said. "I'm only going to be here one night. Then we're moving to Casa Esperanza."

Helen and Father Concha glanced at each other. D.Q. did not notice the glance. "I would feel better if you stayed here."

D.Q. stared at her. The woman stood her ground. Pancho thought he would not like to get in the ring with her.

"Let's take it a day at a time and see how you feel," the Panda said. "If you don't feel well from the treatments, it may be easier for you to be here. It's an option to consider."

"Can you check to see if Pancho can stay with me tonight?" D.Q. asked Father Concha.

Father Concha and Helen looked at Pancho. Pancho nodded to both of them. "It's okay with me," he said.

"I'll go check." Father Concha seemed happy to have something to do.

"May I?" Helen pointed at the green chair Pancho had just vacated. Pancho moved out of the way and headed for the door.

"Don't go," D.Q. pleaded.

"I'm going to get my things."

"Later, please."

Helen sat down. Pancho stood between D.Q. and his mother, not knowing where to go. He went over to the empty bed, jumped up and let his feet dangle. Helen crossed her legs. D.Q. was looking away from her, his eyes fixed on the distant mountains. There was a remote control on the table next to Pancho's bed. Pancho grabbed it and turned on the television. He pushed down the volume until it was barely audible, then propped the pillow against the backboard and leaned back to watch the screen. It was a daytime soap opera. He couldn't hear the dialogue, but it was a relief to have something to look at, like having a cereal box to read during breakfast.

"I really need you to sign the guardianship papers," D.Q. said calmly.

Helen glanced quickly toward Pancho. He pretended to be absorbed in the soap opera. She spoke softly but firmly. "I understand that's what you want."

"It was what we agreed on."

"We agreed that you would be in Albuquerque for a month."

"And I am here and will be here for a month. But sign the papers now." His voice rose up a notch.

"If I sign the papers, who's to say that Father Concha won't yank you out of the clinical trial before it's over, or even before it begins? You agreed to give me a chance to help you and do what I think is best for you, the way a mother would do in a normal family situation."

"A normal family situation?" D.Q. asked sarcastically.

"Daniel, we need to concentrate on your healing. We need to direct all our energies to you getting well." She took her hands from her lap and placed them on the armrests of the chair. There was a long pause when she seemed to be waiting for D.Q. to say something. Pancho quietly began to surf the channels. He stopped when he saw a Tom and Jerry cartoon. "It is not helpful to dwell on the past," she said.

"I have an idea," D.Q. said, perking up. "What if you sign the papers and we leave them with a disinterested party? At the end of the month, that person gives the papers to Father Concha. That would address your lack of trust in Father Concha, wouldn't it? Although it's hard for me to understand how you trusted him enough to leave me with him seven years ago, and you can't trust him to keep his word for a month now."

"Daniel . . ."

There was a knock on the door. A tall, distinguished-looking man with black hair entered the room. "Hello, Helen," he said immediately upon entering. "Good to see you again." He nodded at Pancho, then turned to D.Q. "Daniel, I'm Dr. Melendez." He walked over to the window, dragged a chair to where D.Q. was sitting, and sat down. "How are you feeling?"

"Just great," D.Q. said.

"Good," Dr. Melendez responded. "That's the kind of fighting spirit we want from you."

Pancho got off the bed. This seemed like a good time to escape. He was embarrassed to be in the room.

"Don't go," D.Q. said.

Dr. Melendez and Helen both looked at Pancho. Pancho froze in mid-step. He sat back down on the bed.

Dr. Melendez leaned forward. "I want to go over what we are going to do today and tomorrow. You should know that we are very familiar with your case. I got your records from your doctor in Las Cruces, and I understand fully the treatment you've been receiving to date. Here at Children's, we have had some success using a combination of drugs to supplement the radiation therapy. In the next day or so, we hope to get a fix on the program we'll use as well as the optimum dosages. Any questions so far?"

D.Q. grinned as if he could see through the doctor's cheery facade. Pancho thought he looked like a cornered boxer. There was no way he would be able to overcome the energy and willpower of the people in front of him.

Dr. Melendez continued, "There will be some side effects beyond those you have experienced from the radiation. But here again, we've made some strides with medication to counteract negative side effects." He waited for D.Q. to ask questions. There were none forthcoming. "Well, we should get started as soon as possible."

"How long does the treatment last?" D.Q. asked.

Dr. Melendez looked at D.Q. as if he didn't understand the question. "How long?"

"The clinical trial. How long does it last?"

Pancho could see confusion in the doctor's face. He turned toward Helen for help. "The usual protocol is three months. Two weeks of treatment with two weeks off. Then after that, it is continuous as needed."

"Where is Father Concha?" D.Q. asked nervously. "He needs to be here."

"I'll go get him," Pancho said.

"No, stay here," D.Q. said, full of urgency. "What do you mean, 'continuous'? I was told it lasted two weeks."

"That's correct," the doctor said. "The first phase is a high-intensity phase that lasts two weeks."

"And then?"

"We let you rest for a couple of weeks, we evaluate the effects on the cancer if we can, if the effects are detectable, we see how your immune system is holding up, we make adjustments to the treatment as necessary, and we continue for two more weeks."

"But only if the treatment is effective. I understood that at the end of a month, you would be able to see if the treatment is working."

"I thought —" Dr. Melendez began to say to Helen.

She nodded. "Daniel, at the end of the month, we will see where we are. That's a fair statement to make, isn't it, Martin?"

"Martin?" D.Q. asked.

"Stu is Dr. Melendez's lawyer."

"Oh, man." D.Q. placed his hands over his eyes.

Dr. Melendez reached out to touch D.Q.'s shoulder. D.Q. leaned out of his reach. "Should we proceed with today's schedule?"

Pancho wasn't sure to whom this question was directed. He wondered whether Father Concha had stayed away on purpose.

"We'll be okay," Helen said.

"Good. I'll get things ready." Dr. Melendez left the room without looking at D.Q. or Pancho.

Helen stood up and went over to D.Q., whose face was still hidden. "Daniel, I know you don't trust me. I am not even sure I deserve your trust. But I'm going to say this anyway. In return for your willing cooperation in this clinical trial, I promise you that at the end of the month, if there are no hopeful signs, if there is no measurable improvement, I will turn guardianship over to Father Concha."

D.Q. dropped his hands and slumped down in the chair. He looked like all the fight had been sucked out of him. "What is 'hopeful'? What is 'measurable improvement'? What is this success that your doctor keeps mentioning? Is it a permanent cure? Not that I have any legal choice, as you know, but I agreed to turn myself over to you and your clinical trial for one month. I did it because I wanted to make sure I could say to my own conscience that I tried everything there was to try. The agreement was, you'd either grant guardianship to Father Concha or sign emancipation papers in return for one month: two weeks of chemo and two weeks of recuperation with you. Not for one month provided this or provided that. If at the end of one month, a cure or an extension of life with some kind of quality seems possible, then Father Concha will make the call as to future treatment. That's what I was led to believe would happen here. I kept my end of the bargain. I am here. We gave you the emancipation and the legal guardianship forms to sign and you did not do it." He closed his eyes for a moment and then he straightened himself up in the chair. "But don't worry. I'm going to go through the 'initial phase,' as the good doctor calls it."

"All right," she said. She seemed like she wanted to say more or like she hoped D.Q. would say something else to her.

"Helen," D.Q. said, "would you mind leaving us? I need to undress."

"No, certainly not. I'll leave you now. Good-bye." She turned toward Pancho. "Nice to meet you."

Pancho nodded.

Just as she opened the door to leave, D.Q. said, "Helen, I think it would be better if we didn't see each other. It's too distracting. I need to focus on the healing process, as you say."

The fair skin on her face turned red, from hurt or anger, Pancho didn't know. "You are still coming to stay with us after the initial treatment session."

"Yeah, that was the deal. Good-bye, Helen."

CHAPTER 14

Pancho and Father Concha walked side by side toward the van. D.Q. had been wheeled out on a stretcher to start the medical procedures. Father Concha had obtained permission for Pancho to stay with D.Q.

"Have you ever been in a hospital before?" Father Concha asked.

"No." He didn't think identifying his sister's body was what Father Concha meant by "being in a hospital."

They passed by a children's playground. Plastic horses of various colors were stuck on thick springs. People had gone to a lot of trouble to make this hospital *not* look like a hospital.

"What's going to happen to D.Q.?" Pancho was just trying to get a clearer picture of when and how he could carry out his plan.

Father Concha slowed down as if he didn't want to rush an answer. "Are you asking whether the clinical trials have any chance of succeeding?"

"No."

"No?"

"What will happen to him after the treatments? Where's he going to end up?"

"Ahh. Where's he going to end up?" Father Concha slowed down even more. The harder the question, the slower he needed to walk.

"It doesn't look like his mother will let him go."

"No, it doesn't look that way." Father Concha stopped walking. They were on a sidewalk leading to the parking lot. People in back of them began to go around them. There was a concrete bench a few feet ahead, the kind where people sat while waiting for a bus. Father Concha walked toward it and sat down. Pancho waited a moment and then sat next to him. He thought Father Concha was going to continue speaking, but he had turned silent. Pancho wanted to ask why the mother had left D.Q. at St. Anthony's, but the question could be taken to mean that he was willing to get involved in D.Q.'s life, and he was already in deeper than he cared to be.

"It is not easy to get involved with someone in D.Q.'s situation," Father Concha said.

"You mean someone who's dying."

"I would say someone who is trying very hard to live purposefully."

"Sucking out all the *meollo* from the bone."

"*Así es*," said Father Concha. It was the first time Pancho had heard him speak Spanish. He hoped that was all he was going to say in Spanish because his Spanish was not all that great.

"I'm not getting involved." It came out as a warning, which was fine with him.

Father Concha did not respond. He stretched out his legs. Pancho noticed that the priest's socks did not match: The left sock was blue and the right sock was black. The black loafers were worn out and needed polishing. Father Concha joined his hands across his stomach, like someone about to take a nap. Pancho saw him close his eyes. Just when he thought the priest had fallen instantly asleep, he heard him say, "How long were you thinking of staying with us?"

Pancho looked at him quickly, surprised. Father Concha's eyes were closed. It was possible that D.Q. had said something to him, but what? All that D.Q. knew or had guessed was that Pancho had his own reasons to come to Albuquerque. He had to stop thinking that everyone knew exactly what he was up to.

"How long do you want me to stay?" Lying and pretending required an energy he preferred not to waste.

Father Concha nodded. He seemed grateful for the honest answer. "If you could stay with him while the treatment lasts, that would be good."

"Until he goes to his mother's."

"He's going to need you more than ever when he's with her."

"Need me for what? What am I supposed to be doing other than pushing him around? I don't get it."

Father Concha pulled his legs in and sat back on the bench. His voice was even-tempered. "You don't get it?"

"No. I don't know why he needs me. If he wants moral support or whatever, he's looking in the wrong place."

"I don't think so."

"Is that what he's looking for? What does he want from me?"

Father Concha stuck both hands under his armpits and

lowered his chin. He twitched his nose and mouth like someone about to sneeze. "What do you think about death?"

Pancho jerked his head back like someone had hit him with an invisible jab. "Death? It happens. People die all the time. It doesn't bother me anymore."

"It doesn't scare you?"

"Hell no! Why would it?" He thought suddenly of the revolver in his backpack. Then he thought of his sister. The idea of death filled him with anger, hatred, a suffocating urgency, remorse even, but there was no fear anywhere. Then he realized: *Maybe that's what D.Q. wants*. When he turned, he saw a mysterious grin on Father Concha's face.

Father Concha took a wallet from his back pocket. He opened it and lifted out all the bills inside. Pancho could see they were all twenties. "It's three hundred dollars," Father Concha said, handing him the money. "One hundred for you, and the rest to spend with D.Q. Do some fun things when he is up to it. There are many interesting places to see in and around Albuquerque." Pancho held the money in his outstretched hand as if it were contaminated. "You are owed more, I know. You will be paid for your time as agreed. It's all I could get right now."

Pancho lowered his hand. Putting the money in his pocket right then somehow felt inappropriate. He tried again to calculate how much he would be owed by the end of the month at thirty dollars a day, but he quickly gave that up. Whatever the amount, it would not be enough. He had not given much thought to what he would do after he found Bobby. He had an image of getting on a bus and going to Mexico. But he knew it was unrealistic to think that he would survive in Mexico. People came from Mexico to the

United States looking for jobs, not the other way around. It didn't really matter what happened afterward. He would go someplace and try to survive. The point in time where he met Bobby face-to-face — that was all of the future he allowed himself to contemplate.

"You shouldn't have many expenses. Everything has been taken care of at Casa Esperanza. If you need anything else, you can call this number." Father Concha took a card out of his wallet. Pancho read it.

"He won't want anything from his mother."

"I'm giving you her phone number in case *you* need to get in touch with her."

"Must be an Anglo thing," Pancho said, finally stuffing the money and the card in the side pocket of his pants.

"The wrangling between mother and son?"

"Yeah. It's weird."

"It's something that's hard for you to imagine, isn't it?"

"She must have really screwed him for him not to want anything to do with her. She seems like an all-right lady." He tried to recollect the image of his own mother, but all his memory could come up with was a faded photograph of a woman in a wedding dress, holding a bouquet of daisies.

"She is a mother, and her perspective toward his treatment is that of a mother who does not want to lose her son. You can understand that, can't you?"

Pancho shook his head. He understood where she was coming from all right. What he couldn't understand was how a parent and child could get separated in the first place.

Father Concha said, as if trying to fill in the gaps of Pancho's understanding, "Seven years ago, when she brought Daniel to St. Anthony's, it was only supposed to be for a summer. We don't take kids that young, normally. But Helen was an old friend and I made an exception. She was in a bad state of mind. Her husband had just died and she was suffering from a mental illness. Then the summer turned into a year, and a year into two, and things slowly began to turn around for her — marriage and a successful career as an artist. She visited Daniel frequently as soon as she was able. When Daniel was fourteen, she wanted to take him with her, but he refused to the point of becoming ill. I don't know how to describe it. He did not like the rich, comfortable life his mother offered him in Albuquerque. He was happy at St. Anthony's. He was thriving there, doing well in school. We forced him to spend holidays with her and her new husband, but he always wanted to come back. She had every right to make him stay with her, but she sacrificed her wishes for his happiness.

"Then came the diagnosis of cancer six months ago. It is different now. He is her responsibility. She sees it as her duty as a mother to make sure he gets the best treatment available. She has too much at stake not to fight for him. And . . . she has fought internal battles of her own and won. She knows how important it is to want to live, to have the right attitude. She honestly wants to give this hope to Daniel. She believes that his best chances of survival are with her."

"She thinks he can make it?"

"She believes it with all her heart and soul."

Pancho paused to think. All that he knew about D.Q.'s illness had come from D.Q. Maybe the kid was overly pessimistic. He himself knew the results of going into the ring believing you could win versus the self-fulfilling effects of thinking you were going to get beat. What did he know about D.Q.'s illness? But then again, why should he care? He decided to ask the question anyway. "Does he have a chance? Do you think he can make it?"

Father Concha twitched his nose again. "I believe that with God, everything is possible."

Pancho narrowed his eyes. It was the kind of answer that said nothing.

Father Concha read the dissatisfaction on Pancho's face. "We need to believe that it is possible . . . even if the statistics of the disease indicate that it is not likely." Pancho looked away from his intense gaze. After a few moments, he felt Father Concha touch his forearm. The touch remained until he turned to face him. "He needs *you*. He needs a friend like *you*. Wherever it is you are thinking of going, it will still be there in a few months. Think about it."

Pancho grimaced. He could almost feel heavy iron chains begin to coil around his feet. He jumped up from the bench. "I need to get my stuff," he said.

"Wait one more second. You said that it didn't look like his mother will let Daniel go after the treatments are over. Daniel is seventeen, like you. His birthday was last month, like yours. He's not a child anymore. He's still a minor, but more and more hospitals and judges are taking into account the determination of young people with regard to their medical treatment, especially with end-of-life decisions. I don't know how to say this. I'll try. I believe in what Helen is doing now, but it could be that a month from now, I won't. A month from now, I might be more inclined to let Daniel determine what is best for him. I promised him that. If she doesn't let him go, I will support whatever you two decide."

Pancho didn't know how to respond. Why would he have anything to do with any decision involving D.Q.? He wasn't even sure he understood everything that had been said to him. It didn't matter. He wasn't planning on being around a month from then.

CHAPTER 15

Behind the hospital, by the emergency generators, in a place that looked like no one had ever set foot there, he dug a hole through the crusted earth and buried the plastic bag with the revolver and the bullets. Then he grabbed his backpack and headed to the cafeteria. He had a couple of hours to himself while D.Q. was being examined. He wanted to read his sister's diary, the parts he hadn't already read.

He found an empty table in the corner of the cafeteria. He was digging in the backpack for the diary when he heard a voice.

"Hello there."

The voice came from behind him. He leaned back and craned his neck until he saw D.Q.'s mother, her smiling face hovering above him like a sun. He tried to get up, but she placed a hand on his shoulder and pushed him down gently. She asked with a motion of her eyes and hand if she could sit down. He nodded and slid the backpack under his chair.

She had a tray with two white mugs of coffee. She took one of the mugs and placed it in front of him. "I saw you back here and thought you could use a cup of coffee. You strike me as a coffee drinker."

Pancho nodded his thanks, then raised the mug to his lips and slurped the coffee. She had come upon him unexpectedly and he needed time to observe, to figure out the kind of punches she was likely to throw.

"Do you take cream?"

"No," he said.

"Have you been to Albuquerque before?"

"Once."

She took a sip from her coffee, keeping her eyes on him as she did so. "Daniel wanted you to come to Albuquerque with him."

"I had a choice. I think." He didn't say this to make her smile, but she did. Her eyes were a pale green, as if time and troubles had diminished their original brightness.

"My son must think very highly of you if he wanted you to be with him."

"He doesn't know me." He didn't need anyone's admiration. Nor did he feel like fooling anyone into thinking he was something he was not. "I've been at St. Anthony's all of one week."

She shrugged her shoulders. "That wouldn't prevent Daniel from wanting you to be with him. By now he knows all he needs to know about you, I'm sure."

"Oh yeah?" He let a smirk form on his face. It occurred to him that maybe he would rob the lady blind once they moved into her house. That would show her how well her son knew him.

"When Daniel was nine, I used to catch him staring at a mirror, just standing there for ten, fifteen minutes without moving, without even blinking. I used to watch him from a distance. It wasn't some kind of precocious vanity on his part. It was as if he were trying to figure out the identity of the person in the mirror."

Pancho remembered the boxers at the gym practicing their moves in front of the wall-length mirrors. He would watch where they kept their eyes. The good boxers looked at the motion of their hands and feet as if they were someone else's hands and feet. The bad ones couldn't keep their eyes away from their faces, trying on different menacing looks, eating themselves up. He understood what D.Q.'s mother was trying to say. A mirror, if used properly, was a tool.

She pressed on, animated now, like she had finally found someone who would let her brag about her son. "And he keeps a journal, you know. I still have some of the early ones. There's no explanation for where he got the ideas and images for what he wrote. There was one entry that floored me when I read it. He wrote that the reason God created the world was because He was lonely. He wanted others to love Him, but He didn't want to force them into it. So in order to make sure that there were souls that chose to love Him, He made the world such that He was kind of hidden. Then He put people on earth and gave them some clues about how to find Him. That way, some could choose to look for Him and some could ignore Him. And He could be sure that those who persisted in looking for Him truly loved Him." She shook her head in disbelief and waited for Pancho to respond. "This was written by a nine-year-old," she added, clearly hoping for some kind of reaction.

Pancho stared at her. He noticed tiny creases around her eyes. He remembered what Father Concha had said about her and he wondered what kind of mental illness she had. There was something on the edge of crazy in the way she spoke. She and her son had that in common.

He pushed the coffee mug away from him with his index finger. It had been a day with way too many heavy conversations, the kind where you had to pay attention in order to understand. He wanted to go back to the hospital room, lie on the extra bed, and watch television. He glanced in her direction to see if she had finished talking. It didn't look that way. She was staring at the wall in front of her, deep in thought. She was a striking woman, elegant, refined. The kind of woman who made you want to be polite. His father called that type of woman "a Country Club Lady." "We gonna be doing an addition for a Country Club Lady today, so mind your pleases and thank-yous." That's what his father used to tell him. Then he remembered the Country Club Lady who refused to pay them because she did not like the location of a skylight, even though Pancho himself had seen her pick the spot where she wanted it. "I'm not giving you one dime," she had said to his father when he handed her the invoice for the work. "You're lucky I'm not getting my husband to sue you for a new roof plus emotional suffering." The memory triggered a current of prickly energy in his arms. He clenched his fist and waited for the impulse to disappear.

She was speaking again. "What do you think makes a young boy have those kind of thoughts?"

"I don't know," he said, annoyed, still feeling anger from the memory.

She continued, appearing not to notice his tone of voice. "Daniel's father died when Daniel was nine. One day soon after,

I was with Daniel in our little apartment and I felt like I was going crazy. I guess I had a few drinks. I put him in the car and we just took off. My head was exploding. It's hard to explain. Anyway, I crashed the car against a tree. I think it was an accident. I'm not sure to this day whether it was an accident or whether some craziness inside me made me swerve. I broke a collarbone. Daniel struck his head on the dashboard. Later they told me that his heart actually stopped in the ambulance on the way to the hospital, but the paramedics revived him. He was in a coma for a week."

She swallowed, and her eyes reddened. Then she continued, "Daniel was never really the same after that. It's like he saw things while he was in that coma. It was after the accident that he started writing in the journal, spending long periods of time staring at trees or at the stars. As if he was seeing things for the first time and everything was unbelievably beautiful. Maybe it was the accident that made Daniel so unique. Maybe that's why he perceives the world so differently from other boys his age. Of course, being stuck with a mother like me probably had something to do with it also. Not long after that, I was diagnosed with bipolar disorder. I had to check myself into an institution. Do you know much about bipolar disorder?"

"No." *And I don't want to know,* he said to himself. He pushed his chair back to signal that he wanted to leave. There was an intense look on her face that reminded Pancho of D.Q., only the mother's intensity was different, more complicated. It was tinged with fear and hostility.

"A mother with bipolar disorder is not the best of mothers. The day I crashed, I was having a manic episode, I'm sure of it now. It became clear to me that the best thing for Daniel was to be away from me. That's when I remembered Father Concha, my classmate from high school."

It occurred to him that D.Q.'s mother wasn't just making conversation. She wanted something from him. Father Concha not too long before had asked him to be D.Q.'s friend, as if he could choose to be someone's friend just like that. But D.Q.'s mother was not asking something for D.Q.; she wanted something for herself. He didn't have to be polite to Country Club Ladies anymore. He decided to go ahead and ask.

"Is there something you want?"

She bent down to her purse on the floor next to the chair. It was a soft white leather purse with a shoulder strap and a clasp that reminded Pancho of the buttons on D.Q.'s cowboy shirt. She opened it, and for a moment, Pancho thought she was going to offer him money, perhaps to disappear out of D.Q.'s life. Maybe she saw him as an obstacle to her designs to keep D.Q. in Albuquerque. The idea made him chuckle.

She laughed, a knowing kind of laugh. "Sorry, I have to get a tissue."

Mind your pleases and thank-yous, his father had warned. But his father had been too kind. People took advantage of him. Even after the Country Club Lady with the skylight had threatened to sue him, his father had simply said, "I'll leave the invoice here and trust you to do what is right. Thank you." Then he calmly walked away. Pancho had stood next to his father then, feeling enough humiliation for the both of them, imagining what it would be like to bludgeon the Country Club Lady's skull with his brand-new hammer. When they were in the truck, he said, "She's lying. She told us exactly where she wanted the skylight and that's where we put it." "I know," his father responded. "If I make a stink, it will be worse." "No, it won't. If you make a stink, they won't do it again."

His father turned toward him. "It doesn't work that way with people like her. If we make a stink, she'll make sure I don't get any more work. That's all right. You run into people like that now and then. It's part of the job. It's not worth getting all aggravated about it. Besides, you reap what you sow. She sowed nastiness, she'll reap nastiness. We sowed kindness, we'll reap kindness." Only it turned out that his father was wrong, dead wrong. Kindness had gotten both his father and his sister first taken advantage of and then killed.

He saw her wad the tissue in her hand and then speak. "I just want him to live. I don't want him to give up. I want him to believe that he can beat the cancer. That's what I want."

"I meant what do you want from me?"

"I know Daniel well enough that if he wants you with him, it's because he trusts you. You must be the kind of person that he feels comfortable being around. I can see why. I can see you are very much like him. You're solid, just like Daniel."

Fat chance, he thought. He and D.Q. were different species, not even from the same planet. But he decided not to correct her. To do so would involve more words, and he was sick of words.

"We, my husband and I, live a very comfortable life. We have ample means, and all of them are at Daniel's disposal. My husband is a lawyer, and he's convinced I'm within my rights as a mother. If there were a better treatment being offered someplace else in the States or in the world, we'd fly Daniel there. No expense would be too great. And it's not just Western medicine. I know a sacred healer who healed me. I think he can help Daniel as well. We all need to be working as a team to fight this terrible thing. We must stop at nothing."

He watched her become more agitated as she spoke. What she was talking about, she obviously firmly believed, and no one was going to convince her otherwise. What he couldn't understand was whether she was asking for his help or warning him to stay out of her way.

"I'm sorry," she said. "As you can see, it's hard for me to be dispassionate about this. I know Daniel believes that I'm doing all this out of some kind of guilt for having left him at St. Anthony's." She looked at Pancho as if asking whether he thought that as well. He didn't flinch. "Maybe there's some of that. But you know what? Who cares? Who cares what my motives are? Leaving no stone unturned is still what is best for Daniel. All his talk about preparations and getting his own room to die in, I know about all that, and it is wrong. I don't believe in it. It is no good. It is a slow form of suicide!"

He saw her face turn red and watched her pound the table with her fist. It wasn't a hard pound, but it was enough for him to see that there was anger in her. The red blush of her face slowly disappeared as he waited for her to speak again. He made an effort not to smile. He enjoyed watching her get angry.

"Well, I'm sure you didn't expect to hear all this today. You must be tired too."

He made a gesture with his hands that said, *What difference does that make?*

She smiled at him appreciatively, maybe for listening to her.

Then she looked at a small watch, glittering with diamonds, on her left wrist. "I have to go meet Dr. Melendez. He said he would have some initial information about Daniel and the treatment." She placed the white purse in her lap and grabbed the shoulder strap with both hands. Her eyes rested gently on him. "I don't know you other than the little that Father Concha told me. I know you're all alone. You are welcome here too. You'll be welcome at our home when you and Daniel come. You'll be welcome for as long as you want. Everything we have is at your disposal as well. You asked me a little while ago what I wanted from you. I want you on my side. I want you to help me help Daniel. I want you and Daniel to stay with me here in Albuquerque for as long as it takes or go wherever we need to go to fight this disease with all we've got. You like honest talk. I can tell you do. Well, there it is."

He nodded. He preferred "no talk," but "honest talk" wasn't bad.

"Does that nod mean you agree to help?"

"I'm just here for the ride," he said.

"So you didn't choose to come. You're here. Why pass up the opportunity that has fallen in your lap? Think carefully about it. *Tú comprendes* what I'm saying?"

"Yeah," he said to her. "I understand what you're saying."

CHAPTER 16

After D.Q.'s mother left, he walked out of the cafeteria, took the elevator to the ground floor, and stepped out of the hospital. It was no longer the right time to read Rosa's diary. Maybe tomorrow. He hung the backpack on his shoulder and began to walk. He took a right on Lomas Avenue and sped up, with no intention of going anywhere in particular. He was walking to rid his mind of all the words that D.Q.'s mother had flung at him, which made him feel like the inside of his head needed a good cleaning.

He walked for an hour and then stopped at a place called MaxDonald's. It was a restaurant in a small, half-empty, dilapidated strip mall. The mall had a convenience store, a video store, and a place that sold insurance. The front window of the restaurant advertised in sloppy white letters the best jalapeño burgers in Albuquerque.

Pancho opened the door and paused. Rather than a restaurant, the place looked like a kitchen with a counter and a few tables. A fat man sitting on one of the stools at the counter turned and looked at him as he came in. Two couples around one of the tables stopped talking. He went to the table closest to the counter and sat down. A woman came from around the counter with a glass of water. She pulled a menu from her apron and gave it to him. He didn't open it. He told her he wanted a jalapeño burger and a Coke.

"You wanna get the plate or just the regular burger?"

"It doesn't matter what you put it on," he said. Someone near him laughed.

"Ha-ha, that's very funny. The plate comes with Max Country Fries and a large soda. It's a better deal than if you just get the burger and Coke."

"All right," he said. He looked around to see who had laughed. The fat man at the counter was eyeing him, a smirk on his face. Pancho waited until the man went back to his hamburger and then sized him up. The man was around twenty-five and had a haircut that had started out as a Mohawk. He had a thick football player's neck and arms that had at one point lifted weights, but the rest of his body had gone soft with too much grease and beer. The man's biceps bore a tattoo shaped like a crown of thorns. There were huge drops of sweat on his face. Pancho looked up and saw an air-conditioning unit high on the wall. It was rattling and a yellow ribbon tied to it was fluttering, but the air coming out of it was as warm as the air outside.

He took the three hundred dollars that Father Concha had given him and fanned the bills in front of him like a deck of cards. He held them like that until he was sure the fat man had seen the denominations on the bills. Then he took out his wallet and placed the bills inside. He folded his hands and waited. On the wall opposite the air conditioner that didn't work, there was a Coors beer clock shaped like a waterfall spouting out of some rocks. He wondered what time it would be before he got back to the hospital. He wondered if he even had to go back. Why not find a place to stay, track down Bobby tomorrow, and get the whole thing over with once and for all? *Why pass up the opportunity that has fallen in your lap?* D.Q.'s mother had asked. He smiled to himself. He tried to remember if an opportunity had ever fallen into his lap before, but nothing came to mind.

The waitress brought him an oval plate with a jalapeño burger and the Max Country Fries, which were nothing but regular fries in the shape of a pig's tail. He took a bite out of the jalapeño burger. The fat man had finished eating and ordered another beer. He was taking slow swigs from the bottle and looking in Pancho's direction as if he were waiting for him to finish eating. As soon as Pancho pushed his plate away, the man grabbed the beer bottle by the neck and waddled over to his table.

"Mind if I join you?" the man said. He pulled out a chair and sat down before Pancho could answer. The couples got up to leave. Pancho and the man were the only customers. The waitress was yelling into a cell phone. "You're not from around here, are you?" The fat man looked down at Pancho's backpack.

"Nope," Pancho said.

"I didn't think so. Not too many Mexicans come in here."

Pancho looked around. There was country-western music on the jukebox and no Mexican-looking people in the place. "I saw the sign for the jalapeño burgers. I thought it might be okay."

The man nodded. "You visiting here?"

"Yeah," Pancho said, smiling. "I'm visiting." He knew what was going to happen before the evening was over, and he was going to enjoy it as much as possible until then.

"Listen, you want a beer or something? I can get you a beer if you want."

"Thanks, man. I don't drink." He tried not to sound rude.

"You don't drink? I never met a kid your age that don't drink. You're bullshitting me, right?"

"No."

The man lifted the beer bottle as if to toast to Pancho's health and then he tilted his head back and drank the rest of it. He shook the empty bottle in the direction of the waitress. "What do you do for fun? You smoke weed? You must do something for kicks."

The waitress came over with another beer. She looked at Pancho's plate. "You didn't like the food?"

"I wasn't hungry," he responded without looking at her.

"Hey, bring this guy a beer. Put it on my tab."

"He ain't twenty-one," she told the fat man.

"Put it in one of them dark glasses and don't make any foam when you pour it." The man winked at the waitress. She made a face like she didn't like the idea and went away. The man looked around as if to make sure no one was listening and then leaned across the table. "Let me give you a little piece of advice." He lowered his voice to a whisper. "You shouldn't flash your money like you did when you first came in. You never know, you know what I'm saying?"

"Yeah, you're right. You never know who's watching." Pancho tried to make it a joke, but it went over the man's head. All day long he had been struggling to understand what people were trying to tell him. It was a relief to finally know exactly what was going on.

"That's right, man. There's some bad elements here in Albuquerque."

"Whereabouts?"

The man stopped with the beer halfway to his mouth. "What?"

"Whereabouts are the bad elements?" Pancho asked.

The waitress came and put a big plastic cup in front of him. He looked into it and saw the foamless beer.

"Drink up," the man said, pointing at the plastic cup with his chin.

"Thanks, I don't drink."

The man's eyes narrowed. The grin froze and then the lips tightened. *There*, Pancho thought, *there's the hate.* "I'll pay for it. And I'll buy you another one," Pancho added.

"It's not polite to turn a person down when they buy you a beer. Around here, that's an insult."

"I don't mean any insult," Pancho said. "I don't drink, that's all."

"Why the fuck not?" Droplets of spit landed on Pancho. He took a napkin from a dispenser on the side of the table and wiped his face. It came to him that this man might kill him before the evening was over. They would go outside and the man would want his money, and maybe the man had a gun tucked in his pants, or maybe the man would overpower him and strangle him before he had a chance to land a punch. He was amazed at how all right he was with any of those scenarios. It made him feel almost friendly toward the man, like here was someone he could talk to at last.

120

Pancho moved the beer to one side and put both of his elbows on the table. "There was this Anglo guy, his name was Jeff. He worked with my father at the Sears Auto Center back in Las Cruces. My dad was in charge of batteries and he changed the oil on cars and he patched flat tires. There was no one who could patch a flat or change a battery faster than my father. But he didn't do any heavy-duty mechanic stuff. The guy Jeff did that." The waitress had left behind his Coke and he took a sip. "My name is Pancho." He stretched out his hand. "What's yours?"

The man looked at the outstretched hand with suspicion. "They call me Billy Tenn," he said, floating a fat hand toward Pancho, "'cause I'm a hillbilly from Tennessee."

"Billy Tenn. Nice to meet you." He sat back. The man seemed like he was anxious to hear the rest of the story. "This guy Jeff who used to work with my dad. He was an alcoholic. He wouldn't like show up drunk at work, but he'd keep vodka in a big water bottle and he'd go through one of those every day, just sipping little sips all day long. My dad found out and talked to him about it, but this guy Jeff, he had five kids, the oldest one was maybe ten, and my father didn't want to tell the supervisor about the guy's drinking problem because then the guy would lose his job." Billy Tenn leaned to the side of the chair and spit. He wiped his mouth with the back of his hand. Pancho stopped talking.

"Go on, I'm listening," Billy Tenn said, still clearing his throat.

"My dad used to come home and tell me about this guy Jeff. Every day the guy would make mistakes, and my dad had to cover up for him. He would forget to tighten bolts on tires or he'd be doing a safety inspection and forget to inspect the brakes. He would have gotten fired except that my dad would constantly check up on him. My dad was doing two jobs really. Those little sips of vodka made the guy more and more careless every day."

"You guys want anything else?" The waitress was standing beside them. She looked at the untouched glass of beer.

"How much do I owe you?" Pancho asked. "I'll pay for him too."

She took out a pad from the front of her apron and then fished around her ear for a pencil. She didn't find a pencil, so she flipped the tiny pages from the pad and appeared to add the whole sum in her head. "Nineteen dollars even," she said. "He had two beers before you got here."

Pancho took out his wallet and gave her a twenty. "You want change?" she asked.

"Sure."

She didn't seem happy with this answer but slapped a one on the table. Billy Tenn's eyes were glued on Pancho's wallet. Pancho held the wallet in his hands a few moments before putting it back in his pocket. He looked at the waterfall clock. D.Q. was probably back in the hospital room by now. He wondered what D.Q. would do if Billy Tenn killed him and he never made it back. The kid was going to die in a few months, but Pancho would have beaten him to it.

"You mind?" Billy Tenn had finished with his bottle of beer and was now reaching for the plastic glass.

"Help yourself." He thought that here he was, minding his pleases and thank-yous with this drunk, and he couldn't bring himself to do so with D.Q.'s mother.

"Go ahead and finish your story 'cause I gotta have a smoke pretty soon. I left my smokes back in my car."

"Go ahead. I'll finish it when you get back."

"I can wait." He seemed afraid that Pancho would take off on him.

"There's not much more to tell. One day, Jeff was working on one of those dump trucks they use to haul gravel to construction sites. He raised the bed to grease it and he asked my dad if he could lube the hydraulic arm that lifts the bed. So my dad went in there under the bed with the lube gun. Meanwhile, Jeff's replacing a filter, only he's not too stable because he's been hitting the vodka like he always does, and he stumbles and on his way down, he grabs on to a hose. Turns out the hose fed hydraulic fluid to the arm that held up the truck bed. Without the fluid, the arm collapsed, and the truck bed fell on top of my father. His head, his chest, they were both crushed. They told me he probably didn't even know what happened to him. They wouldn't let me see his body."

"Oooh, shit! That's bad!" There was a look of half disgust and half laughter on Billy Tenn's face, as if he had just imagined what the crushed head must have looked like.

Pancho stared at him. He kept staring until he could tell that the man was getting uncomfortable. Then he spoke again, almost in a whisper. "Ever since that day, I swore I wouldn't drink."

"Shit, man. That's heavy." Billy Tenn gulped the remainder of the beer. "Let's go outside. I need a cigarette."

"I'm not done yet."

"What?"

"There's another reason why I don't drink and never will."

"Man, I'd love to hear it, but I need to get me that cigarette."

"Can I ask you a question?"

"What is it?"

"How much is point-zero-one milligrams of alcohol in a person's blood?"

Billy Tenn, who had begun to stand up, sat down again.

"Shit, man, that's not even one beer. I can tell you 'cause I've been DUI a couple of times, and you're not even legally drunk unless you got point-oh-eight milligrams in you. We're talking blood. Breath is different. Why'd you ask?"

"Something I read someplace. Not even one beer, huh?"

"It's nothing, man. It's the smallest amount that can be detected. I happen to be an expert on this, not 'cause I wanted to be." Billy Tenn burped. "Excuuuse me."

They sat there face-to-face, looking at each other. Then Pancho picked up his backpack and stood up. "You wanted to go outside? Let's go."

He stepped out first, the big man following him. "My car is out back," Billy Tenn said. "That's where I have my cigarettes."

"All right."

They walked side by side around the mall toward the back, where two brown Dumpsters stood open and overflowing with garbage. There were no cars parked back there. They were alone.

"I guess you know I need some money," Billy Tenn said. "I'm sorry about your old man, man. Honest. But this is business."

"Yeah."

"I guess you're not going to hand it over easy."

"I can't. Most of it is not mine. What's mine I need."

"I could probably let you keep some of it."

"I can't."

Billy Tenn reached into his blue jeans and took out a shiny silver object. With a flick of his thumb, the object turned into a switchblade. Pancho moved the backpack to his left hand and raised it as a shield. Billy Tenn edged forward and began to make invisible circles with the switchblade. The sky was a dark blue, violet almost. A light on a pole by the Dumpsters flickered on. Pancho thought that if he got killed, he had nothing on him that would connect him to D.Q. The kid would be worried about him if he didn't show up soon. Billy Tenn lunged at him. Pancho deflected the thrust with his backpack. He could hear the knife tear through the canvas and hoped it didn't damage his sister's diary. Billy Tenn began to breathe heavily. Pancho saw individual drops of sweat bead on his upper lip and on his forehead. Sooner or later, the sweat would flow into his eyes, and when it did, Pancho would make his move.

He could not hold the backpack high enough. The knife came at him one more time. Billy Tenn grabbed the pack and tore it away from Pancho's hand. There was a fixed smile on his face, a fake smile, like the smile on a Halloween mask. Then, with a speed that Pancho did not think possible for a heavy man, Billy Tenn feigned a thrust to one side and brought the blade sideways, cutting a line through Pancho's shirt and across his chest. The sensation that raced through his flesh was almost delicate, what a laser burn would probably feel like. The blood soaked the white T-shirt before the cut began to burn.

"Give me the money. What you wanna die for?" Billy Tenn said.

The drop of sweat that Pancho had been watching rolled down Billy Tenn's forehead and through his eyebrows and curved itself inside the eye. Billy Tenn blinked and raised his hand to his eye. At that moment, Pancho flung his right arm forward as far as it would go. He heard the nose bone crack, a sound as light as the snap of a pencil breaking in half, but that was all it took. Pancho knew Billy Tenn's brain was flooded with a white pain that blotted out all thought, all memory, all knowledge of past and future. He heard the knife drop and then the gagging and choking as the blood filtered down his nasal cavity to the throat. Now Billy Tenn was on his knees, and a second after that, he was doubled on the ground, holding his face and moaning. "Oh, oh. Oh. Ma nose. You broke ma nose."

Pancho picked up the knife and tossed it toward the Dumpsters. He reached into Billy Tenn's back pocket and lifted out his wallet with two fingers. He took out a twenty-dollar bill to reimburse himself for the beers and dropped the wallet on the ground. Then he grabbed the backpack with one hand, and with the other hand on his chest, he began the walk back to the hospital.

CHAPTER 17

Back on Lomas Avenue, a few blocks from the restaurant, he took off the blood-soaked T-shirt, tore it, and tied it around the cut. Then he took his New Mexico State sweatshirt from the backpack and put that on. He went into a drugstore and bought a small bottle of hydrogen peroxide and a roll of gauze. Behind the drugstore, he looked at the slit across his chest. It was straight and thin, like the kind of mark his father used to make with a plumb line just before he sawed a long piece of wood. He poured the bottle of peroxide on the cut and tied the full roll of gauze around his chest as tight as he could. Then he walked very straight to keep himself from breathing deeply, because the cut was deep enough to hurt every time he did so. If he kept the cut closed, the bleeding would stop.

It was nine P.M. when he walked into the hospital. He looked at the front of the sweatshirt and made sure that blood had not seeped through. A sign said visiting hours ended at eight, but no one stopped him or even seemed to notice him.

D.Q. opened his eyes as soon as Pancho stepped into the room. "There you are," he said, as if Pancho had just popped up in a dream he was having.

"Go back to sleep," Pancho said. The only light in the room came from a table lamp next to D.Q.'s bed.

"I wasn't asleep." D.Q. groped around his bed until he found a remote control pinned to the upper part of the mattress. He pushed a button, and his torso tilted slowly up. "I like these beds," he said. Then he pushed another button, and his feet went up.

Pancho went into the bathroom with his backpack and changed into a St. Anthony's T-shirt and shorts. The gauze around his chest was only slightly pink. He came out and put the sweatshirt and blue jeans on the chair next to his bed. Then he jumped on top of the bed.

"Go ahead and turn on the TV if you want," D.Q. said from the other side of the curtain.

Pancho crossed his arms. The pain from a knife cut was not as bad as the pain from a fist. He could feel the cut's pain and still think. "Naah," he said. He waited a few minutes, expecting D.Q. to ask him where he had been.

"I've been cleared for takeoff," D.Q. announced.

"What?"

"They're all set to start the treatments tomorrow."

"We're staying here then."

"We'll be moving into Casa Esperanza tomorrow afternoon. After the first treatment."

"Mmm." Pancho closed his eyes. A minute later he heard the curtain that separated his bed from D.Q.'s pull open. D.Q. was standing there in the funny nightgown. He went over to the chair next to Pancho's bed, placed the sweatshirt and blue jeans on the bed, and sat down. Apparently there was going to be more talking before the day was over. Pancho found it strange that this prospect did not bother him. Tonight, for some reason, there would be something comforting about listening to D.Q. Pancho tried to sit up, but the pain stopped him.

"Push the back of the bed up with that gizmo there on the table. You'll be more comfortable that way."

"I was hoping maybe I could get some sleep," he said.

D.Q. tapped his index finger rapidly on his knee. He looked like he was sending a frantic telegraph message. Pancho folded his arms and shut his eyes tight. He knew that wouldn't stop D.Q. from speaking. "You look like you sat on an anthill. What's the matter?"

"Well . . ."

The reason for D.Q.'s uncharacteristic inability to talk came to him in a flash. Pancho smiled. "It's the girl," he said, putting a hand on his chest. "You're worried about the girl. María."

"Marisol," D.Q. corrected him. Two red circles had appeared on his pale cheeks. Pancho had never seen anyone blush like that before. It was good to know that underneath all his highfalutin talk, D.Q. was just another regular kid.

"It's not like that," D.Q. said, recognizing what was behind Pancho's smirk. "It's different."

"You wanna get laid." He was going to say *before you croak*, but he stopped. He closed his eyes and concentrated on breathing through his nose because it was less painful.

"When you meet her tomorrow, you'll understand," D.Q. said with confidence.

"I understand," Pancho muttered, still with his eyes closed. You could call it true love or whatever, but when you stripped the pretty words away, it boiled down to the same simple need. Then he remembered what D.Q. had said back in St. Anthony's about coming to Albuquerque. He said something about Albuquerque being part of the preparations. "You came to Albuquerque to see her," Pancho said with his eyes closed.

There was a long pause before D.Q. spoke. His tone was different, more personal. "I thought we would have more time before we tackled this subject. It may be too early for you to hear this. But I guess we have to grab the moment when it comes." He stopped.

"Go ahead," Pancho said. "I hear better with my eyes closed." With luck, he would fall asleep while D.Q. talked.

"Okay. Here it goes. You're half right. I didn't have much choice about coming and participating in the clinical trials. Helen was dead set on it. That's a funny phrase, isn't it? 'Dead set.' I wonder where it came from? You awake?"

"Yeah."

"Don't fall asleep. This is important. What's the matter, you have heartburn? Why do you keep making faces and touching your chest?"

"I get gas every time I hear you talk."

"Ha-ha. I mean I had to come and let myself be a guinea pig even though I honestly don't think anything good is going to come out of the treatments. Maybe a little more time, who knows? But you're right, there was a part of me that *did* want to come to Albuquerque."

"You wanna get laid," Pancho said again. *I would want to get laid if I knew I was going to die,* he thought. And then he thought that he had come very close to dying that very night, not more than two hours before. He thought of Julieta, the only girl he had had a romantic experience with, if you could call it that. Immediately, he felt a longing. Something warm pushed its way out from his chest and floated up in the air.

D.Q. ignored his remark. "Remember that passage by Thoreau that I read to you and Father Concha on the way here?"

"The *meollo*," Pancho said. "That's what the girl Marisol is to you."

He heard D.Q. laugh softly. "What if everyone is given a task we're to work on and if possible complete while we're living on this earth? What if before we are born and assigned bodies, all our souls stand up in a line in heaven, and as we get ready to come down, an angel gives us a little slip of paper that says what we have to do? Only the message is written in a language that we forget how to speak as soon as we get down here. But the message on that little piece of paper is still deep inside us, and our job is to remember, to recollect it, and then go about doing what it says."

My task is to find Bobby, Pancho said to himself, suddenly remembering.

"The task is different for everyone but it is also the same," D.Q. continued. "That guy Thoreau went to the woods to find out what his task was. I came to Albuquerque."

"Does she know you have the hots for her?"

"Must you be so crude?" Pancho couldn't tell whether the anger in D.Q.'s voice was real or pretend. If it was real anger, that was good too. The kid should come down to earth. "And no, I've never told Marisol how I feel about her and I'm not even sure I will. It doesn't matter. When I'm around her, I'll find out what I need to do."

"Just being around her is not going to be the same as getting the *meollo*. You should try jumping in her pond instead of just walking around it." That was a nice way of putting it, if he said so himself.

"Just wait until you meet her tomorrow. She's not the type of person you can be crass about. But now that we've started this line of discussion, I want to continue it, in a responsible way if at all possible."

"Yeah, let's grab the moment by the balls." What was the matter with him? It was like the slit on his chest had punctured his seriousness and now all kinds of pent-up silliness were coming out.

"What's gotten into you? And what's the matter with your chest, really?"

"I had a bad taco."

"They brought you a tray of food here. Nice piece of baked chicken, peas, and mashed potatoes. I told them to leave it for you, but they took it away when you didn't show up."

"I went for a walk." He was glad to have made it back, but he didn't tell D.Q. that.

"Let me try to finish, okay? What if I kick the bucket tonight and you miss out on the wisdom I'm about to share with you? Thinking about all the things I think about would be a waste unless I pass them on to someone. All of this, by the way, is written down in the Death Warrior Manifesto. But it's better if you get it firsthand, straight from the source."

Pancho felt the weight of sleep touch his eyelids. Good. Sleep was going to come despite the pain. "Make it quick," he said. "I'm getting sleepy."

"Listen, I got to tell you this." D.Q. spoke faster. "The task that was given to me, my message on that little piece of paper, it has to do with Marisol. She's the one. I know that's where the main business is going to take place because that's where I'm most scared to go. And for some unknown reason, it has to do with you too."

"Shit," Pancho said, half asleep. He wished he hadn't been thrown into the group, but he didn't think he could do too much about it. Not just then anyway.

"It's not like I'm terribly happy about it either. Look at me. What am I supposed to hope for with Marisol? Do we fall in love and I die a couple of months later? And what if we do fall in love? What does that love look like? How am I supposed to act around her? I have no idea. I'm clueless here. And look at you. I'm sharing my most vulnerable secrets with you and you're snoring."

There was a pause. It could have been a minute or it could have been an hour. Then Pancho felt someone tug at his feet and in a dream, he saw D.Q. untie the laces of his red sneakers and take them off his sweaty feet. He got those sneakers one day at the mall when Rosa wanted to buy him a birthday present. She took three ten-dollar bills out of her Mickey Mouse wallet and paid for them, and she giggled and said that now he looked like Goofy. Then he felt the softness of a blanket cover him and he sank into a darkness that was not lonely.

CHAPTER 18

She's nothing to write home about. Those were the words that flashed through his mind when he first saw Marisol. She was standing at the entrance to Casa Esperanza, holding the hand of a bald-headed girl. He and D.Q. had just gotten out of the blue hospital van, and D.Q. tugged at his arm. "That's her, that's her," he whispered.

She waved and started toward them, pulling the girl behind her. "D.Q.!" she exclaimed when she was halfway down the front path. Then she let go of the girl's hand and embraced D.Q. It was a warm embrace, the kind you give a friend you haven't seen for a long time.

D.Q. muttered, shocked, "You remember me."

"Sure, why wouldn't I?" Her voice overflowed with energy and humor. Pancho had never heard a voice like that coming out of a teenage girl.

"It's been awhile," D.Q. said, his own voice trembling.

"Can you take me to the jungle gym?" The bald girl lifted her arms, waiting for Pancho to pick her up. Pancho looked down at her, frozen in place.

"You must be Pancho," Marisol said, smiling. To Pancho's questioning look, she said, "Father Concha came yesterday to drop off your things. He told me both of you would be coming." Then she knelt and spoke directly to the girl. "Tell Pancho your name and ask him nicely if he will take you to the playground."

"My name is Josie. Can you take me to the playground? Please." She held out her hand.

Pancho looked at Marisol and then at D.Q. and then back at Marisol. "I think she wants you to hold her hand," Marisol informed him.

"Where's the jungle gym?" he said to the girl. He kept his hands by his side.

"It's back there." Josie pointed toward the back of the house.

"Finally, you met your match." D.Q. tried to sound upbeat, but his voice was weak. Marisol took D.Q.'s arm and led him toward the front door.

"Come on, I'll show you where your room is," Marisol said to him.

Casa Esperanza was a sprawling Mexican-style adobe house with green cactus and small trees surrounding it. Pancho imagined it was the kind of house that was naturally warm in the winter and cool in the summer.

"Are you going to live here?" the girl asked. She grabbed his hand and led him toward the back of the house.

"Yeah," Pancho said. "Shouldn't you have a hat on or something?" The top of her head still had a few strands of fine, light brown hair.

"It's okay," she said. "The sun is good for me. It has vitamin D."

Behind the house stood two wooden jungle gyms with yellow canvas pup tents on the top platforms. Four large cottonwoods covered the playground with luscious shade. There was no one else there. Josie let go of Pancho's hand and began to climb up a ladder on one side but stopped on the second rung. "Can you help me get up there?" Pancho grabbed her by the waist and lifted her up to the top rung. She went into the tent and then poked her round head out. "You have to come up," she told him.

"I'll wait for you over there," he said, pointing at the wooden fence.

"No, I'm scared. You need to come up here."

What was it about cancer that made people so bossy? He climbed up the ladder and sat next to her, gathering his knees to his chest. He looked to see if there was blood on the front of his T-shirt. "What are you looking at?" he said irritably when he felt her penetrating eyes on him. "Don't you have parents?"

"They're taking a break from me." She took her finger and began to poke him in the arm as if trying to determine whether he was real or not. "I didn't let them get hardly any sleep last night."

"Stop that." He flinched his arm away.

She floated her hand in front of her, wiggled her fingers, and then snapped her thumb and her middle finger. She did it again. "Guess what this is?" Wiggle and snap. Wiggle and snap.

"I have no idea."

"It's a butterfly with hiccups!" she squealed, and then repeated the procedure with her hand. "Get it?"

"Why don't you go down the slide or something?"

"I like it up here. It's cool. Get it? It's cool."

"How old are you anyway?"

"I'm eight and three-quarters," she said, suddenly turning serious. "People think I'm younger when they first see me. But then when they hear me talk, they think I'm older." She turned out the palms of her hands and tilted her head sideways. "Go figure."

"Go figure," he said. He saw the leaves flutter outside and then felt a breeze. In the distance he could see the green grass of a golf course. He was surprised to find so much green. The picture of Albuquerque that had begun to form in his mind consisted of ugly buildings dumped on top of miles of asphalt and cement.

"My real name is Josefina," she said. "I don't mind people calling me Josie. Which do you like better, Josie or Josefina?"

"Neither," he said. He tried to remember when he last thought about Bobby. It seemed like a long time ago. When was it? When he went out for a walk last night? When he sat in the restaurant, before the fight? The next time he went with D.Q. to the hospital, he would get the revolver and bring it here. He would hide it there on the edge of the golf course. He wanted the gun to be always accessible.

"I like Josefina when my grandma calls me that, but I like everyone else to call me Josie. My grandma doesn't speak English. Her name is Josefina also. Do you have a grandma?"

"Nope."

"She died?"

"Probably."

"I have one grandma and two grandpas that already died." She held up one finger on one hand and two fingers on the other. Then she moved all the fingers on her right hand like she was saying bye-bye to someone.

What was taking Marisol so long? But then again, she never said that she was going to come and get the girl. Maybe he had been suckered into taking care of her for the rest of the afternoon. What else was there to do? He needed to start looking for Bobby with the red truck, but that required a phone booth with a phone book.

"Are there telephones in the rooms?" he asked the girl.

"Nope."

"How about TVs?"

"No, but there's a big TV in a room with a carpet and comfy sofas and chairs. And there's lots of movies you can watch. My favorite is *Casper the Friendly Ghost*. Have you seen that?"

"Yeah. Everyone's seen that. Is that all they have, kids' shows?"

"Mostly. Usually the kids watch TV and the grown-ups sit in the dining room having coffee and talking about the kids. Are you a grown-up or a kid?" She examined him.

"What do you think I am?" he said testily.

"Mmmm. Let me think. You are a . . . big kid!" She thought that was extremely funny.

"Is that girl Marisol gonna come get you any time soon?"

"Marisol is my second best friend. My first best friend is Donna. She has leukemia too."

"Where is she?"

"I don't know."

"How can she be your best friend if you don't even know where she is?"

"She just left, that's all. Silly." She banged on his thigh with her closed hand. When he looked down, she was wrinkling her nose and puckering her lips as if she had just smelled something bad. "Who's your best friend?"

He was going to say "no one," but he stopped himself. Was D.Q. a friend now? Can a person be your friend if you don't understand what he's saying most of the time? What if you're not even sure you like him? What if you're sleeping in the same room? What if he's pretty much about the only other human being you have regular contact with?

The girl seemed to detect his trouble in coming up with an answer. "Marisol can be your best friend too if you want. She's a lot of kids' best friend. I don't mind. I think Marisol is pretty, don't you?"

Nothing to write home about, he thought. Not that he had anyone at home to write to. He didn't even have a home. He tried to remember Marisol's face. On second thought, maybe she *was* pretty. She wasn't beautiful like the nurse Rebecca, but there was something about her. "I didn't notice," he finally said.

"Marisol is taking me to the zoo. Maybe tomorrow if I don't feel sick. You can come too if you want. I saw a picture of the zoo. They have lizards and all kinds of poisonous snakes. I like scary animals the best. What's your favorite animal?"

He used to have a dog whose name was Capitán, but they called him Capi for short. Unfortunately, Capi liked to rummage in the neighbors' trash cans, sometimes spilling the contents on the street. They used to get anonymous notes on their front door telling them "The dog will meet a fateful end unless he's reined." His father had to look at an old dictionary to figure out some of the words. They figured that the only person who'd use words like that was Mr. Rafferty, an old man who lived in a sparkling trailer at the end of the park. It was the same Mr. Rafferty who drove by one day when his father was hoisting up the flag and yelled out the window of his station wagon that Mexicans had no business flying the American flag. That was the only time Pancho had seen his father yell at another person in anger. "I served this country too and got wounded for it, you ignorant old fart! Don't tell me I can't fly my flag. What the hell's the matter with you?" Old Mr. Rafferty sped away.

A week later, they found Capi dead under their trailer, a puddle of vomit next to his mouth. His father never said anything, but Pancho knew old Mr. Rafferty had poisoned him.

He snapped back to the present. "Dogs," he said. "I like them best."

"Guess what? Once I get through with the treatments and I start getting well again, I'm going to get a puppy."

The idea of revenge for Capi's poisoning had never even crossed his mind. It would have been so easy to spray the old man's trailer with graffiti or pour sugar down the gas tank of his white Cadillac. It was strange that not only did Pancho and his father not talk about revenge, they didn't even think about it. It was as if the option of revenge did not exist, could not even be imagined. How strange that a feeling once so foreign to him now gripped him with such persistence. He could not imagine living without avenging his sister's death.

"They have Bengal tigers and polar bears all in the same zoo right next to each other, but polar bears like it cold and tigers like it really hot. Maybe they have an air conditioner for the bears."

A flock of blackbirds descended in a blur and landed on the branches of the cottonwood closest to them. They chirped and cawed chaotically. Josie stuck her fingers in her ears and shut her eyes. For a moment it sounded as if they were inside a ball of cracking ice. Josie hid her face against his chest, and Pancho automatically put his arm around her. Then there was the simultaneous flutter of a hundred wings, and the birds burst out of the tree as fast as they had come.

"Ayyy!" Josie cried out. "That was scaaary!" She was still holding on to him.

"Okay, okay," he said. He pried her fingers from his ribs. "Let's get down. They're liable to come back and eat you up."

"Really?" Her eyes lit up with delight.

"Yeah, birds love little bald heads that look like eggs."

"Let's slide down." A yellow S-shaped tube connected to the edge of the tent functioned as a slide. Josie crawled to the edge and then sat down. "You have to come with me," she commanded.

"You go ahead, I'll follow you."

"No, you have to hold me because I'm afraid."

"What are you afraid of? It's just a slide."

"I'm afraid of being inside closed spaces. I'm closophobic."

That's another thing that cancer people have in common, he thought. *They like to use big words.*

CHAPTER 19

They spurted out of the slide and ended up seated on the sand, one behind the other. "Let's do it again!" Josie said immediately.

Pancho picked himself up and dusted himself off. Just then, Marisol emerged from the back door. Josie ran to her and jumped into her arms.

"I brought you a juice box," Marisol said. They walked off toward a wooden bench under one of the cottonwoods. Pancho turned and began to walk away. "Where are you going?" Marisol called after him. He stopped without turning around. "D.Q. is taking a nap. Come sit down."

He turned and saw them on the bench and hesitated. He tried to think of something he could tell her he had to do, a place he needed to go, but nothing he could say came to mind. He took small steps back toward them. Josie was sitting on Marisol's lap, sucking on a straw. Marisol beamed as if he were doing her the greatest honor by coming to sit next to her. He sat tentatively on the edge of the bench, ready to take off at any moment.

Josie took the straw out of her mouth. "Guess what? We were up there on the slide and all these birds came and he said they were liable to eat me!"

"No way! He said that?"

"Yeah! He said they liked my head because it looked like an egg."

Marisol shook her head and shot him a look of disbelief. He glanced away quickly.

"Can he come to the zoo with us?"

"*He* has a name. What's his name?" Marisol asked.

Josie stuck a finger in her nose and said, "I forget."

"Pancho. His name is Pancho," Marisol said, removing the finger from the nose.

"Pancho," Josie whispered. She laid her head on Marisol's shoulder. Her eyelids closed and opened in slow motion. "Can Pancho come to the zoo with us?"

"Why don't you ask him?" She put her hand on Josie's head.

"You ask him," Josie said, and closed her eyes.

A moment later, she was already dozing, her mouth slightly open, one arm limp by her side. Pancho waited until he saw her chest rise with her breath. "She's asleep," he said, surprised.

"It's the chemo," Marisol said. She removed the half-full juice box from Josie's grasp. "The same thing happened to D.Q. He was awake one second and sound asleep the next. That's good."

"Yeah, that's good," Pancho said. Although he had no idea why it was good. He was still on the edge of the bench. He pushed himself back slightly to avoid sliding off. He could feel Marisol positioning Josie so that the girl's body stretched along the bench with her head in Marisol's lap. Marisol was wearing khaki shorts, and her skin was light brown, like his. She had white sneakers on. He folded his arms and leaned back, accidentally touching her arm as he did so. "Sorry," he muttered.

"You and D.Q. should come to the zoo with us," she said. "If D.Q. feels up to it, it would be fun."

"If he feels up to it," he repeated.

"Were you with him today when he received the treatment?"

"I sat next to him." D.Q. had sat in a chair that looked like a barber's chair while a yellowish liquid that looked like antifreeze flowed into him at the rate of one bag per hour. D.Q. watched the liquid leak into him and did not say a word. "What's it feel like?" he had asked D.Q. when it was all over. "It burned a little," was all he had said.

"It's good that you're here with him," she said.

"Yeah," he answered. He held back from telling her that he didn't have much of a choice.

"You live with him at St. Anthony's?"

He turned and looked directly into her eyes. She might not have been anything to write home about, but there was something about her face, especially her eyes, that made him want to keep looking. It was like seeing a face he had glimpsed someplace before but could not remember where. She held his gaze comfortably, and it was he who finally looked away, embarrassed by the fact that he was staring.

"Of course you live with him, that was a silly question," she said when he didn't respond.

"I've only known him for a week."

"You don't have to know him very long for him to make an impression. He's very unusual."

144

"Unusual?" he asked. He instantly regretted sounding like he was interested in how she felt about D.Q.

She stroked Josie's head gently as she spoke. "He's the first person my age I met with cancer." She bit her lip but smiled when she saw that he was looking at her. "There's something unusual about him, don't you think? Not unusual as in weird, but as in out of the ordinary. Like he's in touch with another dimension the rest of us can't see. I don't think I've ever met anyone with such strong faith."

"Faith?"

"Don't you think?"

"I never heard him talk about faith."

"I never have either," she said thoughtfully, "but you can just tell."

"You work here long?" He didn't want to talk about matters he didn't understand.

"This is my second summer. And I worked here last year after school and on weekends, and I guess I'll do the same next school year."

"What do you do exactly?"

"A little of everything. I want to be a nurse after I graduate from college, so this is good preparation for that. Mostly I try to spend as much time as I can with the kids. I help the parents find the social services they need. I do some of the paperwork when Laurie, the director, gets overwhelmed. I even cook sometimes."

"You get paid?"

She laughed. "At least you didn't ask me what everyone else asks me."

"What?"

"Usually people want to know if I find the job depressing. You know, being with kids who have cancer. And yes, I get paid. Not much, but I get paid."

"I'm supposed to be getting paid too," he said. "Just for hanging around D.Q."

"Hey —" Her face lit up with an idea. "Why don't you help me with the kids? They like you for some reason." She glanced down at Josie and then she grinned. "D.Q. will be sleeping quite a bit during the day. You can help me then."

"No, I don't think so."

"What else are you going to do all day?"

"I brought a book."

"One whole book?" she teased.

"I have some places I need to go."

"I need someone to give the kids a ride in the rickshaw. It's only for an hour or two a day. You can pick the times."

"I don't know. Maybe."

"I'll take that as a yes. I can tell you're an athlete; this will keep you in shape."

He felt his face redden. No one had ever called him an athlete before. He had never participated in any sports at school, but before his father died, not a day went by when he didn't jump rope or hit the bags. It struck him as funny that he never saw it as staying in shape or as something an athlete would do. It was simply something that felt good.

"What's a ricksha?"

"Rickshaw. It's not a real, real rickshaw. A rickshaw is a cart for carrying people that's pulled by another person, like a taxi. They have them in China and India. What we have is a bicycle that pulls a two-wheeled cart with a seat. The kids love riding in it. There are paths by the golf course that you can take. It's lots of fun."

It came to him that he had once pulled a wagon behind his bicycle. He was thirteen and Rosa was sixteen, and the wagon was much too small for her, but she managed to sit on it cross-legged. They had left the trailer park and were on the way to the convenience store down the road when a red Thunderbird convertible pulled up beside them. The four high school kids in the car began to jeer and make obscene remarks at Rosa. She waved and smiled at them. He pedaled faster and they increased their speed. He slowed down and the car slowed down. One of them offered Rosa a beer and she replied with her usual, "I'll die if I drink, so help me *Diosito*." This struck the boys in the car as hilarious. Then the boy on the passenger side leaned out of the car and spoke to him. "Hey, kid, what's the matter with your girlfriend?" "She's not my girlfriend!" he replied angrily. But he wasn't angry at the jeers and catcalls. He was angry that anyone could think Rosa was his girlfriend. "Hey, don't get upset, guy," the boy in the car said. "What's the matter with her? Is she re*taaa*rded?" There was a burst of laughter from everyone in the car. Even Rosa thought that was very funny. "Hey, honey, show us your boobs!" the boy in the backseat called. Pancho stood on the pedals of the bike and pumped with all his strength. The wagon behind him jerked and Rosa fell. When he looked back, Rosa was sitting on the sidewalk, laughing and lifting up her blouse. He jumped off the bike, rushed toward her, and tried to pull her shirt down, yelling at her to stop, until the Thunderbird finally roared away. "Those boys were funny. Pancho, weren't those boys funny?" Rosa asked, still sprawled on the sidewalk.

He had not thought about that incident since it happened. Now, sitting there on the bench under the cottonwood with Marisol and the sleeping Josie, the memory of what he said to Rosa ripped through the forgetfulness where it had been concealed. "You're nothing but a *puta*, you know that? You're just a big *puta*! I wish you were dead!"

He bent over on the bench and put his hands over his ears to stop the sound of his own voice.

"Are you okay?"

For a moment, he did not know who was speaking. He straightened and cleared his head with a shake. "Yeah," he said, recognizing Marisol. "You think I could use that rickshaw to do some errands?"

"Of course. Help me carry her in. I'll show you where it is."

He stood and lifted Josie from the bench. The girl opened her eyes, closed them again, and then plopped her head on his shoulder. He followed Marisol to the back entrance of the house.

CHAPTER 20

The "rickshaw" was parked inside an enclosure that housed air conditioners and water pumps. The handlebars were rusty and the front wheel was flat. He could not imagine anyone getting any pleasure out of riding in that rickety thing.

Afterward, they went inside the house. She took him past the TV room and the dining room. A man and a woman sitting at a table drinking coffee stopped talking when they saw the sleeping child on Pancho's shoulder. Past the dining room, they entered a hall with blue wooden doors on both sides. The floors were carpeted and they made no sound as they walked. The whole house seemed to be enveloped in a peaceful silence. She stopped in front of one of the doors and pointed at it. He understood that was the room he would share with D.Q. Delicately, he transferred Josie to Marisol's shoulder.

"Most of the kids will be out playing around four," she whispered, and winked at him as she left.

He opened the door softly. The room had two single beds, a

night table with a lamp, a rocking chair, a desk with another chair, and a chest of drawers. The curtains on the window were only half drawn and a ray of light fell on the curled-up figure of D.Q. on the bed farthest from the door. Pancho closed the door and dropped his backpack on the empty bed.

"What else are you going to do all day?" Marisol had asked him. He sat on the edge of the bed and took off his sneakers. The Panda had asked him to stay with D.Q. for two weeks, until the end of the treatments. He saw countless seconds and minutes and hours stretch before him like a line of ants that went on forever. He had never thought of time as an emptiness that somehow needed to be filled. But filled with what? "I brought a book," he had told Marisol. He had one book that took him months to read.

He lifted up his shirt and looked at the bandage around his chest. It was clean. He flopped back on the bed and turned sideways to look at D.Q. He watched until he saw him breathe. Here he was wondering what he was going to do with the innumerable minutes and hours and days that stretched before him, and there was D.Q., who probably knew he had a definite number of days left. What if he could trade places with D.Q.? Maybe it wouldn't be so bad, to know for sure that the boredom and emptiness had an end.

Then he closed his eyes and imagined that he had killed Bobby and that he was caught like he knew he would be. He was lying on a cot in the prison cell where he would spend the rest of his life. He was seventeen now. Assuming that he lived to, say, seventy . . . How many years was that? Whatever that came out to, you'd have to multiply it by 365 days to figure out how many days that would be, and then whatever that number came out to, you'd multiply it by twenty-four to figure out the number of hours you'd have left. He stopped that line of thinking because it made him dizzy. What would probably happen is that he wouldn't last that long in prison. He'd get into a fight sooner or later with another prisoner and that would be the end.

He rolled on his side until he reached the edge of the bed and he lay there looking at the floor. Then he rolled to the other side and lay there staring at the green parrot he had carved. D.Q. had placed it on the night table that separated the beds. He felt weak, as if a boxing opponent had spent round after round banging away at his kidneys. Those body shots gradually drain the legs and arms of strength, and the mind eventually loses its will to fight. Ever since he met D.Q., people had been taking body shots at him. D.Q., Father Concha, Marisol, the little bald girl, Helen, they all pummeled him with words and requests that weakened his focus on finding the man who killed his sister.

There was a moan. It could just as well have been his, but it came from outside of him. After a few moments, it was followed by the sound of gagging and retching. D.Q. had managed to lift his head a few inches off the pillow before spewing out a rush of white liquid. His eyes bulged out and then his head fell back on the pillow, and out of his mouth came the gurgling sounds of someone drowning. Pancho stood up and rushed to the bed, tipping the desk chair over. He grabbed D.Q. by his underarms and sat him up, then tilted D.Q.'s head forward to drain the liquid from his mouth. Another wave of vomit rose and erupted over both of them. The vomit was warm, like the glass of milk his father used to drink before going to sleep.

He sat on the edge of the bed, partially soaked, waiting for the next bout, while D.Q. tried to come back from wherever he was. There was one more heave, but the only thing that emerged was a giant burp. "Excuse me," D.Q. said. "I didn't mean to burp in your face." Pancho wiped his face with his arm. "Oh. I guess that's not the only thing I did. You should have just let me be."

"You were choking on your own puke."

"Lovely." D.Q. lifted up a hand with dripping fingers. "I feel like someone put me inside a bottle of tequila and then shook it. Have you ever gotten drunk?"

"No."

"No?"

"I don't drink." Pancho realized he was still sitting on the edge of the bed. He stood up quickly and began to look around for something to dry himself with.

"We're going to have to change these sheets," D.Q. said. He burped again. "Maybe later. This little scene may not be over with yet. Ohhh. I hate being nauseous. Oops. That's whining, isn't it?" He scooted to the side of the bed that wasn't wet and began to unbutton his cowboy shirt. "Can you get me a sweatshirt from the top drawer?"

Pancho came out of the bathroom with two pink towels. He threw one to D.Q., then he went over to the dresser. D.Q. had already put his clothes in the top two drawers. He found a dark blue sweatshirt and threw that to D.Q. as well, hitting him in the face. It occurred to Pancho that his whole wardrobe consisted of the pair of blue jeans, the New Mexico State sweatshirt, and the two sets of St. Anthony's T-shirts and shorts that D.Q. had given him a week before. He emptied the contents of his backpack into the bottom drawers. He put on a new T-shirt and went over to his bed. Just as he was sitting down, he saw a plastic wastepaper basket next to the desk. He grabbed it and dropped it next to D.Q.'s bed. "Puke in there," he told him.

"Could you get me a washcloth with cold water? I think it would help." D.Q. was gripping the bed as if it were some kind of roller coaster.

Pancho muttered under his breath as he went back to the bathroom. "What are you going to do while you're here?" Marisol had asked. *I'm going to be cleaning up D.Q.'s upchuck,* he should have told her. When the water got as cold as it was going to get, he soaked the washcloth and squeezed half the water out of it. Then he went over to D.Q.'s bed and waited for him to open his eyes. He was not going to put the washcloth on his forehead like some kind of mother hen. "Thanks," D.Q. said, when he finally saw him standing there.

Pancho watched D.Q. shiver. There were some shelves in the bathroom with extra linen. He grabbed two white sheets and a pink wool blanket. "Can you stand up for a minute while I change the sheets?" D.Q. nodded. He lifted his legs slowly off the bed, then stood holding on to the windowsill. He looked like he was about to crumble. Pancho lifted the wet sheets. The mattress had a rubber covering. He wiped it dry with the towel and threw a clean sheet on top of it. He motioned to D.Q. that he could lie down again and gave him the wool blanket.

"You know what I really could use is a sponge bath," D.Q. said as he propped the pillows on the bed. Pancho glared at him. "Just kidding." D.Q. grinned.

Pancho took the bundle of wet sheets and placed them by the door. He smiled to himself when he remembered picking up the wet towels at the gym where he used to work. He was no stranger to all the smells the human body could produce. He sat down on his bed. D.Q. groaned. "You should have taken the bed closest to the toilet," Pancho said.

"I thought it would be good to look out the window," D.Q. answered. "But you're right. We should probably trade. Oh. Oh." D.Q. leaned his head over the side of the bed and reached the wastepaper basket just in time. After a minute or so, he came up and sighed. There was a container of pills and a glass of water by the side of the bed. He shook out two pills, popped them into his mouth, and washed them down with water. "These are supposed to help with nausea."

"I can call someone," Pancho said.

"No. We have to stick through this. If it seems like I'm too sick to handle this on my own, they'll put me back in the hospital and . . ."

"Yeah, I know." Pancho lay back on the pillow. "You want to be near your girlfriend."

D.Q. coughed. "She's not really my girlfriend," he objected meekly. "What do you think of her?"

"If I had to choose, I'd take the one that we first saw back at the hospital." He tried to remember her name, but the only name that came to mind was Julieta's.

"Oh, brother! Did you get a chance to talk to Marisol?"

"Yeah."

"So?"

"She called me an athlete."

"Get out of here!"

"She wants me to help her with the kids. Giving them rides in this rickshaw thing."

"Really? That's . . . good."

Pancho smiled inwardly. For a moment, he thought about being serious. The kid was sick. But Pancho was enjoying himself. It had been a while since he felt like he was having fun.

"She wants me to go to the zoo with her." He glanced sideways long enough to see D.Q. getting mortified.

"Oh." Then D.Q. whispered, "She didn't say anything to me about the zoo."

Pancho folded his hands behind his head. "Yup. Maybe tomorrow. While you're at the hospital getting your treatment."

"Tomorrow?"

Pancho waited as long as he could before he burst out laughing.

"You shithead," D.Q. said, catching on, embarrassed.

"Don't worry. I'm not her type. She likes smart guys like you."

"Why? Did she say anything? You need to tell me exactly what she said."

"She said it was a shame you were all skin and bones 'cause she liked a little muscle."

"Stop! Don't fool around like that! What did she say?"

Pancho told himself to stop joking around. D.Q. was getting too agitated. Any moment now, he could toss his cookies again. "All right." There was something Marisol had said that sounded strange to him. Yes, now he remembered. "She said you were from another dimension." He concentrated. "She said you were unusual but not weird."

"You're still pulling my leg, right?"

"No."

"She said I was from another dimension? What does that mean? Like from the Twilight Zone?"

"I think she meant it in a good way."

"Tell me the context of how she said it."

"There wasn't any con*test* to it. She just plain said it. She was admiring you. Like you knew stuff that most people don't." Then he remembered what he most wanted to remember. "She said she'd never met anyone with so much faith."

"She said that? Honestly? Those were her exact words?" D.Q. asked as he stood up.

Pancho had never seen D.Q. so energetic. He looked like he was going to start jumping up and down on the bed any second now. "Yeah. Those were more or less her exact words."

"You sure she used the word 'faith'?"

"Yeah."

"Maybe she used the word 'fate' and you misunderstood. Maybe she said, 'I never met anyone with so much fate,' you know, F-A-T-E. If she said that, then that would mean something totally different."

Pancho was getting lost. "I don't know what you're talking about. She said, 'I never met anyone with so much faith' or maybe she said 'such strong faith,' I forget now. But it was 'faith,' however you spell it. That's the word she said exactly. I told her I never heard you talk about faith."

"You did?"

"Yeah."

"And then what did she say?"

"She said she hadn't either, but she could just tell anyhow."

"Oh, God." D.Q. grabbed his head with his hands. Pancho couldn't tell whether he was extremely happy or in extreme pain. "What else? Tell me what else."

"That's about it. She showed me where the rickshaw is. Then she told me how to get to the gas station so I can put some air in the tires. Maybe I can find some oil for the chain too."

He watched D.Q. walk in front of him with his hand across his mouth and go into the bathroom. A few minutes later when he came out, his face and hair were wet. He might have poured water on his head or maybe he was sweating. He walked silently back to his bed, deep in thought, and sat down, leaning against the backboard. "Just because I don't talk about it doesn't mean I don't have it."

"What?" Pancho had no idea what "it" was.

"Faith."

"It don't matter to me one way or another what you have."

"Faith can mean many things."

"No, it can't." The words were out of Pancho's mouth fast, before he even realized he had said them.

"What do you mean?" D.Q. seemed taken aback.

Pancho searched for words to explain why he said what he said. "It doesn't matter."

"Tell me. Try to tell me, please. What do you think faith is? Tell me."

Pancho spoke irritably, still fighting to find the right words. "Faith's what makes you pray. It's why people say the Rosary and light candles to Jesus and Mary and all those saints. It's what you go to church for. It's why you're good when you want to be bad. It's what you think is gonna happen to you after you die." He exhaled, relieved that he could express what he had never considered before.

D.Q. blinked a few times. He sat still. "The kind of faith I have is different. I'm not sure how."

Pancho stared at D.Q. in disbelief. He had never imagined that D.Q. would ever have trouble finding words. Then he said, "The girl already thinks you got faith. I don't know whether she thinks you got the regular kind or your own kind."

D.Q. didn't answer.

"That's good, right? If she said that, it means she's given you some thought. Maybe she'll give you more than that." Pancho wanted to go back to the joking. A D.Q. who didn't talk was making him more uncomfortable than a D.Q. who did.

"Yes," D.Q. said. "It's good."

But if it was good, why didn't D.Q. seem all that happy about it? The silence continued, so Pancho asked, "What did you and Marisol talk about the last time you were here?"

It was the right question to ask. D.Q.'s face lit up again. "That's just it. We talked about ordinary things. I told her about my life at St. Anthony's. I told her I was in Albuquerque to get a second opinion on my illness to make sure that the treatment I would be getting in Las Cruces was the right one. I don't think I was too depressing, as far as I can remember. That's why what she said about me having strong faith is so significant, assuming you're telling the truth, and I believe you are, because I don't think you're capable of making something like that up." D.Q. grinned. Pancho wondered whether he had just been insulted. It was all right if he had been. It was good to hear D.Q. shoot off his mouth again. "So if we just talked about ordinary things and she thought I had strong faith or much faith, it means she felt something as we were talking, don't you think?"

"I think when you have the hots for someone, you end up fooling yourself into believing all kinds of things."

"Listen to you. I suppose you have lots of experience with women."

"I got enough."

"Pssh." D.Q. waved his hand like he didn't believe him.

It was a true statement as far as Pancho was concerned. He didn't say he had *a lot* of experience, he said he had enough. He thought of Julieta. He thought he was in love with her at certain moments during the night he spent with her. The next morning, the love was gone. That was his experience and that was enough. It was enough to know that when you want someone, you don't think straight and you for sure take what the girl says to you and twist it up inside of you. "How long did you all talk for?" Pancho asked skeptically.

"You're looking at this the wrong way," D.Q. countered. "It wasn't what we talked about or how long we talked. It was the *connection*. Something happened. Whatever you want to call it, I came back to Albuquerque because of *it* and she recognized something in me because of *it*."

"She recognized you were mental." Pancho poked his brow with his finger. D.Q. rolled his eyes.

"Tell me again what she said about the other dimension. You didn't do a very thorough job reporting *that* part of the conversation."

"Let me think." Pancho squinted. He scratched his head. Then he noticed that the cut along his chest was itching as well, a sign that it was healing. He saw Marisol's face in his mind and found it pretty in a quiet way. He knew that D.Q. would treasure every word he said, and this filled him with the responsibility to be precise. He spoke very slowly and carefully. "She said that . . . that you were in another dimension. No, that you touched another dimension. She said *touched*. That it was like you were in touch with another dimension most people don't see. But I don't know whether she said 'most people don't see' or 'most people don't feel.' I don't remember which exactly."

"You did great. Thank you. That was great. That was very helpful."

D.Q. was looking out the window again, away from Pancho. Even so, Pancho could tell there was a smile on his face. He knew D.Q. was imagining Marisol. The image of Marisol's smooth, caramel-colored legs came to Pancho and he smiled as well. Then, out of nowhere, the image of D.Q.'s mother appeared. There was something that Marisol had said that reminded him of D.Q.'s mother, but what? Then he remembered. The mother had also said that D.Q. was unusual, that after the car accident, it was as if he had seen something while he was in the coma. It was funny how fast thoughts were suddenly coming to him. Now he remembered what Julieta had said about Rosa. *She was special, like she didn't belong in this world.* The idea that D.Q. and Rosa were both special, maybe in similar ways, struck him as funny.

He looked at D.Q. D.Q. was still gazing out the window, grinning to himself the way Rosa used to grin. The kid was thinking about what Marisol had said about him. He didn't look all that special just then, Pancho thought. Just another kid in love.

CHAPTER 21

In the first four days of treatment, D.Q. went from bad to worse. The initial schedule had called for two four-day stretches of treatments with a three-day break, but it had to be modified to four two-day treatments with one day of rest in between. Dr. Melendez told D.Q. that if the side effects got too bad, they could reduce his daily dosages but increase the total number of treatments, but D.Q. would only agree to an additional day of rest.

Pancho knew that D.Q. wanted the treatments over and done with. While they lasted, all he could do was hang on. Every day, he talked less and less, and what little talk he did was directed at physical necessities: drinking, eating, sleeping, and all the bathroom stuff. All the talk about Death Warriors had stopped. He still made an effort to crack a joke now and then and Pancho never heard him complain, but there was no doubt that the kid was in bad shape. The only thing that seemed to matter to him were the afternoon walks he took with Marisol, for which he appeared to save all his strength.

Pancho went with him to the treatments in the mornings, then spent the afternoons giving rickshaw rides to the Casa Esperanza kids. He was supposed to take them around the block, but after a while he began to explore the surrounding streets. The kids didn't complain. He could squeeze two of them in the rickshaw's seat, but he preferred taking one at a time. The kids sat in the back and watched the scenery pass by. When they tried talking to him, he ignored them. They soon got the message that the ride was for looking and not talking.

The first evening he was at Casa Esperanza, when everyone else had gone to sleep, Pancho had looked for and found a telephone book in the TV room. He counted five construction companies that had names ending in "and Sons." He wrote the names down with their telephone numbers. That was the first step in his plan to find Bobby. The second step was to call each company and ask if a Bobby worked there to try to get his full name.

On the third afternoon, Pancho found a giant white-and-red umbrella in a storage closet. It was almost the size of one of those picnic umbrellas that people back at the trailer park left up year-round. He sawed off one-quarter of the umbrella's aluminum pole and then braced it to the side of the rickshaw with a steel clasp, so the passengers would always have shade regardless of what direction the rickshaw was traveling or the angle of the sun. People at Casa Esperanza, especially the mothers, seemed obsessed with the angle of the sun.

When he finished rigging it up, he opened the umbrella. A gust of wind almost lifted the rickshaw off the ground. Pancho admired the umbrella and the precise positioning of the patch of shade. He picked up the hacksaw and the screwdriver from the sidewalk and put them back in the toolbox.

"What is *that*? It looks like some kind of mushroom," someone said behind him. It was a young man, a year or two older than him. He wore a button-down shirt as neat as a one-by-twelve piece of clean wood. "This must be Casa Esperanza," the young man said.

"Yeah," Pancho answered. "This is it."

"You work here?" the young man asked.

Pancho didn't feel like explaining his situation, so he said yes. But then he thought that he did work at Casa Esperanza, as a matter of fact. He hadn't seen any paycheck for the rickshawing or for keeping D.Q. company, but he worked all right.

They heard a child cry. When they turned to look for the source of the sound, they saw Marisol, her back to them, bending to comfort Kelly. Kelly was one of Pancho's most dependable rickshaw customers. Marisol was wearing her usual khaki shorts and white polo shirt.

The young man said, staring at the bending Marisol, "That is one juicy piece of slender ass."

A ripple of irritation entered Pancho's toes, pricked its way painfully through his body, and came out his mouth. "Why do you say that?" he asked.

"Excuse me?"

"Excuse me?" Pancho said, mimicking. "What if that was my sister?"

The young man narrowed his eyes, then recovered when he saw Pancho's question was hypothetical. "She'd still be a nice piece of ass even if she *were* your sister."

"Pancho, can you help me?" It was Marisol calling him.

"Is that Marisol?" the young man asked Pancho.

"That would be her," Pancho said. Marisol was coaxing Kelly toward the rickshaw.

"That's hot. I'm supposed to talk to her about a job," the young man said. Pancho looked at his hungry eyes and then at Marisol. Was he missing something? Was Marisol more attractive than he gave her credit for? Had he lost the ability to notice a beautiful girl?

Kelly and Marisol were now standing in front of them. Kelly was crying softly. The young man's eyes were riveted, without shame, on Marisol's breasts. How long had it been since he hit someone, Pancho wondered, and how long would he have to wait for another opportunity like this one? Not that he cared about Marisol, but it would be good to teach the guy some manners. He could tell Marisol was uncomfortable. "Kelly is afraid of the umbrella," she said to Pancho.

"I'll put it down." He moved toward the rickshaw.

"Are you Marisol?" the young man broke in.

"Yes," she answered.

"I'm Sal." He stretched out a stiff right hand, which Marisol barely touched. "I'm applying for the live-in college student position in the fall. Laurie said I should come over today. I'm supposed to see her and talk to you."

"She's inside," Marisol said.

"She said you're the one I should really talk to since you pretty much run the place. It would be great to get the lay of the land, so to speak. Is there someplace private we can go?"

It was a beautiful sight to see, the smile that appeared on

Marisol's face. Pancho thought that even if he lived a hundred years, he would always remember it. She could see slime up close and recognize it for what it was, and he liked that.

"I'm busy now, as you can see."

"Come on, just show me around for ten minutes."

"I'm not the person to talk to, really."

"It sure looks to me as if you are."

"I'll go inside and get Laurie," Marisol said, still smiling. She knelt carefully on the ground to talk to Kelly. "Will you let Pancho put you in the rickshaw and take you for a spin? He'll let you touch the umbrella so you can see it's nothing bad."

Kelly shook her head no.

"No? Why not?"

"You need to come with me the first time."

"Okay, it's a deal." Marisol straightened herself up.

Sal tried again. "Listen, maybe you have a telephone number I can call later?"

"I don't think so," Marisol said. Then to Kelly, "Just stay right here, I'll be right back."

When she was halfway to the house, Pancho said to Sal, loud enough for Marisol to hear: "Hey, Sal, can I ask you a favor?" Everyone turned to look at him. He had put down the umbrella, and now the rickshaw separated him from the group. "Can you bring Kelly to this side? I need to tighten something here."

The front door to Casa Esperanza opened at just that moment and Laurie, the director, stepped out of the building. Pancho was the only one who saw her. Sal seemed bewildered by Pancho's request. Kelly stuck her thumb in her mouth and looked toward Pancho.

"Just bring her," Pancho said to Sal. "You can do that, right?"

Sal shot him a *fuck you* look, bent down, and grabbed the small girl by her shoulders. He picked her up as if he was showing off his strength. Kelly began to squirm and cry. Sal held her away from him and she wriggled out of his grasp and dropped straight down to the ground. Marisol and Laurie rushed toward her. Sal stood there motionless like the idiot he was. The women picked up and consoled the little girl. Pancho came over to the group and Kelly eased comfortably into his open arms. He gave Sal a kind of sexy wink as he took Kelly over to the rickshaw.

Sal tried to recover. "Hi, you must be Laurie," he said, stretching out his hand. When she didn't take it, he said, "I'm Sal. I'm here for the college student live-in program. We spoke earlier."

"Glad to meet you," she said, but there was no gladness in her voice. "Let's go inside."

"Marisol!" Kelly was patting the space next to her on the passenger seat. Marisol got in without looking at Sal, who, Pancho saw, was still incredibly hoping for some kind of recognition from her.

Men are such assholes, he thought, even though he was a man himself.

"You did that on purpose," Marisol said to him when they were a block from Casa Esperanza. He had not put up the new umbrella yet. He was going to take the rickshaw a couple of blocks first so that Kelly could see it was the same old rickshaw she had been riding in all along.

Pancho adjusted the right-hand mirror on his handlebars so he could see Marisol's face. "Did what?" He knew that if he could see her, then she could see him.

"You asked him to pick up Kelly and bring her to you just so he would look bad in front of Laurie."

"I wish I was that smart," he said, laughing. He saw her looking at him in the mirror as if trying to gauge how smart he really was, and added, a mocking tone in his voice, "I'm no genius like Sal back there."

"That guy was a *pendejo*," she said.

He agreed with her, but for some reason felt like contradicting her. "He wasn't a *pendejo*," he said conclusively. "He was just a *menso*."

"Oh, yeah?" she said, picking up on his tone. "What's the difference, according to you?"

"A *pendejo* is a jerk on purpose. A *menso* can't help himself." He thought that was a very smart response under the circumstances.

"And Sal simply couldn't help being obnoxious?"

"How was he obnoxious? Just because he nearly dropped Kelly on her head, that doesn't mean he was obnoxious."

"That's not why he was obnoxious and you know it." She was getting irritated.

He thought of Sal's comments about Marisol. "He was just being a normal guy," he said.

"Just being a normal guy?" He saw her eyes in the mirror questioning him.

He didn't answer her, but instead, pulled the rickshaw to an empty parking space on the street and got off. He walked to the side and opened the umbrella slowly.

"Balloon," Kelly exclaimed, delighted.

"Where?" Pancho looked up at the sky.

"She thinks the umbrella looks like a hot air balloon," Marisol explained.

"Can we go to the fiesta?" Kelly asked.

"What fiesta?" Pancho said.

"Albuquerque has a hot air balloon fiesta every October. There's hundreds of hot air balloons, all different colors and designs. It's an amazing sight. You and D.Q. should come."

He climbed back on the bicycle seat and began to pedal. He didn't want to talk about the future.

They rode in an uneasy silence. Marisol seemed deep in thought. Pancho felt bad for teasing her about Sal, so he asked, "How did you get involved with children who have cancer?"

She turned her face in the direction of his voice. "I have a cousin who's a pediatric oncology nurse. I've always wanted to be like her."

"Why?"

The question seemed to surprise her. "Why?"

"Why do you want to be like her?"

Marisol considered it for a few seconds. "Aurora, that's my cousin's name, she has this inner strength. It's like nothing can shake her because she's found out who she is and what she wants to do."

Pancho remembered a term his father liked to use. It was the highest praise he ever gave a boxer, for fighting with pride and dignity. "She has *coraje*," he said.

"*Coraje*," she repeated. "That's a good word. I haven't heard that in a long time. I like it."

When they turned back toward Casa Esperanza, he heard her

ask, "Do you have any plans for what you'll do after you finish high school?"

Here we go again with the future, he thought. "I liked working with my father in carpentry," he said after a while. "It was fun."

"I saw the perico you did for D.Q. That's amazing."

"I seen it too," Kelly said. "Want me to tell you what colors he is?"

"Sure." Marisol hugged her tighter to her body.

"He's green all over, except for a little blue under his wings and some red on top of his nose, and his beak and claws are gold."

"What color are his eyes?" Marisol asked.

Kelly stuck her index finger in her mouth. "I forgot."

"They're purple," Marisol said.

"They're not purple, they're black," Pancho stated.

"Sorry," Marisol said, "but you don't know your colors. The parrot I've seen has purple eyes."

"Purple!" Kelly shouted and laughed.

"I know. Whoever heard of a parrot with purple eyes?" Marisol joined in the laughter.

"They are not purple!" Pancho turned around to look at them in pretend anger and almost crashed into an oncoming car.

"Okay, okay," Marisol said. "Just don't kill us."

"Sorry, but the eyes are black."

The silence after that was comfortable, and Pancho did not expect anything more to be said. But about a block from Casa Esperanza, Marisol asked, "Do you really think that guy Sal was just being normal?"

Pancho smiled when he thought that all along she had been thinking about his remark. He said without hesitation, "That guy was a number one *pendejo.*"

He looked in the mirror and saw her smile back. They were in complete agreement.

CHAPTER 22

Two days later, Marisol, Josie, and Pancho waited in front of Casa Esperanza for D.Q. to get back from that morning's treatment. As soon as he returned, they planned to set off for the zoo. But the moment D.Q. got out of the van, Pancho could tell that he wasn't doing too well. His skin was pale yellow, the color of the liquid they were pumping into him, and his legs trembled when he walked.

"I'm okay, I'm okay," he told the group. "I just need to splash some water on my face and I'll be all set." Pancho knew that D.Q. had a couple of good hours before the nausea got really bad.

After D.Q. came out of the house again, he and Josie settled into their wheelchairs. Marisol pushed Josie and Pancho pushed D.Q. slowly up Yale Street to University Avenue. Josie filled the silence with chatter about the animals she wanted to see. She hoped to be there when the seals got fed so she could see them clap and hear them honk. Every once in a while, Marisol would turn to check on D.Q. and D.Q. would assure her that he was perfectly fine. Then, as soon as she turned away, he would cover his mouth with his hand. *I sure hope he doesn't puke in front of her,* Pancho said to himself.

He tried not to look at Marisol walking in front of him, her black hair tied behind her back and swaying softly. So far, he was succeeding in keeping his distance from her. Whenever she approached him, he stiffened and put on a stern face. He even resisted smiling at the small jokes she made as they loaded and unloaded kids from the rickshaw. There was no single point in time when he had decided to keep his distance. He was just following an instinct he didn't understand. Part of it was the ridiculous feeling that Marisol belonged to D.Q. She was like the only thing the kid had. He didn't know why he should care, he just did. And part of it was a feeling like kindness or forgiveness that came over him whenever he was near her. He needed to keep that feeling away from him. It made him soft and he didn't want to be soft.

Still, his eyes were drawn to her. Her beauty was a puzzle he couldn't figure out. Today she was wearing a white polo shirt and blue shorts. The hands that gripped the handles of the wheelchair were firm. She was tall for a girl; the top of her head reached his nose, and he was five foot ten the last time he got measured. He had not seen any boredom on her face. He remembered what D.Q. had said about her the first night at the hospital. *She's not someone you can be crass about.* He wasn't sure what "crass" meant, but he thought it meant something like "cheap," and if it did, then D.Q. was right. There was nothing cheap about her.

They reached the bus shelter on University Avenue. D.Q. and Josie got out of the wheelchairs, and Marisol and Pancho folded them. A woman holding a green pillow on her lap scooted along the bench, and D.Q. sat down. Josie went up to him and stood by his side as if to give him strength. D.Q. whispered something in her ear and she giggled. He had purple circles under his eyes and an ugly cold sore on his bottom lip. Even though it was hot, he wore a blue Windbreaker with the collar turned up and a blue cap set as far down on his head as it would go. There was no way he should be going to the zoo now, Pancho knew. But it was impossible to keep him from coming either. The only glimmer of the old D.Q. that Pancho had seen in the last five days was when they made plans for the trip with Marisol.

"Maybe this isn't a good day for the zoo," Marisol said to Pancho. They cast a sidelong glance at D.Q. Josie was demonstrating the flight of a butterfly with hiccups with her fingers.

"He gets worse as the day goes on," Pancho responded, not looking at her.

"We won't stay too long then."

"You shoulda just taken the girl." He sounded irritated. The traffic on University Avenue was heavy, but there was no sign of a bus anywhere and the wheelchair did not want to stay folded.

Marisol waited for a truck without a muffler to pass by before she spoke. "I know you're not as big a grouch as you pretend to be, so just stop it."

Pancho managed to chuckle. No one had ever talked to him that way before. She was serious, but there was the beginning of a smile on her face. Pancho shrugged his shoulders. *I don't care what you think about me,* is what he meant to communicate to her.

"Here comes the bus!" Marisol suddenly exclaimed, and she went to grab Josie's hand.

They entered the bus through the back door. Marisol helped Josie climb the first step and then she followed with the wheelchair. Pancho tried to grab D.Q.'s arm to help, but D.Q. shook him off. He winked and smiled as he did so, letting Pancho know that there was nothing personal in the gesture. D.Q. climbed the steps slowly. Josie and Marisol had taken a seat near the back. As soon as Pancho and D.Q. were on the bus, Josie said, "Can I sit with Pancho?"

"Are you sure? He's in a real bad mood today," Marisol said teasingly. Josie jumped out of the seat next to Marisol and went to a seat in the last row. She looked at Pancho and patted the seat next to her. D.Q. sat next to Marisol.

"Excuse me, is someone gonna pay or what?" a woman's voice shouted. It was the bus driver.

Marisol reached into her pocket and took out a twenty-dollar bill. She offered the money to Pancho, who was still standing up. D.Q. pushed her hand down. "Pancho has money. He'll pay. Right, Pancho?"

"Yeah," Pancho said. He went to the front and paid the bus driver.

"Thank you, Pancho," Marisol said to him as he walked by. D.Q. was holding Josie's wheelchair. He handed it to Pancho. Pancho took the two wheelchairs and laid them on an empty seat. The only people on the bus were the four of them and the woman with the green pillow, who had also gotten on the bus.

As soon as he sat down next to her, Josie began to talk. She knew all there was to know about the Rio Grande Zoo and she could not keep all of that information inside of her. She told

Pancho about the enormous tongues of the giraffes. Then she caught her breath for a fraction of a second and asked him if he had ever ridden a camel.

"Nope," Pancho said distractedly. He wanted to hear what D.Q. was saying to Marisol. He heard the word "family" and saw Marisol lower her head, as if to consider D.Q.'s words carefully.

"They have camel rides at the zoo. Can you get on with me?" Someone was punching his leg. "Pancho, will you get on the camel with me?"

"No way."

"Why not?"

"I don't know how to drive one." It was the first thing that came to him. He could not picture how one could sit on top of a camel with those humps in the way.

"Someone leads the camel with a rope while you ride on top of it. Silly."

"Oh."

"Now will you ride one with me?"

"No."

Marisol leaned into D.Q.'s shoulder and laughed. He was probably trying to impress her with how smart he was. Maybe he was telling her about that other dimension he was so familiar with.

"Even if you fall into the pit where the tigers are, they won't eat you because they get fed lots of meat every day. They'll only eat you if they're hungry. Still, I'm going to be afraid when I see them. What animal are you the scaredest of?"

"What?"

"I think snakes are the scariest because you can't see them. If a lion tried to come into your room at night, you could hear him most probably, but a snake could slither into the room and then climb into your bed and you wouldn't even know it."

Pancho was about to tell her that snakes also made noise if you knew how to listen for it when the bus stopped and the doors swished open. Three boys got on. They were Pancho's age, but their baggy blue jeans and loose-fitting long-sleeve shirts made them look older. One of them wore a red bandanna around his head. He swaggered onto the bus like he was in charge. The last one had a cell phone he was holding close to his mouth and talking into like a walkie-talkie. Pancho noticed that they didn't pay. The bus driver looked like she wanted to say something, but then changed her mind.

The boy with the red bandanna scanned the bus. He bobbed his body up and down as he walked down the aisle. Pancho could see him focus on the folded wheelchair and then on Marisol. He walked slowly to the empty seat across the aisle from D.Q. and Marisol and lumbered into it. He slid to the edge and stretched his legs across the seat. The other two sat in front of him, each taking a full seat.

The boy with the phone was yelling into it, and the voice coming from the phone was yelling back. Every other word in the conversation was a swear word of one sort or another. Josie covered her ears with her hands. Marisol and D.Q. stopped talking. The boy with the red bandanna kept his eyes fixed on D.Q. and Marisol. He licked his lips, and his eyeballs drifted from side to side as if he were falling asleep.

D.Q. swung his legs out of his seat, leaned over as far as he could, and tapped the arm of the boy with the cell phone. Marisol tried to pull him back, but he just tapped the boy again. Pancho took his hands out of his pockets. He finally managed to catch the eyes of the boy with the bandanna and now they stared at each other.

"Do you mind very much not talking on the cell phone?" D.Q. asked. "The volume and the language you are using are offensive."

The boy looked disgusted, as if D.Q.'s touch on his arm had infected him with some deadly disease. He kept that look for a few seconds and then he turned around and continued to talk. Marisol grabbed D.Q.'s arm and pulled him back into the seat. The boy with the red bandanna and Pancho were still in a contest to see who would look away first. Pancho could feel adrenaline warm his arms, and his heart began to pump at a faster rate. He smiled at the boy.

D.Q. raised himself up and, grabbing on to the handles of the seats, shuffled a few steps until he stood next to the boy with the phone. "Please, there are children and women," he said. He placed his right hand on the boy's shoulder.

The boy with the phone jerked his shoulder away from D.Q. "Don't touch me," he snarled. Josie buried her face in Pancho's arm. Marisol scooted to the side of the seat where D.Q. had been. The boy with the bandanna slowly shifted his gaze from Pancho to Marisol. The bus stopped and the momentum threw D.Q. into the boy with the cell phone.

"Watch it, asshole!" he shouted, pushing D.Q. away.

"I don't want any trouble here! I'll call the cops right now!" the bus driver was shouting. She held a yellow cell phone of her own in her hand. "Do I need to call the cops?"

"It's inconsiderate to the other passengers," D.Q. was telling the boy with the phone. The boy waved the phone in D.Q.'s face. From inside the phone, a crackling male voice called, "What's goin' down, dude?"

"Okay, that's it, I'm calling the cops," the bus driver said.

Marisol stood up and grabbed D.Q. by the arm. "That's all right, we're getting off real soon," she said. The boy with the red bandanna said something in Spanish to Marisol. It made the other two roar with laughter. *"Pendejos!"* Marisol said to the boys.

"Ooooh!" they all moaned at once.

Pancho studied D.Q.'s face. There was no fear there, he was sure of it. There was anger — well contained, but it was still anger. And there was frustration as well: Here was yet another situation he could do nothing about. Pancho felt a sudden pride and understanding for D.Q.; he had the spirit of a fighter even if he did not have the strength to go with it. He smiled as he saw D.Q. loosen himself from Marisol's grip and reach for the cell phone. The boy stood up and kept the phone out of D.Q.'s grasp. It was a situation that could end very badly, Pancho knew, and yet it was still funny. Boys horsing around, having fun, that's almost what it looked like.

He heard Josie sobbing next to him just at the moment the boy with the red bandanna stood up. Marisol turned toward Josie. The boy with the cell phone grabbed D.Q.'s hat and flipped it to the front of the bus. It landed at the feet of the lady with the green pillow, who had a look of terror on her face. Pancho lifted Josie from her seat and put her in Marisol's arms. Marisol pleaded silently with him not to do anything, and he nodded that he understood but it was out of his hands now. The boy with the cell phone puffed his chest and began to bump it against D.Q. He pushed the talking phone in and out of D.Q.'s face.

There was nothing aggressive about Pancho's movements. He acted as if he were amused by the goings-on and wanted to join in the fun. He simply stood behind the boy with the cell phone and when the phone came within his reach, he grabbed the boy's wrist and took the phone out of his hand. Then in one continuous motion, he dropped it and stomped it with his right foot. There was a crack and the noise was over.

Everyone in the bus was silent. Even Josie held in her sobs. They all looked at the mangled phone as if surprised that it could ever be quiet. Then there were a series of sounds all at once: swearing in Spanish, D.Q. calling out "Pancho!" as if to warn him. Then he felt a burning sensation in his ear and he turned to see the boy with the red bandanna clenching a fist. He heard the sound of sirens, but maybe the sound came from inside his head. He had time to swing and the boy with the red bandanna was within easy range, but the image of Marisol pleading silently kept his arms still. Then he felt the boy's hand around his throat, the wetness of spit on his face, a thud in his groin, and a sinking feeling that rose up in his stomach as if he were on a roller coaster. He saw a flash of white light and then darkness.

Marisol's face floated over him. He closed his eyes again and focused all his attention on the touch of her fingers on his neck. If he concentrated on that touch, the pain in his ear and his groin disappeared. He thought how good it would be to pull Marisol to him and have the touch of her whole body take away all his pain. He was stretched out on the ground someplace and she was kneeling beside him, her hand now on his pulsating ear. She was so within reach. All he had to do was open his arms and bring her down toward him. Lose himself in her.

He opened his eyes again, lifted his head, and tried to stand. "Go slow," Marisol said. She helped him sit up. He was in the middle of the aisle, the mangled cell phone at his feet. He looked around. A worried Josie was sitting in the seat above him. A man he hadn't seen before towered over him. He was a policeman.

"How are you feeling?" the policeman asked.

D.Q. and the bus driver were talking to a second policeman. D.Q. seemed agitated. He was waving his arms, pointing at Pancho and then pointing someplace outside.

"You bleeding anywhere?" the policeman said.

"You don't bleed when you get hit in the balls," he said. Then he remembered that Josie and Marisol were within earshot. "Sorry." He glanced at Marisol. She wasn't smiling.

The policeman asked, "Can you stand up?" He offered Pancho a hand. Pancho took it and pulled himself up. D.Q. stopped talking and came over to him.

"What happened to those other guys?" Pancho looked down at the pieces of cell phone.

"They took off when they heard us," the policeman answered. "They were probably packing and didn't want to risk getting frisked."

"Officers, I gotta get goin'. I'm waaay behind schedule," the bus driver said.

"You want us to call an ambulance?" the policeman asked Pancho.

Pancho shook his head. "I'll be all right." He was tempted to feel himself down below. Parts of his body seemed to have ended up in the wrong places.

The policeman bent down to pick up what was left of the phone. "You were lucky today. Those kids were probably high on meth. It makes people violent, crazed. They could have killed you."

"It's my fault," D.Q. said. "I asked them to turn down the noise and then I tried to turn the volume down myself."

"Who busted the phone?" the second policeman asked.

"I did," Pancho admitted.

The second policeman picked up the broken phone parts. "Joe," the first said, "I don't even think we need to file a report here, do we?" He took a long look at D.Q. and then at the wheelchairs. "You coming from the hospital?"

"We're from Casa Esperanza," Marisol answered. "We were going to the zoo."

"That's that place for kids over by the golf course. We can give you a ride back there."

"Can we still go to the zoo?" D.Q. asked. "I mean, if Pancho feels okay." He looked at Pancho.

"I'm okay."

"Yeah!" Josie piped in.

"You sure?" Marisol asked.

"Sure."

"All right. You could probably file assault charges," the first policeman said to Pancho, "but I'm not exactly sure you're all that innocent, you know what I mean?"

It was as if the policeman could see that he harbored just as much violence as the kid who kneed him in the groin. He could not interpret the look on Marisol's face. It wasn't pity. She seemed puzzled by him. *Join the club*, he thought.

"Officer," he heard D.Q. say, "it really was my fault. My friend was trying to protect me."

"You all have a good day, then," the policeman said, his eyes still on Pancho. Then the two men left the bus.

"Let's all sit down now 'cause I gotta make up some time here," the bus driver said. "I knew those kids were trouble. I never shoulda stopped to pick them up. They get on like they own the bus, they don't pay or nothing. What can I do? I'm lucky they don't beat me up." She had her hands on the steering wheel and was looking out the side-view mirror. "Go on and sit down now."

Josie grabbed Pancho's hand and pulled him down to her seat. D.Q. sat behind them, next to Marisol. They were all quiet for a while and then Josie said, "I want to see the chimpanzees first."

CHAPTER 23

They were in front of the tiger pit, waiting to see them get fed. Marisol pushed Josie to where she could see the big cats a little better. Pancho stood next to D.Q.'s wheelchair and looked down. One of the tigers began pacing back and forth on a ledge. Apparently he smelled something, or maybe he just knew it was time to eat.

"Do you think Marisol is mad at us?" D.Q. asked.

"Why?" Pancho continued to peer down. He had never seen a tiger before and was surprised by the size of its paws.

"She seems kind of quiet."

Pancho shrugged his shoulders. He too had noticed something come over Marisol after the bus incident — a distancing where there was none before. She was more subdued and less talkative. D.Q., on the other hand, seemed charged up.

"It wasn't very smart of us, was it? Back there in the bus."

D.Q.'s words reminded Pancho of the numbness between his legs. He adjusted himself slightly.

"Everything still in place?"

"Yeah."

D.Q. continued, "It was stupid. We endangered Josie and Marisol."

"You're the one who started it," Pancho said. He slid down and sat with his back against the ledge. He felt very tired.

"I had no idea it could turn violent."

"Didn't you see what they looked like?" How could someone so smart be so dumb?

"I know, I know. I didn't think I was making an unreasonable request. It was bad enough that he was talking on the phone as if no one else existed. The guy was yelling obscenities."

"Those people aren't reasonable."

D.Q. bit his lip and furrowed his brow. Pancho knew that as far as D.Q. was concerned, the kids on the bus and Pancho were the same — they were all Mexicans. But he had always seen himself as different from the Mexican kids who sniffed glue or tattooed themselves with gang signs. Those kids were wild, angry with everyone, violent. And he was . . . what? He was . . . someone who didn't care what happened anymore. He was going to kill someone in a few days, no matter what. Maybe he wasn't so different after all.

"I should've recognized they were high on something," D.Q. said.

Marisol walked up to them. She spoke to D.Q. without looking at Pancho. "We're going to move on ahead. Do you want to wait here? Are you feeling tired?"

"I'm feeling great," D.Q. responded, full of pep. "We'll follow you. I'm not keen on seeing raw meat." He put his hand over his mouth and made as if he were going to vomit. It elicited a smile from Marisol.

Pancho slowly stood. He positioned himself behind the wheelchair and pushed. He wished he were the one sitting in the wheelchair. The zoo was crowded with groups of children in T-shirts announcing their various summer camps. They ran back and forth in packs from one exhibit to another. Pancho had to dodge baby carriages pushed by parents who were looking everywhere except where they were going. People tried not to stare at D.Q., but they did anyway. They stopped to admire an elephant taking water from a pond and spraying his back. They watched a male lion sprawled totally unconscious in the shade of a red flowering tree. The female nearby kept a sleepy guard. They saw orangutans leapfrog each other and heard chimpanzees screech with terror or delight, Pancho wasn't sure. The Mexican wolves paced back and forth on top of a mound of dirt. They had tall, skinny legs, but they were not much bigger in bulk than Capi, and they kept their heads down, as if they had just been caught doing their business inside the house.

They bought hot dogs and sodas at the Cottonwood Café and ate outside. D.Q. took one bite of his hot dog and stopped eating. He spit what he had bitten into a napkin and folded it. He asked Pancho to get him a cup of ice. Pancho got him one and D.Q. chewed the ice chips. Marisol smiled and listened attentively to Josie. Pancho saw D.Q. look longingly at her and sigh. Pancho took a deep breath and volunteered to take Josie to the camel ride. Just before he left, he saw Marisol edge her chair closer to D.Q.

The camel ride consisted of a man with a white ponytail leading an old-looking camel by a rope while a little kid sat on a special seat located in front of the camel's humps. Josie told Pancho she wanted the camel to kneel down so she could climb on, but the man with the ponytail led the camel to a platform with stairs up to it instead. Josie insisted on getting out of the wheelchair and waiting in line standing up. She was afraid the ponytail man wouldn't let her on if he saw her in the wheelchair and thought she couldn't walk. "Because you hold on to the camel with your legs" — she had read that somewhere.

"How was it?" he asked her when she climbed down.

"It was bumpy. It was like riding on a mountain. I was scared. Could you tell?"

He picked her up and sat her in the wheelchair. "You didn't look scared."

"I was holding the scaredness in. I'm good at that. Sometimes. Except when you were fighting with those mean boys on the bus, I cried then."

"I wasn't fighting," he protested. "Where to now?"

"Can we go find the birds? I want to see the vultures."

"The vultures?"

"Yeah. They're awesome ugly."

"I don't know where the birds are. Don't you want to pet a burro? They're right there."

"That's the petting zoo. That's for little kids. I'd rather see the vultures and then the Tasmanian devils."

"Those aren't real. Those are cartoons."

"Silly. They are so real. They're like dogs. They're from

Tasmania. That's a place in Australia. Do you know why they call them devils?"

"In the cartoon, they look like the devil, with the pointy ears and the fangs."

"Mmmm. And you know what? Almost all the Tasmanian devils are becoming extinct because they get tumors on their face."

"Where'd you learn all this?"

"On the Internet. I think the birds are that way." She pointed to her left.

"How do you know?"

"I saw a sign that said 'Aviary.'"

Pancho had seen the same sign, but he had no idea what "aviary" meant. All those years at home living with his father and his sister, he had never felt ignorant, and yet clearly he was. He never used a computer, except occasionally at school. He did not own a cell phone or play video games. Back home, before everything happened, he thought of himself as bright enough. He knew where his left foot should be when he sent a left hook. He knew how to find the studs behind a plaster wall and how to lay a plumb line straight. He explained TV mysteries to his father and repeated ordinary well-known facts to his sister until they sank in. Now he felt out of place, like he did not belong in this city where even eight-year-olds knew more than he did.

There was an empty bench in front of a cage filled with bright green birds, like the parrot he had carved, only smaller. He sat down. A woman in front of the cage had one of the birds perched on her index finger. A circle of kids surrounded her. "I think that bird talks," Pancho told Josie. "Why don't you go see what it says?"

"Naah. I'd rather listen to you." Pancho thought that at least he was more interesting than a bird. Josie was twitching her nose as if gathering her nerve to ask a question. "Why did you smash that cell phone?"

Pancho covered his face with his hands. "I don't know."

"Maybe you thought that boy was going to hurt D.Q. and you wanted to protect him."

"Could be. But the kid wasn't hurting D.Q."

"You got angry because they were teasing D.Q."

"I wasn't angry. I didn't feel angry. I just up and did it. I don't know why."

"The boy was saying mean and dirty words. He was loud too."

"Yeah."

"I thought you died when you fell. I cried."

"I saw you crying before I fell."

"I cried different tears after you fell. First I cried 'cause I was scared and then I cried because I thought you were dead."

He observed her carefully to see if she was telling the truth. "How can you cry if you don't even have eyelashes?"

She stuck her tongue out. "They fell off. Meany. Just for that, I'm not going to tell you a secret."

"Good."

"I won't tell you even if you give me one million three hundred dollars."

"All right."

"I would have told you too."

"What is it?"

"I'm not gonna tell you. Take it back a thousand times."

"All right, I take it back. Take what back?"

"That I don't have eyelashes."

"I take it back that you don't have eyelashes. You have them. I see two. One there and one there."

"Okay, I'll tell you, but don't tell Marisol I told you."

"I won't."

"Promise?"

"I promise."

"Cross your heart and hope to live?"

"All right. There. I cross my heart and hope to . . . live."

"Marisol likes you."

"Is that it? I already knew that. What did she say?"

"Will you buy me a snow cone?"

"Maybe. If it's not too expensive."

"You were giving a ride in the rickshaw to Phil and Kelly yesterday, and my mom, she said to Marisol, 'He's a hunk, isn't he?' And Marisol, she went 'Mmm-hmmm.' Like that."

"A honk? A honk? That doesn't mean anything. That's how a duck goes. Honk. Honk."

"Not honk. A hunk. And it does so mean something. When a girl likes someone, she calls him that."

"It was your mother who said it, not Marisol."

"Marisol went 'Mmm-hmmm.' That means like 'For suuure!'"

"You know what I think? I think we better go find D.Q. and Marisol. D.Q. is probably starting to get sick about now. Honk. Honk. That's the noise the seals were making."

Marisol and D.Q. were still sitting in front of the Cottonwood Café. From a distance, Pancho could see that they were carrying on a quiet, serious conversation. D.Q. talked and Marisol listened. She held a paper cup in her hands and nothing seemed to exist in her universe other than D.Q.'s words. Now and then, she tilted her head and smiled appreciatively at D.Q. What could he ever say to Marisol that would make her listen and look at him that way? He could not think of one single thing. All he was and all he ever would be was a honk.

CHAPTER 24

He was tightening the brakes on the rickshaw with an old pair of pliers when he felt Marisol standing behind him. "I have some customers for you when you're ready," she said to him.

"I'm ready. I'm just fixing the brakes."

"Brakes would be good," she said. He glanced back just long enough to see her smile. It was the first time she had spoken to him in a friendly way since the incident on the bus three days before. "How's D.Q. today?"

"I just brought him back from the hospital. He's in the room. He was looking for you."

"We were going to go out for our walk."

"He looks too tired to walk."

"Walking helps with the nausea. It's not good to be lying down all the time even if that's all you feel like doing." She paused. Pancho shook his head to let her know he heard her. "It's a good day for a walk. It's not hot."

He gripped the right brake handle tight and pushed the bike

at the same time. The front wheel squeaked. "The brake pads wore out."

"Is it dangerous?"

"Only if I have to stop." He hadn't meant to sound like a smart-ass; it just kind of came out that way.

"We can buy some new ones. I can get Laurie to give us the money."

"It's okay. I don't go down any hills."

"There's a bike store on my way home. I can buy the parts if you tell me what to get."

"It's all right. The bike stops. See." He squeezed the brakes and pushed. The bike screeched and slid, but the front wheel didn't turn. Her presence irritated him, he didn't know why.

He saw her move her head back as if struck by the force of his words. There was neither hurt nor anger in her eyes. Instead, he saw kindness. Or pity. "What?" he said. He didn't need anyone feeling sorry for him.

"Nothing," she said softly. Then she asked, "Who are you anyway?"

"What do you mean?" But he did understand the question. He too had tried to go inside of himself and sort out the different people who lived there. He took a step backward and almost stumbled over the rickshaw.

She moved closer to him. "It's like you're two people," she said, looking into his eyes. "One Pancho is funny and kind and patient with little kids. And another is . . . I don't know, angry. It's like you can't make up your mind what kind of person you want to be. I don't know. Is there something bothering you? Is there something you want to talk about?"

He snickered. "With you?"

"If you want to with me, why not? Or with D.Q. You're helping him so much. Why not let him help *you*?" She moved to one side and leaned against the bike. "D.Q. told me about your sister. I'm sorry."

He felt a pang of humiliation as he imagined D.Q. and Marisol talking about his sorry past. "It's none of D.Q.'s business," he said. He wondered what exactly D.Q. knew about his sister. He had never once talked to him about her. Back at St. Anthony's, D.Q. had said, "Something's eating you, I can tell," and he had mentioned that in Albuquerque they would help each other out. How much did D.Q. know and how much did he tell Marisol?

"D.Q. thinks he's your friend," she said. "Friends talk to each other." She wasn't accusing him of not being a friend, he could tell, she was encouraging him to be one.

"D.Q. likes to talk." And he didn't. That's what he was telling her.

"You do too, with the kids. I've heard you."

He shrugged his shoulders. It was true. Sometimes he forgot himself and the kids would get him going with some kind of foolish conversation or another. It was fun to tease them and they liked being treated like regular brats.

Mrs. Rivera came out of the house, holding the hand of her five-year-old son, Phil. Phil broke loose and ran toward Pancho, arms outstretched. Pancho lifted him, embarrassed. "Which Pancho is it going to be?" Marisol whispered to him as she walked by.

Later that evening, D.Q. was sitting at the desk writing in his notebook, the one that contained the so-called Death Warrior Manifesto. Pancho came into the room and threw himself on the bed. He had been playing a spaceship video game with a ten-year-old named Andrés for twenty-five cents a game and ended up losing eight dollars. The conversation with Marisol and then the loss to the little hustler had put him in a foul mood.

"Listen, I want to read you something," D.Q. said. Pancho grabbed his pillow and put it over his head. "Come on, this won't take very long. We need to make some progress here — in passing on to you the principles of the Death Warrior, I mean."

Pancho groaned.

"The sooner you listen, the sooner I'll stop. You know I'm going to read you this no matter what. Might as well listen to it now rather than having me wake you up in the middle of the night."

Pancho removed the pillow from his face and tucked it behind his head. He was just beginning to get the hang of simultaneously turning, accelerating, and shooting lasers from his spaceship. If the mother had not taken Andrés to bed, he would have recovered his losses, he was sure of it.

"Okay, here goes." D.Q. read out loud:

1. Who is a Death Warrior?

Anyone can be a Death Warrior, not just someone who is terminally ill. We are all terminally ill. A Death Warrior accepts death and makes a commitment to live a certain way, whether it be for one year or thirty years.

2. When does one become a Death Warrior?

There is a specific moment during which you can decide to become a Death Warrior. That moment is when death shows you that you will die.

3. How do you become a Death Warrior?

Once you accept that life will end, you can become a Death Warrior by choosing to love life at all times and in all circumstances. You choose to love life by loving.

4. What are the qualities of a Death Warrior?

A Death Warrior is grateful for every second of time given and is aware of how precious each second is. Every second not spent loving is wasted. The Death Warrior's enemy is time that is wasted by not loving.

5. Why should you become a Death Warrior?

So you can live and die with truth and courage, and because life is too painful when you're wasteful with the time given to you.

"Who are you writing that for?" Pancho interrupted.

"This is the Death Warrior Manifesto. I'm writing it for you. It's what we talked about. " He was sitting on the edge of the chair, the notebook on his lap. "Those are the first five points of the Manifesto. I had lots of pages, but I'm condensing it into the essentials."

"I thought the first rule was 'no whining.' I didn't hear

anything about 'no whining' in there," Pancho said, sniffing the air. He could tell D.Q. had been vomiting. He probably missed the toilet bowl again.

"It's implied in the third principle. When you love life, you don't whine."

"I liked the no-whining rule better. It was easier to understand." Pancho touched his ear, his chest, and finally his groin — all the places that still hurt.

"You look like a third-base coach signaling a batter," D.Q. said. He started to laugh and then the laughter turned to coughing.

When he stopped, Pancho said, "You didn't write that stuff for me. You wrote it for Marisol. All that stuff about loving."

"It's for you, honest. I wasn't even planning on showing it to Marisol. These are the principles you'll need to follow to become a Death Warrior. I wanted to put them in writing so you'd have them after I'm gone. I'm hoping you'll be a Death Warrior before then. You need to make a decision in order to be a Death Warrior. You need to decide."

"To love." Pancho tapped his heart melodramatically, like a character in one of the Mexican soap operas that Rosa liked to watch.

"Correct."

"You're full of crap." *D.Q. and Marisol are perfect for each other*, Pancho thought. *They even sound like each other. Which Pancho is it going to be?* says one. *You need to decide*, says the other. They sounded like the same person, both full of the same corny crap.

"I sure am." D.Q. grabbed on to the side of the chair and stood. "Speaking of which." He walked into the bathroom, leaving the door slightly ajar.

"Shut the door," Pancho ordered.

"I can't reach it," D.Q. whimpered.

Pancho swung his leg and slammed the door shut with his foot. It was around the time of the evening when D.Q. started to fall apart. He could hold his bodily functions more or less in check during the day, but as soon as night came, his body began to crumble. He came out of the bathroom with a white towel around his neck.

"Shut the door," Pancho ordered again. "It smells."

"Sorry. It's the chemo." D.Q. closed the door.

Pancho watched him shuffle over to the bed. "What does all that have to do with being a warrior? That crap you just read. It has nothing to do with being a warrior."

"I was just getting to that part." D.Q. started toward the desk and the notebook.

"Just tell me," Pancho said impatiently. "Warriors fight. Who does your Death Warrior fight?"

D.Q. collapsed back into bed. "The Death Warrior fights against time that is wasted. Time that is wasted by not loving is the Death Warrior's enemy. I say it right there. But I need to expand the warrior theme, I agree. The Death Warrior fights against all that seeks to diminish the value of life. He fights against the death of the spirit, whatever form it takes. The death of the spirit can come when we grasp life more than we should or it can come when we fail to appreciate life, when we are not grateful for it, when we don't even notice we're alive."

Pancho exhaled loudly. It was hopeless to even try to understand.

D.Q. continued quickly, "Like right now. Part of me just wants to give up. The feeling of wanting to give up, of thinking that life as I'm living it now is not worth living, that's a kind of death. That's the kind of death the Death Warrior fights against. I'm a Death Warrior when I struggle against that feeling. Not very successfully right now, I admit." D.Q. burped.

"How are the walks with Marisol?" Pancho asked. It was amazing how D.Q. was well enough to go for walks in the afternoon, and then at night, when Pancho had to take care of him, he turned into a stinking mess.

"They're so good, Pancho. We go to this bench over by the golf course and watch the golfers. It's been so good to be able to get to know her and talk to her. It's been perfect, a real gift." D.Q. took out a pair of pajamas from the top drawer of the dresser and began to undress.

"What do you guys talk about anyway?"

"I don't know. Everything."

"I know *you* talk about everything. What does she say to you?"

"Her plans. Her family. You know how she seemed upset with you after you demolished that kid's cell phone?"

"Yeah."

"She has an older brother who just got out of jail. He was in a gang. Still is, I guess. He did time for selling drugs. So it was scary to her, to see you be violent."

"I'm the one that got kneed in the balls."

"She doesn't understand how her brother could have turned out the way he did. They grew up with loving parents. Her father died three years ago of . . . cancer. But her brother was already on a bad path by then. So you see, that's why she felt the way she did about you."

There was a pause. Then Pancho said sternly, "Don't talk about *me* to her."

"What?"

"You told her about my sister. You don't know nothing about my sister."

"Oh." D.Q. finished putting on the pajamas. The pajamas were light blue with pencil-thin red stripes. Every night D.Q. put them on and every morning Pancho threw them in the wash along with the soiled sheets from D.Q.'s bed. "She asked me about you. She's worried about you."

Pancho jumped off the bed almost in one motion. He stood in front of D.Q., glaring at him. D.Q. stood still, unflinching. "She told me you told her about my sister. What did you tell her?"

"I told her your sister died not too long ago."

"What else?"

D.Q. put his hand on Pancho's shoulder. Pancho flicked it away. "I know you want to find the man you think is responsible for her death. I didn't tell her that, though."

Pancho's hard face softened. "How did you know that?"

"I read your file in Father Concha's office the day you came to St. Anthony's. I went to ask him if he would assign you to be my helper. He had to leave the office for something or other and the file was there."

"There's nothing in that file about the man."

"Actually, Mrs. Olivares's report said that you believed your sister was killed by the man she was with. She said a detective told her you should be watched to make sure you didn't go looking for the man."

Pancho let his body sink to the floor. He leaned back against the bed, drew his knees up, and put his hand on the side of his head. He was a stupid, ignorant fool. He had gone to all the trouble of hiding his purpose and it turned out everyone knew what he was after.

D.Q. sat on the edge of his bed. "The guy you're looking for is in Albuquerque, isn't he?"

"Is that in Mrs. Olivares's report too?"

"I figured that one out myself. I'm not stupid. Why else would you come?" There was hurt in D.Q.'s voice.

"Why else."

"I take it you know where to find him."

"I'll find him."

"But you haven't seen him yet?"

"No."

"I've kept you busy, huh?"

Pancho looked up and nodded absently. The only light in the room came from the lamp on the desk, where D.Q. had been writing his manifesto. He could barely see D.Q.'s face. "What are you gonna do?" he asked D.Q. point-blank.

"What should I do?" D.Q.'s voice was shaky.

"Nothing. You should do nothing," Pancho said without emotion.

"What are you thinking?"

"I'm done thinking. He killed my sister. I have no doubts about that. In one way or another, he killed her."

"Even if the police say there was no foul play?"

"I know for sure he did it. I thought about it a long time. I wouldn't do what I'm going to do if I wasn't sure."

"You need to explain to me how you're so sure. Is it a gut feeling?"

"Yeah. No. It's more than a gut feeling. It's too complicated."

"I got time. Not much, but enough. Probably. If you get started soon." Pancho couldn't see D.Q.'s face, but he could hear him smiling.

Pancho spoke as if in slow motion. "I saw the coroner's report. It said she died of undetermined natural causes. But there at the bottom of the page, I read something. It said that they found alcohol in her blood. Point-zero-one percent. It wasn't enough to make anyone legally drunk. But my sister, she couldn't drink. When she was about seven, one of our neighbors had a birthday party in the backyard, and my sister took a sip from a leftover glass of rum and Coke. About ten minutes later, she fainted. They took her to the hospital and barely managed to revive her. At first, they didn't even know what happened to her. She had no signs of anything life-threatening. All the doctor could figure out was that she was allergic to alcohol. It was a very rare allergy. The doctor said it was so bad she could have died from even that sip. There were no rashes or choking or anything like other allergies. The alcohol would just work its way through her body and then she would lose consciousness and her heart would stop.

"So my sister, she wasn't too smart, but the one thing she knew was that she couldn't drink. Not even one sip. Before that birthday party, my dad liked to have a beer after work. After that, he stopped drinking altogether. Wouldn't even drink outside of the house. He drummed it into her that she would die if she drank until nothing scared her so much as the sight of a beer can. We all spent our lives scared, checking medicines and sodas and all liquids that came into the house to make sure they didn't have alcohol. I never knew there was so much stuff that used alcohol. She wouldn't even touch the empty beer cans at the Green Café where she worked. She'd pick up all the dirty plates from the table and leave the beer bottles there for someone else. She thought that if she got too close to an open bottle, the fumes would kill her, or a drop would get on her hand and then she might stick it in her mouth by mistake. She never drank anything she didn't pour herself. That's how I know she didn't die of natural causes. That's how I know she was killed. The guy she was with made her drink. He must have forced her even though I know she would have told him she couldn't. I know because I know. I know her like my own blood. She *was* my own blood. She'd never drink on her own. 'I'll die if I drink, so help me *Diosito*.' That's what she said to people when they offered her a drink. 'I'll die if I drink, so help me *Diosito*. I'll die if I drink, so help me God.' That's what she used to say to people."

"Did you tell that to the police?"

"The police didn't even want to look for the man who was with her. Think about it. How could they prove that someone forced her to drink? How could they prove it wasn't a mistake? I'm only sure because I lived with her all my life."

"If they can talk to the guy, question him. If they know that the guy knew about her allergy —"

"If the police question him, he'll deny he did anything wrong and I'll never be able to get to him. I'll never know the truth."

"So you plan to do what?"

"I plan to find him."

"Then what?"

"You said back then you were gonna help me. You help me and I'll help you, you said."

"You want me to help you get away after you kill him. Is that what you want?"

"No. I don't care about afterward. I need you to not do anything. That's the only help I need from you."

D.Q. lowered his voice even more. "When we talked back in St. Anthony's about what you had to do, we talked about how we would go through the treatments first and then you would do what you needed to do, and I would help you then. You need to wait until we finish with the treatments and we spend two weeks with Helen. Stu, Helen's husband, is a high-powered lawyer. He can help us bring this guy to justice. By then, you may not want to do this all by yourself, or even kill him."

"It's not gonna happen."

"It's already happening. You're getting closer to being a Death Warrior every day. You won't kill anyone."

"He killed Rosa. I was supposed to be taking care of her."

"What makes you think that snuffing out his life will be that big of a punishment for him? Let him stew in his guilt for the rest of his life. That's a much bigger punishment."

Pancho shook his head. "There's no way around it."

D.Q. gave out a long sigh. "I have faith that you will change your mind."

"Faith."

"I have faith in you. You're not a killer. You're a Death Warrior. Death Warriors don't kill people."

"You don't know me."

"Maybe I know you more than you know yourself. What will change after you kill him?"

Pancho shouted: "Maybe I'll kill him, maybe I won't! I don't know! Whatever I do, it will make things right!"

D.Q. covered his face with both hands. When he uncovered his face, he said, "Look, the guy's not going anywhere. If after the treatments, after we stay with Helen, you still feel the same way, I won't stop you. I'll help you find him. I'll help you get away if you need to . . . afterward. I'll get money from Helen so you can go hide someplace. But we are in agreement that you will wait. Promise me you won't do anything until after we stay with Helen. After that, if you still feel the same way, we deal with your man."

"I'm not asking you to get involved."

"You're my friend. I'm already involved. Two more weeks, more or less, that's all I ask." D.Q. grabbed his stomach. "I need to hear you promise not to do anything."

Pancho nodded.

"I need to hear you say the words."

"All right, I promise," he said, annoyed.

"I have to go again," D.Q. moaned. He stood up. Pancho stayed on the floor. Just before D.Q. entered the bathroom, he turned around and said to Pancho: "In two weeks, you'll be a Death Warrior. You'll be busy killing all the junk Death Warriors need to kill. You're basically almost there. You just need to decide to be one. You need to decide once and for all to live like a Death Warrior."

CHAPTER 25

He dug the revolver and the bullets from the hospital grounds the following morning and hid them under the bed. Then, in the afternoon, while D.Q. was napping and before the rickshaw rides began, he climbed on the rickshaw and rode five blocks to the telephone booth. He took out the piece of paper with the name and telephone numbers of the five construction companies whose names ended with "and Sons." What he decided to do was call a company and ask if Bobby worked there. If they said yes, he would say he had a package to deliver to him and ask for his full name. Then he would see whether he could look up the man's home address in the book. He thought it better if he went to the man's house. And then he would find the man and step into the ring with him.

"Which Pancho is it going to be?" he heard an imaginary Marisol ask as he closed the doors of the phone booth. *I guess it's going to be this one,* he said to her. He took a blank piece of paper and a pencil from his shirt pocket. He studied the other piece of paper and then he wiped his mouth with the back of his hand.

He dialed the first number.

"Jensen and Sons." It was a woman.

"Uhh. Yeah. Can I speak to Bobby?"

"Bobby who?"

"I don't know his last name."

"Hon, I can't help you if you don't have a last name. I got about four Roberts here, and as far as I know, they could all be Bobbys."

"He was in Las Cruces a few weeks ago."

"That's got to be Robert Lewis. Hold on a second, I'll connect you."

Shit. She was connecting him. Should he hang up? He stayed on the line. He took a deep breath. *Stay cool.* It would be a lot easier to stay cool if he didn't have to talk.

"This is Robert."

He gulped. "Robert Lewis who works at Jensen and Sons." He forgot to make it sound like a question.

"Yes, what is it?"

"I have a package for Robert Lewis who works at Jensen and Sons."

"Yeah, this is Bobby Lewis. I work here. What is it? What kind of package?"

His heart pounded. His mind went blank. He was talking to the man who killed Rosa.

"Hello? You still there? What do you need? What kind of package?"

He clenched his jaw and squeezed his eyes shut. He put the receiver of the telephone against his forehead and bit his lips to keep the words he most wanted to say from coming out.

"Hello? Hello?"

"It says here I'm supposed to deliver it to your home at 25 Marisol Drive, but I can't find your house."

"Maybe that's 'cause I don't live at no 25 Marisol Drive. What kind of package is it? Are you from UPS?"

"Yes, sir."

"Who's the package for?"

"A Robert Lewis."

"Well, that's me all right. Where's the package from?"

Silence.

"Hello! Are you still there? Who sent the package?"

"It's from Josie's."

"Josie's? I didn't order no package from Josie's."

"I could return it."

"No, go ahead and deliver it. Probably something my wife bought."

"I can do that. What's the correct address again?"

"145 Handel Road."

"Thank you." He hung up. He noticed that the receiver was moist from the sweat on his hands. He wrote down the man's full name and his home address on the blank piece of paper. He was surprised at himself. He didn't think he was capable of coming up with words as fast as all that. Marisol Drive? Josie's? It was funny the things that came out when you didn't have time to think.

He climbed onto the bicycle and rode back slowly toward Casa Esperanza, the quarters jingling in his pocket. His mind replayed the sound of Robert Lewis's voice. The voice sounded old and tired. He sounded the way D.Q. sounded sometimes, like there wasn't enough air in his lungs to push the words all the way out. Pancho tried to remember some of the words from the Death Warrior Manifesto that D.Q. read the night before. *The moment when death shows you that you will die.* He remembered those words because he had actually thought about them and had concluded that death had shown him that his life would come to an early end, just like it did for his mother, father, and sister.

A car was honking at him. He waved it on with his left hand. He couldn't move any farther to the right even if he wanted to, and there was plenty of room to pass. Still, the car honked. He stopped and turned abruptly to tell the driver what to do with himself when he heard his name called out. A white sports car pulled up beside him, and a dark glass window slid down automatically. D.Q.'s mother lifted her sunglasses and rested them on top of her head. "Hello there," she said, waving. "It's just me. Do you have time for a cup of coffee?" Now someone was honking at her. "Oh, shush!" she said to the car behind her. "It will only take a minute. I'll meet you there." She pointed to the convenience store at the end of the block. Then she waved again, placed the sunglasses back on her nose, and drove away slowly.

Pancho rode into the parking lot of the convenience store. She was waiting for him, standing beside her car with two paper cups of coffee in her hands. He stopped the bike next to her and put down the kickstand but didn't get off. She handed him the coffee. "Sugar and milk all right?" she asked. He nodded, even though he liked his coffee black, and took the cup from her. Her car was sleek and new, the kind that only seats two people. He thought it must be funny to see the rusty rickshaw with its unopened beach umbrella and the fancy car next to each other. He took a sip of the coffee and waited for her to speak.

"This is an interesting contraption." She looked over the rickshaw.

"It works," he said.

"Mmm. It probably wouldn't be that hard to get a new one. There must be places that sell them on the Internet."

He waited again. There must be a reason she wanted to talk to him. What was she doing driving around five blocks from Casa Esperanza anyway? "D.Q.'s not doing too well," he said. "He throws up a lot."

She made an expression like she knew all about it. "Actually, he's doing better than expected. I just came from Dr. Melendez's office. His blood counts are holding up. He doesn't think the side effects are so severe. I mean, he thinks Daniel is doing quite well with the program. He's hopeful that he will be able to continue with the treatment."

Pancho felt like telling her that Dr. Melendez had obviously not seen D.Q.'s pale, green face or heard him retch in the middle of the night or cleaned up after his nosebleeds. He had accompanied D.Q. to nearly all his treatments and sat next to him during most of them and not once had he seen Dr. Melendez. "Continue treatment? He has only two more treatments left."

"Followed by a two-week recovery period. Then after that we'll continue with another cycle of treatments."

"For how long?"

She took a slow drink of her coffee. "Until he's well."

Pancho dropped his head on his chest. He felt like D.Q. would have felt at that instant: deceived, trapped. This lady was never going to let D.Q. go back to Las Cruces. He raised his head again and met her eyes. "You lied to him," he told her.

The smile on her face said she knew she had lied but she didn't care. Nor did she care what he thought of her, he could tell. "You'll like living at the ranch. I fixed up the room over the garage, next to Juan. Have you ever ridden horses?"

"No. I never rode no horses," he said with an edge, pretending he was even more ignorant and backward than she thought he was.

"My husband just bought a young racehorse. You can help Juan train him."

"Who's Juan?"

"He works the ranch. He's been with us forever."

A wave of nausea came over him. He looked for a place to dump the coffee.

"All I ask is that you give me a chance." She was wearing a pink skirt and a white blouse without sleeves. He felt the touch of her hand on his arm — the softest hand that had ever touched him. He glanced down at the hand and she removed it. "You're going to be very comfortable there. It is where Daniel should be . . . while he is going through this."

He remembered D.Q.'s smile, the one he saw on his face whenever D.Q. saw or talked to or talked about Marisol. Wherever Marisol was, that's where D.Q. should be. That's where he would want to be. Pancho got off the bicycle and walked over to the trash can at the side of the store. He dropped the cup inside, still full

211

of coffee, then went back and grabbed the handlebars. He stopped. She was waiting for him to say something. "D.Q. thinks you're gonna pick him up this Saturday."

"Friday at eleven is his last treatment." She sounded businesslike.

"One of the girls who works at la Casa invited him over to her house for dinner on Friday. He'd like to go to that."

"Oh?" She seemed surprised.

"Yeah."

"I made some plans for Friday. I was going to pick you all up after the treatment."

"It will go easier all around if it's on Saturday." Friday afternoon, while D.Q. rested, was the day he was going to check out Robert Lewis's house. Then on Saturday, he would go with D.Q. over to his mother's. He had promised to stay with D.Q. for two weeks after the treatments were over and he planned to honor that promise. After that, all bets were off. But he wasn't pushing a Saturday pickup because of his own plans. He had no intention of going to Marisol's house, even though he had been invited and D.Q. insisted that he should go. He just knew how much D.Q. was looking forward to the dinner. The lady had to understand that Friday afternoon would not do.

"I'll make you a deal," she said, perking up. "I'll pick you guys up on Saturday if you come with me now. I want to show you something. It will take about an hour."

Pancho looked at her suspiciously. She was an attractive woman, her blond hair shining in the sun and her lips a rosy color he had never seen before. He had heard of older women . . . "What for?" he asked, shaking those thoughts out of his mind.

She grinned, as if she could tell from past experience what he was thinking. "I want you to meet someone, someone who can help Daniel. And who knows, maybe he can help you as well."

"I don't need help."

"We all need help, sweetie. Come on. One hour, that's all I ask."

"What time is it?"

She turned her wrist and looked at the tiny, brilliant watch. "It's only two P.M."

The rickshaw rides generally started around four. But sometimes, a few non-nappers were ready to go even earlier than that. "I gotta get this back." He patted the bicycle seat.

"Hold on." She lifted one finger and disappeared into the convenience store. When she came out, she said, "All taken care of." She was waving a key. "We can lock it up by the Dumpster." She motioned for him to follow her.

Behind the store, she unlocked the door to a wooden enclosure and he pushed the rickshaw in next to the Dumpster. Then she closed the door and locked it. She was smiling, happy with herself, it seemed, for her brilliant solution to the problem of the rickshaw. They went back around to the car.

"I need to get back by three. There's some kids expecting me," he said, sinking into the car seat.

She smiled briefly in his direction. He didn't get the sense that his schedule mattered to her. She started the car and shifted into reverse and then first, her movements both smooth and forceful. She waited only a second before she lurched into the street.

There was classical guitar music coming from the radio. She turned it off. He waited for her to tell him where they were going, but she drove in silence, like she didn't even know he was there.

Her hand gripped the top of the steering wheel tightly. He looked out the window. She went up a ramp, got on I-25 South, and pressed down on the accelerator. The car's engine hummed.

There was something uncomfortable about the way the lady was all smiles and friendly one minute and stone cold the next. She was definitely strange. D.Q. was strange as well, but in a different way. D.Q. was always the same weird, a steady weird. You could count on who he was. With the mother, you had this uneasy feeling, like you never knew what you were getting.

They were heading away from the center of town, away from the mountains. A billboard advertised genuine Hopi Kachina dolls, and Pancho thought of Rosa.

After five minutes of fast driving, they got off the highway. The exit sign read RIO BRAVO BOULEVARD. They turned onto a road lined with stores that sold Native American crafts, and drove past a parking lot full of cars. Pancho couldn't figure out what all those cars were doing in a little town and then he saw the sign for a Baptist church. A few blocks later, they turned onto a street with crumbling adobe houses. In front of the first house on the street, a child was trying to keep a tortilla out of reach of a yellow dog. A satellite dish in the backyard was bigger than the house. They slowed down. For the first time, Pancho noticed that a cloud of dust was trailing them. They were on a dirt road. Two men without shirts leaned against the hood of a truck, drinking beer. They stopped talking to watch them drive by.

"Don't worry," she said. "It's safe." Those were the first words she had spoken since they got in the car.

He turned and glared at her. Why on earth would she think that driving through a poor neighborhood would ever bother him? She was the one who should be afraid, with her rich, fancy car and her golden hair. "I don't worry," he said, looking away from her.

"Don't you want to know where we're going?"

He shrugged his shoulders. "I figure I'll find out one of these days."

She cracked a smile and shifted down into second. The engine made an unhappy sound, like it didn't like to be reined in. "I think you're going to like Johnny," she said. A chicken fluttered out of their way.

"Who's Johnny?"

"Johnny Corazon is a shaman. You know what that is?"

"Nope."

"He's a healer, a spiritual doctor. He's going to help Daniel."

"Help him do what?"

She pulled into a driveway and turned the ignition off. There was immediate silence. She seemed to be looking for a way to explain something that was difficult to explain, or maybe she just thought he was stupid. He didn't think the question he asked was all that hard. She turned so that her back was against the car door and she was facing him. "Cure him. He's going to cure him."

"A witch doctor?"

"Not a witch doctor, a healer. Just a gifted healer of body and soul." He kept his eyes fixed on her to see if she was joking. She wasn't. She went on. "The body and the mind are one. What you think and what you feel affect your health. Western medicine, the kind that is treating Daniel back at the hospital, is for his body, but what about his mind? Healing will come when the mind is healed."

"D.Q.'s mind is working pretty good," Pancho asserted. "Most of the time I don't even understand what he's saying." He thought maybe that wasn't saying all that much.

She was silent for a moment. Maybe she was wondering if he was capable of understanding *her*. Then she said, "Daniel does not believe he can be healed. He needs to believe. Johnny Corazon is going to help him believe." She raised her eyes and looked at the house in front of her.

Pancho looked at the house as well. On the brown door, he could see a big red heart with the word "JOHNNY" in black, piercing it like an arrow. The house was not painted or even plastered. Pancho could see straw sticking out of the raw adobe walls. The wooden beams that sustained the flat roof were rotting. He could feel the sweat on the back of his shirt. A giant wooden cross leaned against a fence. It was one of those crosses people carried on their backs during Easter services when they were pretending to be Christ. He sighed. He was paying a high price for D.Q. to have an extra day with Marisol.

"Do you have any questions before we go in?"

"Yeah. What does all this have to do with me?"

She looked dry and cool. The woman did not sweat. "If *you* have faith in Johnny, Daniel will come see him. It's as simple as that."

He chuckled to himself. There it was again, that word. The more he heard it, the less he knew what it meant. He pulled on the door handle, but the door didn't open. The little kids back at the Casa would be looking for him soon. "Let's get this over with," he told her.

"When I met you at the hospital, I was delighted. I thought you

216

would surely be receptive to nontraditional kinds of healing. Your background, I thought, would have given you access to . . . natural medicines like herbs, for example. You must have heard of *curanderos*, right?"

He smiled at the Anglo way she pronounced the word. "*Cure-an-dero?*" he asked, mimicking her pronunciation. He shook his head. Their medicine cabinet, in the tiny trailer bathroom, had Pepto-Bismol for the stomach, aspirin for the head, and hydrogen peroxide and Band-Aids for the rest of the body. That was it.

Someone tapped on his window and he saw a big, brown face on the other side of the glass.

"Johnny!" he heard the woman exclaim. She turned the ignition on and rolled down the window.

"Are you guys coming in or what?"

Pancho's instant impression was that the man had the face of a drug addict. It was either a young man's face that had aged before its time or an old man's face trying hard to look young. The skin on his jaws sagged, his brown eyes floated in a web of red lines, and his greasy, long black hair was pulled back and tied in a braid.

"Hello, Helen!" he said, waving his fingers at D.Q.'s mother. "And you must be Pancho. Pancho! Pancho! Pancho! A powerful name!" Johnny Corazon stuck his hand through the window and held it in front of Pancho's face. Pancho pretended to shake it by grabbing the top of it with his right hand. Maybe at one time it had been a workingman's hand, but not anymore. "Well, come on in. I've been waiting for you." He opened Pancho's door.

"Wait!" D.Q.'s mother said. "I brought you a little something." She reached behind her seat and pulled out a brown paper bag. Two cartons of Marlboro menthol cigarettes were sticking out of it.

"Wonderful!" Johnny Corazon said, grabbing it and inadvertently whacking Pancho on the side of the face. "Oh, excuse me, Pancho," he apologized. "I ran out of smokes this morning. You're a lifesaver, Helen." He moved back so that Pancho could step out of the car.

It occurred to him that he should just start running. He had some money in his pocket. He could offer the men he saw down the street forty dollars to drive him back into town. Or he could just walk back. How long would that take him? It took them about five minutes to get there and the woman was driving around eighty miles an hour. If you drive for five minutes at eighty miles an hour, how many miles have you gone? Why did he keep giving himself math problems when there was no way for him to figure them out? He thought of the time D.Q. had asked him how long it would take to walk from St. Anthony's to the mountains. "On those things?" he had said, pointing at D.Q.'s legs.

He was walking behind D.Q.'s mother and Johnny Corazon, who were whispering to each other. The guy was wearing red gym shorts and yellow flip-flops. Next to him was D.Q.'s mother in her pink skirt, her back very straight, like the queen of some cold country. If he ran now, would he be able to find his way back? Johnny Corazon was holding the door open for him. "Come in, come in. *Mi casa es su casa*," he was saying. Pancho was about to go into the house of a witch doctor wearing gym shorts.

As soon as he entered the house, he was hit with an overly sweet smell that made it hard to breathe. The room was dark except for the light of dozens of flickering candles scattered on shelves, on tables, even on the floor. Against a wall stood an altar with a statue of the Virgen de Guadalupe surrounded by a string of multicolored Christmas lights. The altar had a white tablecloth. Next to the statue, on either side, were two milk bottles filled with large black and brown feathers. The wall behind the statue was plastered with pictures of people. In the middle of the room was a cot covered with a Mexican sarape. A black sofa and an assortment of chairs were arranged around the cot like theater seats.

"Sit, sit." Johnny Corazon moved some chairs out of the way and pointed at the sofa. D.Q.'s mother sat in the middle and patted the space next to her. Pancho grabbed a metal chair instead. Johnny Corazon pulled a chair in front of Pancho and dropped the bag with the cigarettes on the floor. He crossed his legs. "Well," he said, "here we all are." His unblinking eyes fixed on Pancho as if trying to peer down his insides.

"I gotta get back pretty soon," Pancho said uncomfortably.

"Excuse me, do you mind?" Johnny Corazon leaned across and stretched his arms so that his hands were a few inches from Pancho's face. Pancho flung his head back as far as the chair would let him. "I just need to feel your aura for one second." He closed his eyes and spread his fingers. "Oof," Johnny Corazon said. He opened his eyes and put his hands flat on his lap.

"What is it?" D.Q.'s mother asked.

"That's a lot of anger you're packing, son." Johnny Corazon touched his heart as if in pain. Pancho narrowed his eyes. No one had called him "son" since his father died.

"I'm not angry," Pancho said.

"No?" Johnny Corazon stuck his right hand out like he was about to bless Pancho. "Maybe you don't feel angry anymore, but anger is there. It's dried and set like concrete. It's the worst kind."

Pancho looked away. When his father died, his father's friends had sent flowers to the funeral home. He was surprised at how many flowers surrounded the closed wooden coffin. Johnny Corazon's living room had the same sickening smell.

D.Q.'s mother said, "Johnny, tell Pancho about the people you healed." Pancho followed her eyes and saw she was looking at the pictures behind the altar.

Johnny Corazon uncrossed his legs, stood up, went to the pictures, searched for a few moments, and then removed one from the wall. He sat down again and offered the picture to Pancho. It was a black-and-white picture of a boy who looked a lot like Memo back at St. Anthony's. D.Q.'s mother scooted to the edge of the sofa and stretched her neck to see the picture. Pancho handed it to her. "Ahh," she exclaimed, "Esteban."

"Esteban is twelve years old. He had a rare form of lymphoma, a very deadly cancer. He's in total remission."

"Johnny healed him," D.Q.'s mother said.

"No," Johnny Corazon corrected her. "He was healed through me. I don't feel like I'm responsible for the healings. I'm a conduit."

"A what?" Pancho said.

"Powers work through me."

"What kind of powers?"

"Good powers," D.Q.'s mother piped up. Johnny Corazon motioned to her that it was all right, that he could handle Pancho's questions on his own. "Sorry," she said.

"You're anxious. You want to get back. Someone is expecting you. Children perhaps? Don't worry, they'll understand if you're late just this once." Johnny Corazon raised his eyebrows as if to ask, *Did I get it right?*

"Yeah. They're waiting for me." Pancho was not impressed by Johnny Corazon's guess. D.Q.'s mother could have whispered something to him on the way in.

"Okay. You ask what kind of powers? Helen says they are good powers because they bring good results. And maybe they do here, in this room, in this sacred space. But for all I know, these same powers also bring results that we humans would call 'bad.' Esteban there was healed." He nodded toward the picture. "The same power that caused the cells in his body to go wacko caused them to settle down and act normal again. Where is that power? It was in Esteban's own body. It is everywhere. For some reason, it sometimes comes when I ask it to come, and for some reason it sometimes acts in ways we humans call 'good.'"

"Esteban believed in that power, didn't he?" Helen said. "He surrendered to it. Pancho —" She waited for him to look at her. "Remember at the hospital, I told you about the illness that forced me to take Daniel to St. Anthony's?" Pancho didn't answer. He was trying to think of the term she had used, something to do with a pole. "Bipolar disorder, remember? Johnny helped me get better. I owe him my life, really. I think I would have ended up hurting myself or hurting many others if I hadn't met him. He says it isn't he who heals people, but if powers act through him, then as far as I'm concerned, he's the one who heals."

She was beaming at Johnny Corazon. Johnny Corazon winked gratefully at her. The whole scene was making Pancho ill. He tried to picture D.Q. lying on the cot in the middle of the room, and Johnny Corazon waving feathers around him and blowing smoke in his face, or whatever it was that he did to invoke the powers. There was no way that D.Q. would agree to it. Not if his life depended on it, which it did.

Johnny Corazon said, "Don't let appearances deceive you. I know this place looks a little hokey. People kind of expect this kind of atmosphere, so I give it to them. It helps them. I have an Indian outfit and bead necklaces that I can put on if you want me to." He laughed. "I didn't choose to do this. It chose me. I'd rather not have gone through all the humiliation I've had to go through because of this. I'm just a poor Chicano recovering heroin addict, and every day is a battle to stay sober. I'm not going to lie to you. This so-called gift I got is a royal pain in the ass."

Pancho thought of D.Q. If D.Q. were here, what would he say? He would be looking at Johnny Corazon to see whether the guy was a Death Warrior. A question came to him. "Can you heal all the people that come to you?"

Johnny Corazon and D.Q.'s mother glanced at each other. "No," Johnny Corazon admitted — reluctantly, it seemed. "Not always."

"If they have faith —" D.Q.'s mother started to say, but Johnny Corazon cut her off.

"Here's what I do." Johnny Corazon edged his chair closer to Pancho's. Their knees touched. Pancho moved his legs. "It depends on the age and intelligence of the person. I use everything at my disposal, herbs, ancient purification rites, trance sessions, spirit invocations, meditation, plain old talk therapy, acupuncture, homeopathy. I meet with people and sometimes we discover the emotions or the memories that are affecting the body. Sometimes I bring the whole family together. Sometimes we have rituals of mutual forgiveness. I let myself be led by the person's spirit. I practice holistic medicine. Holistic as in 'whole,' because we take in the whole person, heart and soul, and no approach is excluded."

"You ever have kids die on you?"

"Yes. I'm not God." Johnny Corazon seemed offended by the question.

"Kids can get their hopes up high to be cured, and if they don't, then they would be worse."

"It doesn't work like that," Johnny Corazon said quickly. "It's never worse afterward, even when people are not healed. Holistic medicine can even make people tolerate regular treatments like chemotherapy and radiation better. And even if the body is not healed, the person's spirit will be strengthened. I have no doubt about that."

"But so many people do get healed," Helen broke in. "Look at all those pictures on the wall."

"Okay," Pancho said impatiently. "I get it."

"Do you believe that Johnny can help D.Q.?" There was a trembling quality to her voice. "That's the important thing."

Pancho reflected. All he knew was that if he were ill, he would not want to spend time in this dark room that smelled like a funeral parlor. But he didn't say what he was thinking. He just wanted to get out of there. "Sure," he said. "Anything is possible."

D.Q.'s mother smiled, but Johnny Corazon looked concerned. He wasn't convinced that he had won Pancho over, and he was right. "I wish you would come see me again," he said slowly and meaningfully. "Your anger is going to kill you."

"Could be." Pancho stood up. "I'll talk to D.Q. That's what you want me to do, right?"

Johnny Corazon and D.Q.'s mother both rose, but not as quickly as Pancho. Johnny Corazon went to the altar, grabbed something from a wicker basket, came back, and placed it in Pancho's hand. Pancho opened his hand and saw a key chain with a round plastic heart. It was the kind of thing you get out of a bubblegum machine. On top of the heart was a black button. Johnny Corazon flicked it, and a red light began to throb inside.

"For you," Johnny Corazon said solemnly, as if he had just given Pancho a most valuable treasure. "To remind you."

CHAPTER 26

It was Friday afternoon and Pancho, D.Q., and Josie were waiting for Marisol to pick them up. It was cloudy, probably the first cloudy day since Pancho and D.Q. had arrived in Albuquerque. Josie's mother had given her a jacket, which she had taken off, so now Pancho was holding it.

"What time is it? Maybe we missed her," D.Q. said. He was rolling his wheelchair forward and backward nervously.

"It's five," Pancho said. "That's the time she told us to be here." Pancho wasn't happy to be standing there. He had decided to come only after Marisol told him that D.Q. refused to go unless Pancho went. She pleaded with him, "Please, do it for me," and he had fallen for it. So Pancho had to put up with days of D.Q.'s nervousness and anticipation. Helen had left a message that she would pick them up Saturday morning at ten A.M. Pancho's sacrificial visit to Johnny Corazon's had bought them an additional day.

"Look, Pancho." Josie was sitting on the front step of Casa Esperanza tugging at his sleeve. "It died." He had given her the key-chain heart he got from Johnny Corazon and now it had stopped blinking. He took it from her and examined it. There was no place for a battery. When it went, it went for good.

"It was a cheap thing." He moved to throw it away.

"Nooo! It's mine," Josie protested. "I want it anyway."

"Why?" He held it away from her grasp.

"You gave it to me."

"Pancho gave his heart away," D.Q. teased.

"He's not my boyfriend or anything." Josie grabbed the plastic heart. "I already have a boyfriend."

"Maybe we should call." D.Q. was very fidgety. Pancho thought he knew why. The past couple of days, D.Q. had been unusually quiet, thinking overtime. Pancho had caught him talking to himself a couple of times, as if he were rehearsing a speech. He suspected that D.Q. saw the dinner at Marisol's house as an opportunity to tell her how he felt about her.

"She'll be here," Pancho said. "Stop worrying."

"I don't worry," D.Q. said. He said it the way Pancho always said it, like he was way too tough to worry.

"Now what?" Pancho asked Josie. She was rubbing her eyes with her hand. "Why are you crying now?"

"Shhh." D.Q. gestured to Pancho. He reached over from his wheelchair and put his hand on Josie's back. "We'll see each other again, I promise. Santa Fe is not so far. We'll come visit. Or you'll come visit."

"She's not crying 'cause we're leaving," Pancho said, trying to sound funny. "She's crying 'cause the heart doesn't light up anymore."

"I'm not even crying," Josie said.

Everyone was silent. Maybe they were thinking like Pancho that no matter how much D.Q. promised Josie and the other kids that they would see each other again, the truth was that it was unlikely that they ever would.

Pancho took the key-chain heart from Josie's hand. He examined it and saw that the two halves were glued together. He might be able to open it with a razor blade and replace whatever it was that lit it up. Or he could return to Johnny Corazon's house and pick up another one. *Yeah, right,* Pancho said to himself. He had not mentioned the trip to Johnny Corazon's to D.Q. A couple of times he had started and stopped. If D.Q. knew that his mother had no intention of letting him go anywhere after two weeks or two years, Pancho's own plans might be jeopardized. Already he was falling behind the schedule he had set for himself. This was the afternoon when he was supposed to have checked out Robert Lewis's house. Andrés, the kid who always beat him at video games, had, for a fee of only one dollar, gone on the Internet and printed out a map of 145 Handel Road, with directions on how to get there from Casa Esperanza. It was only a half-hour bus ride away, assuming he didn't run into anyone on the bus. He was set to go as soon as they got back from D.Q.'s last treatment at the hospital, but D.Q. never took his nap. Then the kids came and there were rickshaw-ride requests he found hard to refuse since it was his last day. When he came in after the rides, he was too tired to go anywhere. He fell asleep while D.Q., already showered and dressed, waited anxiously for five P.M. to finally come.

"She's not coming," D.Q. said.

"You smell like oranges," Josie said to him.

D.Q. tapped his cheeks. "I might have overdone it a little with the cologne."

"You think?" Josie pinched her nose.

"I should go splash some water on my face. I don't want to smell like a fruit."

"It's better than what you usually smell like," Pancho declared.

"Ha-ha. Josie, is it really too strong?" Pancho fanned the back of D.Q.'s head with his hand. "What are you doing?"

"I'm shooing the flies away," Pancho responded.

Josie jumped up. "I'll be right back. I'm going to get a paper towel with water so you can soak your face."

"No, stay. What if Marisol comes?" D.Q. yelled after her. But she had disappeared inside already.

"Where did you get that perfume? I didn't know you brought any." Pancho sat on the ledge. He peered at D.Q.'s face. "Did you put makeup on?"

"No."

"What's that on your face?"

"It's just a little sunblock."

"There's no sun."

"It's sunblock with some color so it looks like a tan. One of the nurses at the hospital got it for me . . . from the gift shop . . . when she got the cologne." D.Q., who had started out embarrassed, was now laughing.

"It looks like shoeshine."

"I'm too pale. You can see the veins on my face. I look like a skeleton tossed in flour."

"You think smearing your face with caca is gonna make you look better?"

"Is it that bad?"

Pancho took another look. "Only if you're planning on getting kissed."

D.Q. ran his hand across his forehead. There was a light brown tint on his fingers. He shook his head. "I don't know what got into me."

"I can tell you, if you want me to," Pancho said.

"Has this ever happened to you?"

It was one of the few times when Pancho knew exactly what D.Q. was talking about. He considered for a few seconds, then opted to answer with a joke. "I never got it so bad that I was willing to make an ass of myself."

"You're right. I lost track of myself. It's just that after tonight . . . If I can't convince her to come see us at Helen's or visit us in Las Cruces, I mean, tonight could be it."

"She'll come visit you," Pancho told him. He could say that with certainty from all that he had seen of Marisol.

"Us. We need her to come visit *us*."

Pancho saw in D.Q.'s eyes a spark of secret understanding.

"I don't think she likes being around me," Pancho muttered, embarrassed by the thought that maybe D.Q. knew more than Pancho wanted him to know.

"Don't be a dummy. You know that's not true."

"She's afraid of me."

"You may be killing someone. Can you blame her?"

"She doesn't know. . . ."

"No, she doesn't." D.Q. lowered his head. "I have a feeling

that's not why she's afraid of you." His eyes were focused on some distant point.

Pancho felt a pressure inside his head, as if all of a sudden a dozen thoughts were calling for his attention and he didn't know where to turn. He grabbed on to one of them. "I'm not going to be around much longer."

"Me neither," D.Q. said.

Josie came out at the very moment they heard Marisol's car down the block. Josie handed the wet paper towel to D.Q. "You do it," D.Q. said to Pancho. "Hurry."

Pancho squeezed the water out of the soaking towel, then opened it and began to wipe D.Q.'s face. "She's coming, she's coming," Josie was yelling.

"Did you get something to dry his face with?" Pancho asked.

"Oops."

"Never mind. Get away from me." D.Q. pushed him away and dried his face with his sleeves.

The car pulled to a halt in front of them. "Sorry I'm late," Marisol said through the open window. "I had to get a neighbor to jump the car. It wouldn't start."

"You need a new muffler too," Pancho told her.

"Don't complain. It's a piece of junk but it's still my mom's precious car. You're lucky she's letting me use it. I told her there was no way we were taking the bus!"

Pancho pushed D.Q. toward the passenger side. D.Q. was smiling and trying to look calm at the same time. "Pop the trunk open!" Pancho shouted to Marisol.

"Oh, no!" Marisol exclaimed.

"What?" Josie asked, alarmed.

"If I give you the key to the trunk, I have to stop the car and then who knows whether it will start again."

"That's all right. I don't need the wheelchair." D.Q. tried to stand up, but the wheelchair was still moving, and he stumbled forward. "Oh, my God!" Pancho heard Marisol yell. He rushed to D.Q. and quickly lifted him off the ground. He was very light.

"That was exciting," D.Q. said, brushing himself off as he leaned against the car. "I'm okay, I'm okay."

Pancho made a move to help D.Q. into the car, but D.Q. shook his head. Pancho understood the gesture. "I'll take the wheelchair in," he said.

"Are you bleeding?" Josie asked D.Q.

"No, of course not," D.Q. answered. "It was nothing."

Pancho sat in the backseat with Josie. He watched Marisol and D.Q. in front. It was not as hard to imagine them as a couple as it had been two weeks ago. He had been observing Marisol and concluded that someone like her could very well be interested in someone like D.Q. She could get past the way he looked and appreciate D.Q.'s weird mind. She was unusual, like him. There was something about them both that he could not define. He had looked for the word but could not find the right one. It was a calmness they had, a seriousness that lay inside of them, solid and unshakable. No matter how much they joked or laughed on the outside, no matter how silly they acted, the seriousness persisted.

He tried to remember the words that D.Q. had read to him

from the Death Warrior Manifesto. *There is a specific moment during which you can decide to become a Death Warrior.* How did the rest go? He always had trouble remembering the rest. He could remember the meaning, more or less, but he could not recollect the exact words. *Once you know that you will die, then you need to choose life or death. If you choose life, you become a Death Warrior.* But choosing life required seriousness, fearlessness, like Marisol and D.Q. had. They were both Death Warriors.

The thought made him smile. It also made him feel sad. He exhaled. Sitting there, listening to Marisol and D.Q. talking in the front seat, Pancho made up his mind to tell D.Q. about Johnny Corazon after they returned from Marisol's house. Suppose the guy was not a phony. There were dozens of pictures on his wall of people who had been cured. *If you choose life, you need to do all you can to stay alive. You need to give even the Johnny Corazons of the world a chance.* That was the argument he would use to convince D.Q. Besides, if D.Q. stayed in Albuquerque, it would be easier for him and Marisol to see each other.

"Pancho." Josie was speaking to him. "Guess what this is." She fluttered all her fingers and then snapped her thumb and middle finger. Flutter. Snap. Flutter. Snap.

"A butterfly with hiccups," Pancho answered absently.

They were entering a neighborhood of small houses with red-tiled roofs. The front yards had skateboards, bicycles, plastic toys that were carelessly abandoned. Two girls about Josie's age were turning a rope and singing a rhyme while a third one skipped. Pancho had heard Rosa sing the same Spanish rhyme to her dolls. Josie followed the movements of the girls closely as they drove by.

"Hey! What's this?" Pancho fluttered his fingers and snapped them, trying to imitate Josie's movements. She did not respond. The sight of the girls jumping rope had sunk her into silence.

The car stopped and the engine cut off. "We're home!" Marisol announced. She opened her door and got out, but no one else opened theirs. The cream stucco of the walls, the red roof, the geraniums by the door, the closely trimmed grass, the white curtains fluttering out an open window, the Mexican music coming from inside made the house look invitingly happy, and no one moved. "Come on." Marisol poked her head back in the car. "What happened to you guys all of a sudden? It's not that scary."

"Who are those people?" Josie asked, concerned. Pancho peered through Josie's window. He could see two people sitting inside.

"It's just my mother," Marisol assured them.

"There's a man with a crew cut," Josie said.

Marisol raised her head and squinted. "Oh God. It's my brother." Pancho saw her exchange glances with D.Q. "Well, looks like you'll get to meet my brother, Ed."

Marisol went around the car and opened D.Q.'s door. Josie looked at Pancho, and Pancho looked at Josie. Pancho shrugged his shoulders. *There's no way out of this one,* he was telling her.

Josie and Pancho followed Marisol and D.Q. into the house. He wished D.Q. had not forced him to come. Fortunately, he could pretend to be sociable by talking to Josie. He gave her a gentle whack on the back of the head, but she only reached up and grabbed his hand. She turned to look down the street. Despite the music coming from inside the house, they could still hear the rhyme of the girls jumping rope.

Marisol held the screen door open for them, and Pancho's nostrils filled with the smell of Mexican spices. He stepped inside. The light from the setting sun streamed in through the window and made the living room radiant. A green vase with white roses stood on top of a coffee table. The chairs and sofa were covered in quilts embroidered with Indian-looking squares and triangles. In the back, Pancho caught a glimpse of a table set with blue dishes and emerald glasses.

A young man dressed in a white T-shirt and khaki pants and wearing black work boots rose from one of the chairs in the living room. An older woman in a pink apron began to lift herself out of the sofa. Marisol went to the record player and bent to turn down the volume. "It's so loud," she said. "The neighbors are going to complain."

"It's Mamá," said the young man, joking. "She needs it loud, otherwise she can't hear."

Marisol stared at the can of beer on the table. "It's my first one. I swear," said the young man.

Marisol introduced her mother to the group. "So you are Daniel," the mother said, hugging D.Q., who looked surprised. She pronounced his name the Spanish way. The mother hugged Josie as well, but when she came to Pancho, she stopped at a distance and scanned him from top to bottom, inspecting him. "*Y tú debes de ser Pancho*," she said, cautiously offering him her hand. Pancho met Marisol's eyes briefly. She must have told her mother about the incident on the bus.

"This is my brother, Ed, everyone," Marisol announced. Ed stepped up and shook hands. His grip was strong, almost painful.

Pancho noticed the tattoos on his forearms and the bulging biceps and powerful neck of a bodybuilder.

"Ouch," Josie squealed after Ed shook her hand.

"Sorry," Ed said. He made to pat Josie's balding head, but then he changed his mind.

"Let's all sit down," Marisol's mother urged. "Marisol, why don't you get everyone some sodas? We have a little time before dinner, unless you're really hungry."

"We have lots of time," D.Q. said. Pancho laughed, a short nervous laugh.

They shuffled slowly forward, each one trying to determine the best place to sit. Pancho headed for one end of the sofa, but Josie beat him to the spot. He almost sat on her lap, then moved over to the middle. D.Q. picked a place on the other end of the sofa. Marisol's mother perched on the edge of a large lounge chair covered with a blue-and-green Indian quilt. Ed grabbed the can of beer and sat on a smaller chair across from them.

"Marisol, bring the guacamole and the chips!" the mother yelled into the kitchen. "I hope you like green chicken enchiladas," she said to D.Q. "I made some soup as well in case you can't eat the enchiladas."

Pancho liked the straightforward way the lady said that. In the time he had been with D.Q., he had seen many people "pussyfoot," as D.Q. liked to say, around his cancer.

"Tonight I will eat everything," D.Q. declared with confidence.

"I like enchiladas too," Josie chimed in. "But my mother never makes them at home. We mostly always have them at a restaurant."

"Luisa's are better than any restaurant," Ed said.

"Who's Luisa?" Josie asked.

"That's my name," Marisol's mother said, pretending to be angry with Ed. "He doesn't like to call me 'Mother' like all the other sons call their mothers."

"Luisa's a good name. I like calling you that." Ed shook the can of beer. It was empty. He leaned back in the chair. He had been tapping the toe of his boot on the floor nonstop since he sat down.

"Ed, can you help me?" Marisol shouted from the kitchen.

Ed jumped up out of the chair. He crushed the empty can with his hand. "Maybe she'll let me have another one of these. You guys want one?"

Pancho, D.Q., and Josie all shook their heads at the same time.

"Eduardo," Marisol's mother said in a low voice.

"Not to worry, Luisa. Everything's under control."

When he had disappeared into the kitchen, Marisol's mother said, "I'm sorry. We weren't expecting him. He shows up sometimes. Unexpected." She wrung her hands.

Josie pulled on Pancho's arm. He bent down and she whispered into his ear, "Don't get into a fight with that jerko."

He looked at her, shocked — what kind of person did she think he was? Then he smiled.

"I'm glad he's here," D.Q. said. "I wanted to meet him as well."

"Marisol told you," the mother said, lowering her voice. She was about to continue, but then she saw Josie. "He's my cross," she said instead. There were loud voices coming out of the kitchen. "Oh, boy. Excuse me for a second." She stood up. Pancho looked at her pink slippers as she went by. Rosa had some just like them. Sometimes they made a smacking sound when she walked.

"Wanna go outside?" Josie asked Pancho.

D.Q. said quickly, "No, stay here. After dinner, maybe we can all go for a walk. Marisol told me there's a park a couple of blocks away."

Pancho understood that D.Q. planned to talk to Marisol during that walk. What would he say to her? Would he tell her how he felt about her? Yes, Pancho thought, D.Q. would not waste the opportunity. If the brother came on the walk, Pancho would have to entertain him with some kind of conversation. He did not look forward to that.

Marisol came out of the kitchen, holding a tray of soda cans and glasses with ice cubes already in them. Ed followed with the guacamole and the tortilla chips. He cradled an unopened can of beer under his armpit. She set the tray on the coffee table. Ed did the same with the two bowls he was carrying. Josie slid down from the sofa, cracked open an orange soda, and quickly took a sip. "I was sooo thirsty," she said, when she noticed everyone staring at her.

"That's all right. You're entitled." Marisol began to pour soda into the glasses. "I didn't get anything with caffeine."

Ed opened the beer, and foam began to pour out. "Shit!" He held the erupting can away from him.

Marisol made a point of ignoring him. "What kind of music do you like? We have other CDs," she told D.Q.

"I like Mexican music," D.Q. responded. "That's a Mexican corrida, isn't it?"

Pancho crunched an ice cube in his mouth. Josie elbowed him.

"That's very good," Marisol said. It took Pancho a few moments to realize she was not commenting on his ice-crunching ability. "How did you become an expert on Mexican music?"

"I'm not really an expert. Whenever I hear a guitar play like that, I think of corridas. I learned about them at St. Anthony's."

"One time," Josie said, "my dad surprised my mom on her birthday with a mariachi band. She was asleep already when we heard them outside playing. They woke up the whole neighborhood."

"Ooo, that's so romantic," Marisol said to her. Pancho crunched again, this time on a tortilla chip with guacamole. "Is it too hot?" Marisol asked him. He looked at her, befuddled. Why would it be hot?

"She means, is the guacamole spicy?" Josie translated.

"No." He finished chewing what was in his mouth quietly.

Ed, who had been staring at D.Q., said, "So what kind of cancer do you have? If you don't mind my asking."

"Ed," Marisol warned.

"I'm just asking a question."

"I don't mind at all," D.Q. said calmly. "I have something called diffuse pontine glioma."

"I have leukemia," Josie piped up.

"Would you like to see my room?" Marisol asked Josie.

"Yeah!" she said, jumping down from the sofa and handing Pancho her soda.

"Your mouth is colored orange," Pancho told her.

"So is my tongue. See?" She stuck her tongue out at Pancho as she left the room.

"What kind of cancer is *that*?" Ed asked D.Q. There was a slight tone of disgust in his voice.

Pancho saw the physical resemblance between the brother and Marisol. He had her good looks, the same straight nose, the clean forehead and deep, dark eyes. But Marisol's face was inviting, while the brother's was hard to look at directly. And Marisol was nice. The brother was turning out to be a jerko, like Josie said.

"It's a cancer that forms at the base of the brain where the brain and the spinal cord connect, a place called the pons." D.Q. touched the back of his head. "It's not a tumor. It's diffuse, spread out."

"Like a fog," Pancho said, remembering what D.Q. had told him once.

"Like what?"

"A fog. I told Pancho that I sometimes picture it like a low-lying fog."

"How about you? What kind of cancer you got?" Ed asked the question as if he wanted Pancho to take offense.

"I don't got any," Pancho responded.

"He came with me to help me. We're from the same boarding school in Las Cruces," D.Q. said quickly. *Boarding school?* Pancho inquired silently. D.Q. blinked, or was it a wink?

"That's cool. Like you got your own little servant." Ed laughed to himself.

Pancho felt his stomach tighten, then he remembered what Josie had whispered in his ear. He raised his eyebrows at D.Q. *I'm trying*, he was telling him. This time D.Q. definitely winked at him.

"How was prison life?" D.Q. asked.

Ed began to cough, as if his beer went down the wrong way. "What did you say?"

"I was wondering what your time in prison was like?" D.Q. seemed to be enjoying himself.

Ed seemed flustered by the question. He moved his tongue once around his cheek before he answered. "It wasn't hard time. I had friends there."

"How does it work?" D.Q. continued. "What if there are no other members of your gang in prison?"

"There's alliances," Ed answered. "Everybody knows that."

"So you need to find other gang members to align yourself with, if there's no one from your gang."

"I don't have to *A-line* myself with anyone. The alliances already exist."

"So it's not like all the Mexican American gangs against all the Anglo gangs against all the African American gangs? It's more complicated than that?"

"Yeah, it's complicated."

Pancho reached for some more guacamole. So far he was the only one who had eaten any. He crunched away.

"Suppose I do something stupid and end up in prison. What would I need to do to survive? Would I have to align myself with the Anglos or could I make it on my own? If I just keep to myself, let's say, could I survive?"

"Someone like you might survive," Ed snickered.

Pancho thought this was meant as an insult, but D.Q. either didn't see it that way or didn't care. He persisted with his questions. "What about someone like Pancho here? Suppose he did something stupid and he ended up in prison? If he kept to himself, would he survive? Or would he have to join a gang — like yours, for example?"

Pancho stopped crunching and stared at D.Q.

Ed scanned Pancho from top to bottom. Then he said, still looking at Pancho, "He'd be killed within a month if he didn't hook up with an organization."

"Why? Why couldn't he just stay out of trouble and do his time?" Either D.Q. was truly curious or he was doing a good job pretending.

"Because of the way he looks at people. People would want to take him on. He'd piss people off."

"How? How does he look at them?"

Pancho and Ed stared at each other. "Like he's looking for a fight," Ed said.

D.Q. seemed happy with Ed's answer, like that was exactly what he was hoping he'd say.

"Dinner!" Marisol's mother called.

D.Q. struggled to stand up. Ed crushed another beer can as he rose. Pancho remained seated for a moment. He couldn't see himself "hooking up" with an organization and taking orders from people like Ed. He had always supposed he wouldn't last long in prison once he got there. Now he knew for sure.

Fortunately, Marisol's mother didn't ask him any questions during dinner. Every once in a while, she would look at him and make like she wanted to ask him something, but just then Marisol would steer the conversation in a different direction. D.Q. kept up the fantasy about the boarding school where they lived. He made it sound as if it were a place where only a few privileged kids were admitted. Marisol's mother was impressed with the fact that they held Mass every night, and almost all the kids attended without anyone forcing them. Pancho let her suppose that he too was one of those saintly kids.

It turned out that D.Q. was not able to eat the enchiladas. Pancho thought D.Q. was going to vomit right there on the table when the plate was set in front of him. Marisol rushed to take the plate away from him and he accepted a bland-looking bowl of chicken soup instead. Even then, it was obvious to all that D.Q. was suffering, and everyone except Ed hurried through the meal. It was too bad because Pancho could have gone for another helping or two.

After dinner, Josie went back to Marisol's room to play with her old dollhouse. Ed, Marisol's mother, and D.Q. went out to the backyard for fresh air. Marisol volunteered Pancho to help her with the dishes.

He was standing next to her by the sink, drying the dishes, when it occurred to him to ask, "Does your brother have a car?"

"No." She laughed.

"What's so funny?"

"It's just funny what's in your head sometimes. I was wondering just now what you were thinking about and you asked me if my brother had a car."

"I just want to know how we're gonna get back. You need someone to jump your mother's car to start it. If your brother had a car, we could use his."

"Why would you be worried about that at this particular moment?"

"I don't know. Why not?"

She shook her head, smiling. "Are you that anxious to get out of here?"

"I'm not anxious."

Marisol took a dinner plate from the sink with suds, scrubbed it with a sponge, and dipped it in the adjoining sink filled with clear water. Then she gave the dish to Pancho, who dried it with a towel embroidered with blue daisies.

Marisol said, "What were you guys talking about before dinner, when I was with Josie in my room?"

"Prison."

"Oh, great. Of all the times for Ed to show up." She sighed. "And no, he doesn't have a car. He lives in a house with other . . ."

"He's in a gang."

"Yes. Have you ever been in one?" She seemed afraid of what he might answer.

"No."

"Would you ever be in one?" She was scrubbing the same dish she'd been scrubbing for the past minute. He took it from her hand and dipped it in the sink with the clean water.

"No. I can't see it."

"We didn't always live in this house, in this neighborhood. Till about five years ago, we lived in a pretty bad section of town. I guess Ed felt he had to join for his own protection."

"*You* didn't join."

"No. But I didn't have to. My older brother was in a gang, so I was protected. In a way he made it possible for me to go to school and study and be a regular kid."

They continued washing the dishes in silence. Pancho let himself imagine what Marisol would think of him in two weeks if he ended up killing Robert Lewis. Would she be surprised? Would she be talking to him now if she knew what he might do? She seemed relieved when he told her he wouldn't join a gang. He would kill for his sister. That's how he saw it. But the reason he killed wouldn't matter to Marisol, he knew.

He felt drops of water on his face. Marisol had sprinkled them on him with her fingers. "Now where did you go? Still worried about how you're going to get back home?"

"It's still early. Maybe we can walk over to that park that's supposed to be close to your house."

"Okay. But what do we tell the others?"

A shiver of something similar to fear ran through his body. "I didn't mean . . . I meant all of us. You thought —"

"I'm kidding." She pushed him with her shoulder. "Geez! So there is something that scares you! I was beginning to think you weren't human."

"What scares me?" Pancho said.

"Walking alone with a girl obviously terrifies you."

"Not just any girl."

"Mmm. Did you just say something nice to me?" She turned slowly toward him, and he felt himself go red from the top of his head to the very end of his toes. She stayed like that, looking at him, and he felt a force pulling him toward her. He began to yield to it and then he pulled himself back.

"D.Q. is looking forward to walking with you in the park."

"D.Q.?"

244

"Yeah." He concentrated on drying the dish he was holding. "He told you that?"

"Yes. I don't think I'm supposed to tell you."

"Why?"

"He was looking forward to talking to you. He's hoping he'll get to see you again. We're leaving tomorrow for his mother's. He thought this was the last time. He doesn't want it to be the last time but, after tonight, it may be hard for him to . . . see you. He hopes you . . . He'll tell you. That's why he wants to talk to you."

They were done with the dishes, but Marisol remained standing in front of the sink. Then she said, her head down, her hands looking for the stopper that would let the water drain, "What about you?"

"Me?" He sounded scared.

"Yes, you, Pancho Sanchez. What about you?"

"What about me what?" He wasn't as dense as he was pretending to be. He half knew, half hoped what she was asking. But what was he supposed to do? What was he supposed to say? There was no future for him. It was D.Q. who needed all the future he could get.

"What about *you*?" This time she said it softly, almost as if she were all alone and speaking to herself.

He folded the towel and watched the last of the so-called clean water ebb away. "I can't . . ." He stopped himself. *I want to but I can't* is what he wanted to say. He looked at her for a few moments and then said softly, "Come on, let's go to that park."

"Okay," she said. "Wait." There was a calendar attached to the refrigerator with a magnetic strip. Marisol ripped off a corner of the calendar. She went back to the counter and wrote something on the paper with a small pencil. She handed it to him.

"What?" he asked.

"My phone number. You better call me."

He opened his wallet and placed the piece of paper in there, next to Robert Lewis's address.

CHAPTER 27

"Pancho!"

"What?"

"You asleep?"

"Yeah."

"What do you think of Marisol's brother?"

"He's an asshole."

"What'd you guys talk about on the way to the park?"

"I don't know. He wanted to know if I was interested in joining Los Locos."

"His gang?"

"Yeah."

"What you say?"

"I said I'd think about it."

"Think about it?"

"I didn't want to show disrespect. On account of the fact that you're romancing his sister and all."

"Pssh. I hope you're not even considering it. Los Locos."

"I don't know. He made it sound like it was just a regular

business. He said gangs have gone modern now. It's all about the money. And I'll have some protection when I end up in prison."

"You're kidding, right?"

"Yeah, I'm kidding."

"Good. I mean, not that what you might end up doing is much better."

"How'd it go with you and Marisol? You get a chance to tell her what you wanted to tell her?"

Silence.

"Hey, you still there?"

"It went okay."

"You sound disappointed."

"No, it's okay. It'll be okay. I expected it."

"You're making no sense."

"Well. Let's just say that she's going to visit us."

"At your mother's?"

"And in Las Cruces. She has an aunt and a cousin in El Paso, which is only an hour away. What did you and her talk about when you were doing the dishes?"

"Just stuff. You know. About her brother. How they used to live in a bad neighborhood before. Things like that."

"That's all?"

"Pretty much. Why?"

"I don't know. She seemed happy."

"I didn't say anything. We washed the dishes."

"Sure you did."

"What's that supposed to mean?"

"Don't pay any attention to me. I don't mean to sound resentful or anything. I'm glad. I'm glad whatever it was you said made her want to come see us. Of course, it means you'll need to be around when she comes, which I hope you are."

"What I can't figure is why you don't want to stay with your mother. It'd be a lot easier for Marisol to come see you there than to go all the way to Las Cruces."

"It's hard to explain. Maybe it'll be easier to explain it after we've spent some time at Helen's. You'll see for yourself. You wouldn't want to . . . die . . . at a place like Helen's. You'll understand once you're there."

"That's just it. Maybe you need to be in a place that's not good to die, so you'll want to live."

"I want to live. Trust me. It's just that there are some things more important than living at any cost."

Silence.

"There's something I didn't tell you. I saw your mother. I was riding the bike from . . . I guess I was coming back from putting air in the tires or something. She wanted me to go with her to meet someone. So I went. His name is Johnny Corazon. We went inside his house and we talked. Your mother wanted me to meet him because she thinks he can help you. There were lots of pictures on a wall behind a statue of the Virgin, pictures of people he had healed. Or he says powers working through him are the healers. They showed me a picture of a boy who had gotten cured from cancer. I mean, the guy was kind of weird, he had these gym shorts and hair in a braid and he was this old dude trying to look like a kid, but it may be worth a try. I don't think it would hurt. He said it definitely wouldn't hurt. It would only help."

"I don't think I've ever heard you say so much all at once since I met you."

"Sorry."

"So, Johnny Corazon, that's the guy's name?"

"Yeah. He gave me that plastic heart that flashes, the one I gave Josie. He had a whole basket full of them."

"That's kind of funny, isn't it? Little plastic hearts that flash from Johnny Corazon."

"What do you think? You think you might see him?"

"You know what I always wondered? If God wanted to work a miracle and cure me, why wouldn't He just go ahead and do it. Why would he wait for me to go see Johnny Corazon and have Johnny do whatever it is Johnny does?"

"Maybe God wants to see that you believe. That's what your mother thinks. You need to believe first and then you'll be cured."

"Really? I wish she'd tell me how to do it."

"Tell you how to do what?"

"How do I believe? What more can I do? Can I turn on a little switch in my head and after that it's 'Oh, I believe I'm going to be fine'? How can anyone possibly think that I don't want to be cured? Just because I don't want to be caught with my pants down when death comes doesn't mean I don't want to live. That's what a Death Warrior does — he accepts death and gets prepared for death and yet he wants to live with all his soul, with all that is in him. It's not a contradiction."

"Oh, man. Maybe we should get some sleep."

"Besides, who are you to be preaching to me about wanting to live? You're willing to just throw your life away as if it were worth nothing."

"I wasn't preaching anything. I was just telling you —"

"Why don't *you* go see Johnny Corazon and have him cure you? You have an illness too. A cancer that fills your head like a fog. That need for revenge no matter what, what's that? That's a cancer that will sure as hell kill you. At least I didn't bring mine on myself."

"All right."

"It's not all right. What would I not give to be you? I would give up my *brains* to have your body, to have your life, to have life ahead of me the way you have yours. And you don't even realize what you have. You're going to piss this gift away for what? I mean, have you ever stopped to think what your sister would say to you if she could talk to you? You think she wants you to kill this guy? Really? You say you're doing it for her, you say it will make things right, but that's bullshit! You're killing that guy for you, not for her. You think killing that bastard is going to help you get rid of the loss and guilt and self-hatred for not being a good brother. You are so wrong. You're so wrong it's unbelievable."

"I already told you. I thought about all that. I don't have your brains, like you say, but this is one thing where I thought about all there is to think. I expect I'll feel worse after I kill him, if I kill him. I'll feel worse and I'll feel better too. I'm not doing it because of feeling better or worse. That's not what I mean by making things right. You wanna know something else? If I could give you my life, I'd give it to you. I'd say, here, take it. Use it, 'cause I don't have any need for it!"

"Pancho."

"Go to sleep, man."

"They say that diffuse pontine glioma can affect how people act and talk and feel. Back there where the brain meets the spine, that's where all your basic emotions come from. People that have DPG can get wacky as the illness progresses."

"Great."

"I'm just telling you so you'll know."

"Now I know."

"All right."

CHAPTER 28

Helen arrived at ten the following morning. She appeared in the doorway of the dining room where Pancho and D.Q. sat at a round table with a group of kids and their parents. "Hello, Helen," D.Q. said when he saw her.

"Hello, Daniel. Hello, Pancho." Pancho nodded. She was wearing a white pantsuit with a blue scarf tied loosely around her neck. Nothing she wore ever had any wrinkles. He took the last bite of pancakes drenched in syrup and butter. Andrés's mother made the pancakes as a sort of thank-you gift. She also made a fruit salad with mangoes, papayas, and pineapples. Pancho thought she probably bought the expensive fruits with all the money Andrés had won off of him.

"Are we almost ready to go?" Helen asked when she didn't see anyone getting up from the table.

D.Q. rolled his wheelchair away from the table. "Well, good-bye, guys," he said to the group. Pancho pushed his chair back and stood up. Andrés's mother was the first to hug him. Then

Andrés, the little hustler himself, leaned his head against Pancho's chest. In return, Pancho pulled his ear. There were no words spoken.

They went back to their room and got their things. Helen carried the smallest of D.Q.'s bags, and Pancho carried the rest. Pancho was folding D.Q.'s wheelchair in the driveway when he remembered Josie. He had not seen her all that morning. He put the wheelchair in the back of Helen's SUV. The same group of people who was with them at breakfast was standing by the entrance, waiting to wave good-bye. "Have you seen Josie?" he asked Andrés's mother.

"No. That's strange," Andrés's mother said. "I'll go check her room."

"I know where she is!" Andrés said. "She's hiding." Andrés pointed to the back of the house, and Pancho knew exactly where to go. He motioned to D.Q., who was already sitting in the front seat, that he'd be right back, and D.Q. motioned for him to go on and take his time. Helen was sitting in the driver's seat, a frozen smile on her face, her two hands gripping the top of the steering wheel.

Pancho went around back and climbed up the ladder of the jungle gym. She was crouched inside the tent, hugging her knees against her chest. "Now what?" he asked, poking his head in. She looked away without answering. "Don't tell me you're crying?"

"Nooo!"

He clambered in and sat in front of her. "D.Q.'s mother is out there waiting for me. She's going to take off without me if I don't get back."

"Good," she said. "I mean, that's not good."

"You want me to go?"

"Yes."

"Marisol's going to take you and Andrés to the movies in the afternoon when she comes in."

"I don't wanna go."

"I guess I don't want you to go either. I think Andrés likes you."

"Yuck!"

"Yeah. Better stay away from him."

She looked at him finally. "We're leaving for Santa Fe tomorrow."

"Your mom told us this morning. Your tests came back. Your cancer's in revision."

"Remission, dummy."

"That's what I said. You're gonna be okay. You're gonna get your eyelashes back and everything."

"I *have* eyelashes! They're just white. See?" She batted her eyelids, like she had something in her eyes.

"D.Q.'s mother has a horse."

"So?"

"Maybe you can come visit."

"All the way from Santa Fe?"

"Is it far?"

She rolled her eyes like she couldn't believe how dumb he was. She opened up her hand. "Here." It was Johnny Corazon's plastic heart. "It doesn't work anymore."

"I gave that to you."

"I don't want it anymore."

"Okay." He took it from her. "I guess I better go." He lifted himself from the floor so he could crawl backward and then descend. He turned to look at her one final time just before he went down the ladder. Her lip was quivering and her eyes were bright red. He opened his arms and she came to him. He held her head against his chest and he opened his eyes as wide as they would go in order to keep them dry. She wanted to say something, but he pressed her tight. "Shhh. Don't say anything." He let go of her and started down as quickly as he could.

"I want my heart back," she said between sobs.

He still had it in his hand. He went up a rung and gave it to her. His vision was blurred as he walked back. He stopped beside the house and wiped his eyes with the sleeve of his T-shirt. He clenched his jaw shut. This was ridiculous. He didn't cry after his father died. He didn't cry when Rosa died. Why now? Hot snot was flowing out of his nose and he could feel waves of pain rising up and getting stuck in his throat. He thought of Rosa. Had he ever been playful with her like he'd been with Josie and the other kids? Had he ever felt the loneliness of loss he was feeling now?

He didn't know how much time it took for all that to come out of his system. He half expected D.Q. and his mother to be gone by the time he came around to the front of the house. But they were still there, sitting in the SUV with the windows open, talking calmly. He looked down, keeping his eyes away from them, when he entered the car.

"Ready?" Helen asked pleasantly. D.Q.'s conversation, whatever it was, had made her happy.

"Sorry," he said. The four or five people still standing at the entrance waved at them. The last thing Pancho saw as they pulled away was the rickshaw beside the house.

They were on the highway for a while before he realized that D.Q. was acting strange. Strange wasn't the word; D.Q. was always strange. D.Q. was acting different, like nothing had ever happened between him and his mother. Helen was talking about the treatments and how well they had gone, according to Dr. Melendez, and D.Q. was taking it all in. He almost seemed to be agreeing with her. She was saying that they would not be able to tell, of course, whether the cancer had been arrested or diminished in such a short period of time. But Dr. Melendez was happy that D.Q.'s white blood cell count had remained steady. It meant that he would tolerate further treatments well.

"But we can discuss that later," she said tentatively, like she didn't want to push her luck too much, "after you rest for a couple of weeks."

"A couple of weeks," D.Q. repeated absently.

Now Pancho remembered that D.Q. had looked different all morning. He was like a party balloon with half its helium leaked out, his head listing a little to the side. Pancho had noticed the difference at breakfast and attributed it to sadness at not getting to see Marisol for a while. But now as he listened to him, he thought the Death Warrior sounded like he had lost a battle, if not the war.

They were on I-25 North heading toward Santa Fe, leaving

downtown Albuquerque behind. The morning was crisp and the air rushing in from D.Q.'s open window was like a playful slap on his face. Two weeks from now, he would leave Helen's house and D.Q. for good and go directly to see Robert Lewis. After that he'd keep going, he didn't know where.

"Pancho told me," he heard D.Q. say.

"He did? I really think you'll like him. I'll have him come to the house for the first visit, but later, you'll need to go to his house. Johnny says that makes a difference."

"Fine."

Pancho leaned forward. He thought he had heard D.Q. say "Fine."

"So you'll see him?" Even Helen was looking at D.Q. as if something was wrong with him.

"Why not."

"Pancho will tell you. He's a little bit of a character." She was looking in the rearview mirror, searching for Pancho. He moved closer to the door, out of her field of vision.

"You might want to pull over there for just one second." D.Q. lifted a hand weakly and pointed at the emergency lane of the highway.

"We're about five minutes from home," Helen said.

"Please." Even without looking at his face, Pancho could tell that D.Q.'s eyes were shut tight.

Helen swerved and came to a stop faster than Pancho expected. D.Q. opened the door. A buzzer sounded. "Your seat belt," Helen reminded him. D.Q. tried to find the buckle, gave up, leaned out the door, and vomited.

"Oh, Daniel," Helen said.

Pancho got out and waited for D.Q. to finish. Then he leaned in and unbuckled him. He swung his legs outside the car. "Don't step in it," D.Q. said to him.

"You got more?"

D.Q. nodded. Pancho took him to the side of the car. He had found out during their stay at Casa Esperanza that it was easier for a person to vomit standing up than sitting down. He held D.Q. by the abdomen while he was bent over. Cars whizzed by. One idiot honked. Pancho placed his hand on D.Q.'s back. Vomit splashed on his pants and sneakers. D.Q.'s knees twitched as if unable to sustain even the little weight they held.

"You done?" Pancho asked after a while. D.Q.'s eyes were closed, saliva dribbling from his lips, but he nodded. Helen sat frozen in the driver's seat, a scared look on her face. *Had she ever seen a chemo patient throw up?* Pancho wondered. Even when they didn't have anything inside to throw up, the violent retching continued just the same.

Pancho sat D.Q. back in the front seat. Helen tried to wipe his mouth with a Kleenex, but D.Q. moved his head away from her hand. He leaned his head as close as he could to the open window. Helen waited for an opening and sped away.

"Did you take your antinausea pills?" she asked him.

"He took them," Pancho answered when D.Q. remained silent.

"Johnny gave me some herbs for your nausea. As soon as we get home, I'll have Renata make you a tea. You'll be good as new in no time."

Good as new, Pancho repeated to himself. What was wrong with the lady? Something was not right with her, but Pancho didn't know exactly what.

Pancho wanted to pay attention to the roads so that he would know which way to go when he left, but soon his mind wandered. Scenes from the past two weeks flashed before him. There was the fat guy called Billy Tenn asking him, knife in hand, "Why you want to die?" There was Marisol waiting for D.Q. so they could go for their daily walk. Had he really thought that she was nothing to write home about? There he was sitting next to D.Q., watching cartoons while D.Q. had his eyes closed, a pale yellow liquid flowing into his arm. Now he was pedaling the rickshaw up a small hill with Marisol and Josie in the back, Marisol pretending to get angry when he told her he wasn't used to pulling so much weight. There was Andrés maneuvering his spaceship — magically, it seemed — so that instead of being pursued, it was now shooting red lasers at Pancho's rear. There was D.Q. bumping into his bed in the middle of the night on yet another trip to the bathroom. Why did he never make D.Q. take the bed closest to the bathroom, the hell with his being close to the window? There was Josie's mother announcing to the breakfast table, her voice trembling, that Josie's cancer was in revision — at least that's what he thought he heard, and he knew it was good news because people at the table cheered. He looked for signs of envy in the faces of the other mothers, but he didn't see any.

"Here we are," he heard Helen say. She said it as if now, finally, everything would be just fine.

It wasn't like any kind of ranch that Pancho had ever seen. The house looked more like a small castle. It even had a tower rising from one of the corners, white like the rest of it, with a red tile roof. The house was in the middle of a field about the size of the trailer park where Pancho used to live. A white stucco fence lined the front of the property, low enough that the house was not hidden from the street but high enough, Pancho imagined, to keep a horse from jumping out. The rest was bounded with a log fence. They stopped by a black iron gate. Helen pushed a remote control on the visor, and the gate swung open. She drove down a long pebbled driveway and turned the car off in front of a separate four-car garage. The garage itself looked like a house large enough for a family to live in. Pancho could see an air conditioner in one of the upper windows.

Helen nudged D.Q.'s shoulder. "We're here, Daniel," she whispered, like she was afraid of waking him.

"Oh, no," D.Q. mumbled.

"I'll get Juan to help you out." She started to open the door.

"I think I left the perico back in the room."

"The what?"

"I checked the room before we left. We didn't leave anything," Pancho said.

"What is the perico?" Helen asked.

"I was holding it in my hand last night, when I couldn't fall asleep. It's in the bed under the sheets."

"What is it?" Helen turned to Pancho.

"It's a wooden parrot," Pancho told her.

"We gotta go back and get it," D.Q. said. His voice was weak but determined.

"A wooden parrot?" said Helen.

"Did you strip the beds?" D.Q. asked Pancho without turning around.

It took Pancho a few seconds to realize that D.Q. was saying *strip* the beds and not *rip* the beds. "No. Was I supposed to?"

"We have to get back there before they clean the room. Otherwise it might get thrown away. Let's go, Helen."

Helen looked at D.Q. "What's so special about this wooden parrot?" she asked Pancho.

Pancho shrugged his shoulders.

"Helen, please!"

"Can we call someone to look for it, and if it's there, to hold it? I'll send Juan to pick it up."

"We can call someone," Pancho said quickly. "I'll call Marisol."

D.Q. looked up. "How do you have her phone number?"

"I —" Pancho began to answer.

"I need the perico," D.Q. cut him off. He sounded delirious.

"Okay, let's get you inside." She tapped the horn twice.

Pancho stepped out of the SUV and opened D.Q.'s door. D.Q. seemed to be measuring the distance between his seat and the ground. Pancho grabbed him by the armpits, lifted him off the seat, and stood him on the ground. He supported him until he was sure D.Q.'s legs would hold. An older-looking Mexican man in a white short-sleeve shirt and gray pants appeared by his side and offered to take D.Q.

"Juan, there's a wheelchair in the back," Helen said to him. Juan scurried to the back.

"I can walk," D.Q. said. "What's everyone making such a fuss about?" But Pancho could see his legs tremble like they were about to buckle. In the space of one night, D.Q. had gone from more or less okay to bad. Worse, Pancho thought, was not that far off.

"Don't be silly. Let Juan take you in the wheelchair. We just built a new ramp up to the back door."

Pancho expected D.Q. to question why they built a new ramp when he was only going to be there two weeks, but D.Q. didn't say anything. He waited for Juan to bring the wheelchair. "Hello, Juan," D.Q. said as he sat down.

"Hello, Señor Daniel," Juan answered with a slight bow of his white head.

"This is Pancho." D.Q. pointed at Pancho.

Juan gave Pancho a smile and Pancho nodded back. There were deep creases at the edges of Juan's eyes, probably from having to smile all the time, Pancho thought.

Pancho turned around to get his backpack. "Leave your things in the car," Helen said. "Juan will take them to your rooms later." Pancho grabbed the pack anyway. He wasn't going to let the revolver out of his grasp.

"Rooms?" D.Q. asked. "What rooms?" He stopped the wheel-chair by grabbing the edge of the wheels.

"Your room, the one you always stay in," Helen answered.

"And Pancho?"

"I thought he'd be more comfortable with Juan."

"Oh, Helen!" D.Q. was shaking his head in disbelief. "What a piece of work you are."

"Daniel—" She stopped herself. "Please don't talk to me that way."

They all stood in the space between the garage and the side of the house. D.Q.'s knuckles were red from gripping the wheels of his chair. Juan was smiling like an idiot. In the distance, Pancho could see a brown horse trotting around the boundaries of a corral, looking for the gate.

"Pancho is staying with me." The veins in D.Q.'s neck were sky blue and bulging.

Helen's face was red. "In your room?"

"Yes."

"I've made plans for a night nurse to come in. I don't think . . ."

D.Q. grabbed the sides of his head. It looked as if he were trying to keep his skull from exploding. "Helen. I don't need a . . . night nurse. I . . . need . . . Pancho. That's . . . why . . . he's here."

Pancho looked at D.Q., surprised. He remembered what Marisol's brother had said about D.Q. having his own servant.

The wheelchair moved forward, catching Juan off guard.

"There's only one bed in there," Helen said behind them. D.Q. wasn't paying any attention to her. She turned to Pancho. "I just thought you'd be more comfortable in Juan's apartment. The apartment has two bedrooms. You'd eat with us, of course. But you could also cook in your own kitchen if you wish. Or eat Juan's cooking, which is out of this world. You guys can watch the Spanish channels. Wouldn't you be more comfortable with Juan?"

"Could be," Pancho said, still thinking about D.Q.'s words.

They went up the ramp at the back of the house. D.Q. motioned for Juan to stop at the top. The far boundary of the property seemed to be the same place where a rocky formation began its slow transformation into hills and then mountains. Close to the house, there was a swimming pool in the shape of an S. A red barn stood next to the corral and now Pancho saw two more horses. They looked older and more subdued than the horse that pranced round and round the corral. "That's Caramelo," Juan said, pointing at the restless horse.

"Isn't he beautiful?" Helen asked D.Q. She was beginning to calm down. "This will be so good for you. Look over there." She pointed at a grove of piñon pines halfway down the property. "Stu had a contractor build you a screened-in porch in the shade of the trees. We ran electricity out to it and installed a hammock, because I know how much you like hammocks. There's even a bathroom. You can sit out there and breathe in all that fresh air."

"While I go to the bathroom?"

"I didn't mean that." She tried to smile.

"It's cold out here, isn't it?" D.Q. crossed his arms.

Helen and Pancho looked at each other. They were in the shade of the house, but it was a warm eighty-degree day. Helen opened the screen door, and Juan pushed D.Q. inside.

They moved through the kitchen with its dozens of copper pots and pans hanging from a structure in the middle of the ceiling. They passed a room with a small table for four, and then another room with a table long enough to seat sixteen. Then they were in a long hallway with rooms on both sides. At the end of the hallway, there was a wheelchair on a steel platform. The platform was connected to a steel tower that rose to the top of the stairs.

"It's an elevator, basically, with a special battery-operated wheelchair that can be detached. We had this installed so you wouldn't have to climb the stairs," Helen announced. "Isn't it nifty?"

"Nifty," D.Q. said, unimpressed. He transferred himself to the motorized wheelchair. Helen buckled a seat belt around his waist and pushed a green button. D.Q. began a slow ascent.

Pancho tried to carry the wheelchair upstairs, but Juan didn't let him. "No worry. I get it," Juan said. He had a heavy Mexican accent. He was an old man, Pancho noticed, much older than his father. His dark brown arms were thin and sinewy, like the roots of pecan trees. Juan folded the wheelchair and placed it underneath the stairs, out of view.

"He won't need that anymore," Helen said.

Helen, Pancho, and Juan climbed the stairs. They reached the top at the same time as D.Q. Helen walked up to the wheelchair and detached it from the platform. Then she moved a black lever on the right armrest. The chair rolled forward and hummed. "What do you think?"

She had thought of everything. Pancho was sure that D.Q. was thinking what he was thinking: There was no way he was getting out of there in two weeks. But D.Q.'s face was expressionless. "Try it," Helen urged. "Juan, help him." Juan seemed to jump every time Helen called his name. Whether he jumped with fear or eagerness to please, or both, Pancho didn't know.

"I can do it." D.Q. put out his hand to stop Juan. "I'm not an invalid yet." D.Q. pushed the black lever, and the chair zipped forward, the wheels leaving a trail in the lush green rug. D.Q.

266

went down the hall, tried to turn left, and crashed into a corner. "Oops," he said. "This isn't as easy as it looks." He set the wheelchair in reverse, straightened out, and turned the corner. Helen touched the scratch on the flowered wallpaper as she walked by.

D.Q.'s room was blue: blue curtains, blue bedspread, blue walls. Only the carpet was white. The bed was bigger than any bed Pancho had ever seen. On the wall in front of the bed hung a flat-screen television. D.Q. went immediately to the window and opened the curtains. Pancho knew that D.Q. liked daylight. At Casa Esperanza, D.Q. never closed the curtains during the day, or at night for that matter. D.Q. turned the wheelchair around and surveyed the room. Pancho looked out for the mountains, but all he could see were other large houses and the interstate highway in the distance.

"We can put Pancho's bed over there." D.Q. pointed at a desk with a computer. "We can move the desk under the TV."

"You're going to be so crowded here."

D.Q. ignored her. "Juan, is there a bed for Pancho that you can move in here?"

Juan was standing by himself out in the hall. He looked at Helen and waited for her to nod before he spoke. "I can bring cot that folds. It has good mattress. Thick mattress. I get it?"

"Go ahead," Helen said, giving up. "There are some sheets in the closet of the guest room next door."

Pancho put the backpack on D.Q.'s bed. "I'll help with the bed."

"Is okay," Juan said. "It has wheels."

"Well, I guess I'll let you boys get settled. Juan will bring your bags. Is there anything you'd like to do?"

"Sleep," D.Q. answered.

"Yes. Rest for a little while. We'll have lunch around noon. Then maybe . . . well, we can talk later, after you rest." She looked at Pancho, inquiring with her eyes what he was going to do.

"I'll go take a look at that horse." It was the first thing that came to his mind.

"Help me get in bed," D.Q. said to him. "I'll see you in a while, Helen."

"Should I ask Juan to wait to put the bed in until after your nap?"

"No, he can bring it right in."

She seemed at a loss as to what to do or say next. "I'm so very happy you're here," she said.

"I know," D.Q. said softly. "I'm glad you're happy, Helen." It sounded to Pancho as if he meant it.

"Until later, then."

Pancho exhaled loudly as soon as she left the room. D.Q. said, "She sure is trying, isn't she?"

"Trying what?" Pancho went over to the bed and pulled back the bedspread.

"I can't believe I left the perico at Casa Esperanza. You'll call . . . someone about it."

"Yes, I'll call Marisol and make sure it doesn't get lost. She can bring it over when she comes to see you."

"Juan can go get it. Tell him I said so."

"All right." Pancho knelt down and untied D.Q.'s sneakers. He helped him stand up. "Those pants are full of puke."

"That was embarrassing. Puking in the middle of the freeway. Poor Helen." D.Q. unbuckled his belt. He let his pants drop down and then stepped out of them.

"What's that on your legs?" Pancho was looking at blotches of red skin on D.Q.'s thighs.

"Dry skin. The whole machine is breaking down. Would you mind rubbing some cream on my legs?"

"I'm not rubbing nothing on you."

"It's hard for me to do it and they're very itchy."

"Hell no." Pancho picked up the pants with his thumb and index finger and threw them across the room. He helped D.Q. pull his shirt over his head. "Why are your legs so shaky?"

"I'm slipping down the Karnofsky scale fast."

"The what?"

"It's a scale the medical profession uses to gauge where a terminally ill person is on his journey toward the inevitable. At a hundred the illness is there, but it has no symptoms. At zero, well, you can imagine where I'll be at zero."

"Zero is zero."

"Correct." D.Q. stretched himself out on the bed. Pancho covered him up.

"Whereabouts you think you are now?"

"On the scale? I think I was about eighty until yesterday. Then last night I sank to around sixty for some reason."

Marisol, Pancho thought. D.Q. had said she was coming to visit, but something else must have happened that D.Q. wasn't telling him. "What's thirty like?"

"Around thirty you start wearing diapers."

"Shit."

"Exactly. And guess who will have to wipe my ass?"

"Don't look at me. I'm not wiping you." Pancho took his backpack from the bed. He looked around for a safe place to put it. He opened one of two sliding doors. The closet was full of hanging shirts and pants. He put the backpack on the floor inside, then he pulled the chair from the desk and sat on it.

"You want to hear a real tragedy?"

"I thought you wanted to sleep."

"I will. I'll tell you this and then I'll sleep."

"I should probably help that guy Juan with the bed. He looks like he's hitting twenty on that scale."

"Juan? Juan just looks frail. I was visiting here last year before I got ill and I tried to help him out in the barn. I couldn't keep up with him. He's been with Helen since Helen married rich."

"She married the lawyer."

"Yeah. Good old Stu. Stuart is his name but he likes to be called Stu. He does quite well, as you can see." D.Q. closed his eyes for a few seconds, opened them, and then closed them again. "You know that pretty nurse, Rebecca? The one that made your heart go wacko every time you saw her?"

"I know who she is."

"She rubbed my legs with cream once."

"Get outta here!"

"I'm serious. It was at the beginning of this week. Monday or Tuesday, I'm not sure. You went out someplace. I had just finished with the chemo treatment and she noticed that the skin on my arms was dry. I told her it was worse on my legs. They were all red and blotchy. She asked me if anyone had taken a look at them and I said no. So she made me put on one of those nighties, and when she came back she said she was going to rub some cream on my legs. I was a little embarrassed. I mean, what if, you know, what if I had a natural reaction to her touch."

"You mean, what if you got a hard-on?"

"I was afraid of that."

"You're making this up."

D.Q. continued speaking, his eyes still closed. "She rubbed cream on my legs. All over my legs, from my ankles all the way up, all around. She came this close to touching my private parts." D.Q. lifted his hand from under the sheet and held his thumb half an inch away from his index finger. "The tube of cream, whatever it was she was using, fell on the other side of the bed, and when she reached over to get it, one of her beautiful, soft breasts touched my arm."

"Man, you're dreaming."

"It's the truth, Pancho. It's the truth. Don't get me wrong. I'm not foolish enough to think that she was attracted to me. She was being kind. She was giving me the pleasure of her touch. Not because she felt sorry for me or anything. Just out of kindness."

Pancho waited for more to come, but D.Q. had stopped talking. Just as Pancho started to get up, D.Q. spoke again. "But nothing happened. Isn't that the cruelest thing you ever heard?"

"What did you expect? You think you were going to get laid right there in the hospital room? People walk in and out all the time."

"No, I'm not talking about that. I mean, nothing happened to me. There was no natural reaction in me. Nothing. I felt her soft hand all over my thighs. I felt her breast. Nothing. The radiation. The chemo. The cancer. They zapped all the sap out of me.

Maybe you were right. Back at St. Anthony's when you said that life sucks. Maybe you were right."

Pancho wanted to say something funny, to tease D.Q. somehow, but he couldn't think of anything to say. He waited a few minutes until he thought D.Q. was asleep. Just as he started to leave, D.Q. spoke again. "Don't forget the perico," he said.

CHAPTER 29

Out in the hall he met Juan pushing a roll-up bed. "He's asleep," he told him. "Leave it, I'll set it up later." There was a look of doubt on Juan's face, as if he were considering the consequences of not following Helen's precise instructions. "It's okay," Pancho assured him.

"Is okay," Juan said. They turned around and walked side by side. When they were going down the stairs, Juan asked tentatively, *"Hablas español?"*

"No," Pancho answered.

"No?" Juan was surprised. "How can it be?"

Pancho shrugged his shoulders. He didn't feel like explaining to Juan that his father only spoke to him and Rosa in English. He wanted his kids to be Americans. Rosa knew more Spanish than Pancho did because she learned it by watching telenovelas.

At the bottom of the stairs, Pancho stopped for a moment, not knowing which way to turn. Juan motioned toward the way they had first come in. Pancho remembered that he needed to call

Marisol to inquire about the famous perico. "Is there a telephone I can use?"

"Sure. There many phones. Even outside there's phones. Let's go outside, you be more private there. I show you around."

"Okay." *Outside is good,* he thought. He felt like he had dropped ten points down that death scale that D.Q. talked about ever since he stepped inside the house.

They went outside and Pancho breathed deeply. They were on a terrace overlooking the grounds. Caramelo was still circling the corral. Pancho walked to the farthest end of the terrace and looked down at the pool. Sunlight shimmered on the light blue water. Juan came and stood next to him. "Is a lot of work taking care of all this. I take care of pool, horses, garden. *La Misses,* she likes lots of green, but this is desert. We have well just for grass and plants. Another well for house. But underneath two wells, water comes from same place, no? How does water down there get full again? It never rains. No snow. Is not normal to try to grow plants and grass here in desert. Cactus, *nopales,* that's okay." Pancho kept staring at the surface of the pool. "The water in the pool we buy. Big truck comes every year. Come, let's go down."

They stepped away from the edge of the terrace and walked toward a stone stairway next to the newly built wooden ramp. "*El joven* Daniel is very ill, no?"

"Yeah."

"*La Misses* is very happy to have him here. All last month she put in the ramp, the elevator. I painted a room in my apartment. She said you stay there. Good, I like company. But Daniel wants you to stay with him. You must be good friend to him."

Pancho sighed. Two weeks. That's what he had promised D.Q. He wondered if he could make it in this place for two weeks. It wasn't so bad outside, though. He would need to find something for his body to do. At Casa Esperanza, the endless rickshaw rides kept him tired and therefore calm. But here? He remembered the huge pile of rocks he had seen on the side of the driveway as they drove in. "What are those rocks out by the driveway for?"

"Ahh. Those rocks." Juan shut his eyes and rubbed the top of his head with his hand. "Those rocks are gonna kill me. *La Misses* wants to build a stone wall around the pool. But no truck can go back there. So they dump the rocks in front and I haul rock back there. One, two rock at a time. My back. I'm old, you know. Seventy-two."

"I'll help you move the rocks."

"Nooo. You a guest here. You relax, keep Daniel company. You two sit by the pool or in the *kiosko* we built out by the piñones. Is cool out there."

"I need to work."

Juan disappeared into the space underneath the stone stairs and came out with a tattered straw hat in his hand. "For sun." He put the hat on. They walked toward the corral, following a stone path through a garden of desert flowers.

"Where's the husband?"

"The who?"

"You know, *La Misses*'s husband."

"Ah. *El Señor* Stu. He works all the time. Travels. He in New York now. I'm in my apartment watching TV or asleep when he comes in. I hear his car. Even on Saturdays and Sundays he works." Juan made a face. People working on Sundays was something he would never be able to understand. "He's nice, don't get me wrong. But *La Misses*, she wears the pants in the house."

"Yeah." Pancho stopped. A bee was buzzing around his head. He stood still and watched it land on his arm. His father once told him that bees can smell when you're angry or afraid of them and then they sting you in self-defense. If he concentrated on the spot where the bee was, Pancho could feel the touch of its tiny legs walking calmly on his arm. He realized that he did not feel any anger. He had always imagined that he would confront Robert Lewis out of anger or with anger. Where had the anger gone? It had disappeared, but the decision to make Robert Lewis accountable for his sister's death had not. That decision was still there. Pancho could feel it, solid, inevitable.

Juan put his finger on Pancho's arm in the path of the bee. The bee climbed up onto Juan's finger. Juan brought the finger close to his mouth and blew on it. The bee flew away. "You not afraid of bees," Juan said, as if discovering something about Pancho.

"You neither," Pancho responded. His father used to blow bees away from his finger just like Juan.

"They still sting me. When I cut flowers, they mad. They think all flowers are theirs." This time when he laughed, Pancho noticed that he had a tooth missing.

At the end of the stone path and the garden with the wildflowers was another path that led to the corral. The corral was farther away from the house than it first appeared. They climbed onto the first rung of the fence. Juan clucked his tongue at Caramelo.

The horse snorted and shook his head. "He's *testaduro*, that horse," Juan complained. "How you say *testaduro*?"

"Stubborn."

"So you understand Spanish, but you don't speak it." Juan took a cube of sugar out of his pocket. The horse sniffed the air, moved toward them, and then jumped away.

"He's wild."

"He's young. They wild when they young. Like you." He smiled as if he knew something. "You can help me train him."

"How do you do that?"

"Tomorrow I show you."

"I'm not much of a rider."

"Don't worry. It'll be a long time before we ride him. Tomorrow and for many days, we throw a rope around his neck and we let him run like that with the rope until he gets used to you. Then you begin guide with the rope. You get closer. Like that, little by little."

"How long does it all take?"

"A few weeks. There's no hurry. A little each day."

"We're only gonna be here two weeks."

"Two weeks? *Dos?*" Juan seemed confused.

"*La Misses* didn't tell you?" There was some sarcasm in Pancho's voice.

"No. She say you here to stay."

Pancho jumped down from the wooden fence of the corral. "I better go make a phone call."

"We go to my place. I show you." Juan stepped down slowly, holding on to Pancho's shoulder. They walked back. "Why you want leave here for? This is nice easy place to live. You and Daniel live here."

Pancho looked at the house. It looked like a palace in the distance. A Spanish palace in the desert. Why would D.Q. not want to live here? *It's not a good place to die,* he remembered D.Q. saying. Despite the pool and the grass and the plants that Helen had forced out of the ground, the place was still a desert, dry, desolate. Not that Las Cruces was much different. And yet there was something about this house that seemed dark and *closophobic*, like Josie used to say. The horse back there knew it. He was going crazy running around and around, trying to find a way out.

"You like it here?" he asked Juan.

The question caught him by surprise. "Eh? Me like it? Is a good place for an old man. I have daughter in L.A. Five grandchildren. I go see her for Christmas. I spend my whole life in city working in rich people gardens. In L.A. for twenty years. My wife, Sara, and I come to Albuquerque fifteen years ago, then she die. Three years ago, I come work here. Is okay. Someday soon I take all I save and go back to L.A. I build little room in back of my daughter's house. She and grandchildren take care of me when I'm old." He grinned. "More old."

The entrance to the apartment was up a green wooden staircase in back of the garage. Juan held the door open for Pancho. "*Mi casa,*" Juan said. Inside was one big room that served as kitchen, dining room, and living room. The stove, sink, and refrigerator stood at one end. There was a round table with three chairs by the windows that faced onto the driveway and the air conditioner that Pancho saw when he arrived. A sofa and a recliner sat by the windows that faced the corral. "I show you phone." Pancho followed

Juan into a narrow hallway where there were three doors. "The bathroom," Juan said, knocking on the first door. He knocked on the second door. "My room." When he got to the last door, he opened it and said, "This was going to be your room."

He moved out of the way so Pancho could step in. It was a small room with a single bed, a bureau with a television sitting on it, a desk with a chair and a telephone, a bureau with a mirror on top, and a bedside table with a lamp. For once Helen was right, Pancho thought. He would be more comfortable here.

"I leave you." Juan closed the door.

He stretched himself out on the bed and closed his eyes. He wondered what he used to think about before Rosa died. He didn't think he thought about anything when he was alone. This thinking about things that he had never thought about before started recently — first with imagining and planning how he was going to kill Robert Lewis, but it soon went beyond that. D.Q. and all his happenings, Marisol and the new feelings that she brought, even the Death Warrior stuff occupied his mind. Thoughts came to him out of nowhere. He needed to get in the ring with a better fighter, someone who could knock him out and stop the thinking.

He imagined now that D.Q. somehow accepted the fact that he would be better off staying with his mother. He would get over whatever happened with Marisol and Helen would hire her as D.Q.'s nurse. She would come over every day and Pancho would get to see her. He would not tell her how he felt about her, but she would know somehow. They owed it to D.Q. not to be open about their feelings. Helen would give him a job as Juan's helper, and eventually he'd move out here and this would be his room. Then what? He hesitated about going any further. *D.Q. dies or doesn't die?* Which direction should his imaginings go? D.Q. dies. Pancho stays on as Juan's helper. Juan eventually goes to live with his daughter in L.A. Pancho finishes high school. There must be a high school somewhere around here. He'd have to buy a car. What did Juan use for a car? He starts going out with Marisol. What would he do to make a living? This was an area of his life that he never thought about. He would work in construction as a carpenter. Would Marisol be okay with that? Maybe he would take over Juan's job. Helen would always need a caretaker. And Marisol, they could move into the apartment. She'd drive to town to work. But if you were Marisol, would you want to live over a garage? And when the kids came, there wouldn't be any room for them.

Or D.Q. doesn't die. Johnny Corazon gives him an herb that makes him better. What happens then with Marisol? He'd have to go away. He'd move someplace else so D.Q. would have a chance with Marisol. He couldn't do that to D.Q. Why? Since when did he start caring?

He opened his eyes and focused on the light fixture on the ceiling. He could see dead moths in the bottom. His Rosa. He must not forget about her. Robert Lewis. The only thing about the future he needed to concern himself with, the only imagining he needed to have, was the road that led to Robert Lewis.

The telephone was on the desk. He got up, sat at the desk chair, and took out a piece of paper from his wallet. He dialed. He heard the ring on the other side.

"Hello?"

"Marisol?"

"Pancho, is that you? What a nice surprise. Where are you?"

"We're at D.Q.'s. At his mother's."

"How is it? Is it nice?"

"It's fancy."

"How's D.Q. doing?"

"He's worse. He doesn't look good. He got worse overnight."

"Oh." He could hear her breath, shallow and rapid. "It happens sometimes. All of a sudden, there can be a shift. It may be temporary. He could bounce back."

"He's worried about his wooden parrot. He says he left it in his bed, mixed up with the sheets."

"I was heading out there now. I'll look for it."

"Yeah. I don't know why he likes it so much. It's like he can't live without it."

"If you made it, I can understand why he wants it."

He felt a lump in his throat. There was no reason in the world why he should be getting a lump in his throat at this particular time. What was the matter with him anyway? He was going soft all of a sudden.

"Pancho, are you there? What's the matter?"

He put the receiver away from his mouth and cleared his throat. "Ahh, you think you could bring it when you come visit? D.Q. said you told him yesterday when we were walking to the park you'd come visit."

"I won't be able to come till next Saturday. Can he wait that long?"

"Probably not. If you can hold on to it, I'll see if this guy who works here can go get it. His name is Juan."

There was a pause on Marisol's end of the line. "Did D.Q. tell you what we talked about during our walk to the park last night?"

"He said you would come visit us, ah, him, here and maybe even go to Las Cruces. You have an aunt and a cousin who live in El Paso."

"Is that all he said?" She sounded relieved.

"What else would he say?"

She spoke slowly. "We talked about things, like we always do. We talked about the difference between friendship and love. I told him that what he and I had was friendship." She stopped.

"Oh."

She waited for him to say more. Then she asked, "How's he doing?"

He knew that this time she was asking about D.Q.'s emotional well-being. "He seems hurt. Angry. I've never seen him like that. He's even angry at me."

There was a long pause, then she said softly, "Wouldn't you be angry as well, if you were in his place?"

Pancho felt suddenly uncomfortable. "Yes," he finally answered. Then he said, "So . . . we'll see you . . . next Saturday. Someone will go pick up the parrot. Or leave it in the TV room. No one will take it. Wait. Do you know where his mother's house is?"

"Yes. D.Q. gave me the address. It's a pretty ritzy area on the way to Santa Fe. Everyone knows about it. I'll find it. What time on Saturday? I have to do errands in the morning with my mom. Is the afternoon okay? Around four?"

"Four. That's good."

"Good-bye, Pancho. Thank you for calling me. Don't lose the phone number now, okay?"

"Okay."

He hung up. He felt both lighter and heavier at the same time. He stepped out of the room and walked to the large room of the apartment. Juan was standing over the stove, scraping a black pan with a spatula.

"I made us *chilaquiles* for lunch," Juan said as soon as he saw Pancho. He took the pan over to the plates on the table and deposited half of its contents on one and half on the other. "You like *chilaquiles*? I grow the chiles back there. *La Misses* doesn't know. They mixed up with all other plants."

Pancho sat down where Juan had pointed and waited for him to sit down. They started eating. "What do you use for a car?" Pancho asked.

Juan stopped, the fork halfway from the plate to his mouth. He clearly wasn't used to company while he ate. "The truck. *El Señor* Stu bought a truck. He use it every year one weekend maybe, when he go fishing. Rest of the time I use."

"A truck." They ate in silence for a few more minutes. Then Pancho asked, "Do you think maybe I could borrow it sometime for a couple of hours?"

Juan didn't look up. "You have license?"

"I woulda had one, but . . ." He didn't want to tell Juan that first his father died and then his sister died. He ate the last piece of egg and tortilla from the *chilaquiles*. He shouldn't have asked Juan. He should have figured out where they kept the keys and just taken the truck.

Juan drank half the water in his glass in one gulp. He wiped his mouth with a paper napkin. "You know how to drive?"

"We had a 1997 Ford Ranger. I drove it."

Juan was studying Pancho, squinting, deciding something. "When you want the truck?"

"When it's not a problem. It would be good if no one knew I had it." He tried not to sound like he was up to something bad.

"Probably best time for that is on Saturday afternoon. Saturday evening, I go have a few beers and watch *fútbol* with my friend Rafael at his house in Bernalillo. I go around five. You use truck. You pick me up after. All right?"

"All right."

"But we can't tonight because I don't go to Rafael's house. He's in Phoenix until next week. Tonight I just go for a few beers by myself."

The following Saturday was when Marisol was going to visit. He thought it was just as well if he wasn't around when she came. It would be less painful. "Next Saturday — would be good," he told Juan. He would stay only one week with D.Q. rather than the two he promised, but maybe D.Q. didn't want him around for two weeks anymore.

He waited for Juan to ask him where he would be going with the truck, but Juan only drank the remaining water in his glass. Then he walked over to the sofa and lay down, propping a brown cushion under his head. "You go to college?"

Pancho turned his chair around to answer him. "I'm in high school."

"But you go to college someday, right?"

"Not me. I'm not smart enough for college."

"Shh. *No digas eso.* You smart enough. I can tell a smart horse and a smart man when I see it. You go to college. You want to be like me all your life?"

"That's not so bad."

"Is not if you're me. It is if is you. Don't be stupid. You wanna take orders from people like *La Misses* all your life? I close my eyes for half an hour. Then I go get the perico from the Casa Esperanza."

"How'd you know?"

"*La Misses* told me. You come?"

He thought of seeing Marisol once again. Then he thought of D.Q. "I guess I'll stay," he said.

CHAPTER 30

D.Q. slept the rest of the day, barely waking even for dinner. When Pancho told him that Marisol was coming next Saturday, D.Q. said "How nice, you must be happy" in a voice Pancho had never heard before. He accepted the perico from Juan with a mumbled "Thanks" and went back to bed. Pancho lay awake in D.Q.'s room late that night, listening to his raspy breathing.

The next morning Pancho was hauling rocks from the driveway to an area next to the pool when he heard a car drive up. He looked up from the wheelbarrow and saw Johnny Corazon stepping out of Helen's SUV. He wore a black cowboy hat with a feather sticking out and black sunglasses that hid most of his face. When he saw Pancho, his mouth stretched in a grin of recognition. Pancho looked away. *This is no good,* he said to himself.

"Pancho!" Helen called. "Look who I brought." She sounded as if she thought seeing Johnny Corazon would make him happy.

Pancho dropped the rock he was holding and walked toward them. Johnny Corazon had a green canvas bag slung over his shoulder. Juan stood behind him, struggling with two oversized red nylon suitcases. Johnny Corazon extended his arm to shake Pancho's hand, but Pancho avoided it by taking one of the suitcases from Juan. He grimaced at the weight.

"My medicine stuff," Johnny explained.

You use bricks to cure people? Pancho thought. "This isn't a good idea right now," he told Johnny Corazon. Helen gave him a piercing look but Pancho didn't much care. "D.Q. could use a couple of days to get his strength back."

"Johnny needs to be here right now," Helen said. That was all the explaining she was willing to do. She walked toward the house and the rest of them followed.

Juan stopped to take a deep breath. Apparently the suitcase he still held was heavier than the one Pancho took from him. "I got some sacred rocks in there," Johnny Corazon said to Juan.

He is using bricks, Pancho said to himself. "Give me that." Pancho grabbed Juan's suitcase and allowed Juan to take the suitcase he was carrying. He knew Juan didn't like to appear useless.

As soon as they were inside, Helen said, "Juan, put Johnny's things in the guest room next to my studio." Turning to Johnny Corazon, she said, "There are only two rooms on the third floor, my studio and the guest room. The view is fantastic."

Pancho and Juan exchanged glances, thinking of carrying those suitcases to the third floor.

"Shall we go see Daniel?" Helen asked Johnny Corazon.

The fact that Johnny Corazon kept his hat and sunglasses on inside the house didn't help Pancho's impression of the man. He moved with a kind of nervous energy that did not inspire confidence. He didn't have the solid assurance of the fighter who knows

287

he will have to take a few good, painful punches in order to carry out his strategy. Instead he was jittery, like someone who didn't want to get hit.

But it could be that Pancho was wrong about him. He remembered when Johnny Corazon told him that he had not chosen the medicine, but the medicine had chosen him. If the medicine, as Johnny Corazon put it, could choose whomever it wanted, then it could, likely as not, choose a man who wore pointed, shiny boots and kept his sunglasses on indoors.

"Hello." It was D.Q. He had silently maneuvered the motorized wheelchair to the entrance of the kitchen.

"Daniel!" Helen exclaimed. "What are you doing out of bed?"

"I thought I'd try this." He jiggled the knob with his right hand and the wheelchair moved left and right.

"Daniel, there's someone I want you to meet."

D.Q. slid forward a few inches. "You must be the miracle worker who's going to save me."

Johnny Corazon took off his sunglasses. "I'm no miracle worker, but I'm going to do all I can to help you heal yourself. My name is Johnny Corazon."

"Mmm," D.Q. said, stretching out his skinny arm for a handshake.

"Johnny has agreed to stay with us a few days. Pancho, would you and Juan take Johnny's things to the guest room?"

Pancho hesitated for a moment. He tried to catch D.Q.'s eyes to see if he was okay, but it seemed as if D.Q. was doing everything possible to avoid talking to him or even looking at him. He gave up and nodded to Juan.

As soon as they were out of the kitchen, Pancho took the other suitcase from Juan. This time, Juan let it go gratefully. They began their long climb up the stairs to the third floor. "I don't like it when that guy comes over," Juan confided to Pancho.

"He's been here before?"

"He come over with plants for *La Misses* sometimes. He never stay over before. He smell funny." It was true. Johnny Corazon smelled like those violet candles in his house, plus cigarettes and a bitter kind of sweat. "What he gonna do to Daniel?"

"Cure him. He says."

"*Si Dios quiere*," Juan answered. *God willing.* It was what Pancho's father liked to say as well whenever a wish was made.

There were only two doors on the third floor. Juan opened one to reveal a room with a single bed and a window that went from wall to wall. The curtains were drawn open and Pancho could see a series of rolling hills that gradually turned into mountains. Here and there, houses sat on the side of the hills. He dropped the two bags on the floor. "Nice, eh?" Juan said.

"Nice," Pancho agreed. He wondered why Helen had not given this room to D.Q. It was just the kind of room that D.Q. liked. There was no reason why the wheelchair elevator could not have been built to come up to the third floor.

Back in the hallway, Juan closed the door and looked to see that no one else was around. He put his index finger to his lips and slowly opened the door at the end of the hallway. Pancho stepped in silently. The room was Helen's studio. Curtainless windows curved around a space flooded with brightness. Pancho realized the room was located on top of the tower he had seen when he first arrived. He saw a table with tubes of paint and brushes in jars half filled with water. There was a roll of canvas and pieces of wood, and when he looked further, Pancho found a saw and a small hammer, which surprised him. He didn't think Helen was the type to work with wood and nails and hammers.

While Juan kept a nervous lookout, he walked up to a large easel in the middle of the room. There on the canvas was the painted image of D.Q. — not D.Q. as he was now, but a healthy D.Q. as he might be. His cheeks had color and his lips were not cracked. His thick hair was light brown with shades of gold and his pale blue eyes were happy. The painted D.Q. sat in a chair floating in the light of a sunset with mountains in the distance. Helen was still working on the background, but the painting was almost done.

Pancho moved closer and examined the picture taped to the side of the canvas. It was a photograph of D.Q. when he was ten. Helen had amazingly transformed the picture of the ten-year-old into an accurate portrait of D.Q. as a young man — a young man who didn't have cancer, or one who had it once and was rid of it. And yet, despite the painting's accuracy, there was something unreal about it. It was as if Helen had decided to create her own private version of D.Q., one where she could pick and choose those qualities she liked and dismiss the ones she didn't.

"Who's that?" Pancho asked, moving away from the easel to study a painting on the wall. The painting portrayed a man who looked the way D.Q. would have looked if D.Q. was twenty years older and had thick, wavy, brown hair.

"Thas D.Q.'s father," Juan answered. "*La Misses* talks about him all time. I think she still love him."

Pancho looked away to the finished paintings leaning against the walls. "Look at this," he said to Juan. Juan entered the room softly as if his footsteps might be heard all the way to the first floor. It was a painting of Caramelo galloping wild and free, his tail and mane blowing in the wind.

"*Ay, Dios mio!* Thas good. She got even the white marks on his leg. See."

"You never seen these?"

"I see her take the pictures of the horse, the flowers. She takes paintings out downtown sometimes but always wrapped in plastic."

"Maybe there's one of you in here. Maybe she painted you strong with some meat on your bones. Wanna look?"

"Ha-ha. Thas good. You make a joke. You so serious always. I was thinking maybe you not Mexican." Juan pulled Pancho's arm. "Les go see what they doing to Daniel."

"*Daa-nee-EL*," Pancho repeated, pronouncing it the Spanish way as Juan had done. He saw D.Q., Helen, and Johnny Corazon out of one of the studio windows. They were examining Helen's garden. D.Q. was looking away in the direction of the mountains, clearly not listening to what Helen was saying.

Pancho noticed a half-dug trench that went from the corral to the grove of trees in the distance. Juan saw him looking at it and said, "*La Misses* wants to build a sidewalk all the way up those trees where the *kiosko* is. You see?" He pointed to a green spot in the distance. "I got ready to put in forms to pour the cement."

That's something else I can do this week once I finish with the rocks, Pancho thought. Thinking about how he could use the muscles in his body gave him a strange comfort. If he started the sidewalk on the other end, he could park D.Q. in the shade of the trees so he could watch. Of course, D.Q. might not want to be anywhere near

Pancho. He touched his wallet where he had Robert Lewis's address. He knew all about anger and how long it could last.

Later that afternoon, he snuck into Juan's apartment and picked up a map of Albuquerque that lay with a stack of papers on the table. The names of the streets in Albuquerque were in alphabetical order on the side of the map. He found Handel Road and next to it an 8-R. Letters ran down the side of the map, the numbers along the top. He located the street by drawing an imaginary vertical line from the number eight and an imaginary horizontal line from the letter R. He took a pencil and circled the spot where he would find Robert Lewis. Then he folded the map into a small square and stuffed it in his back pocket.

The next morning, he and Juan started training Caramelo. His job was simply to get in the corral with a loose rope tied around the horse's neck and try to get him to go clockwise. Juan told him to be patient. Just getting the horse to be used to his presence could take a week or more and a horse could smell impatience.

But it was hard for Pancho to be patient. Another week at Helen's sounded like an eternity, especially since D.Q. was acting as if Pancho's mere presence caused him added pain. While Pancho continued to sleep in his room, D.Q. rarely said anything to him other than curt requests, given without pleases or thankyous. He spent almost all his time sleeping, or sitting with Helen and Johnny Corazon, talking. Pancho knew where Juan kept the keys to the truck, and part of him just wanted to take the keys, get in the truck, and follow the map to Robert Lewis's house. He didn't think he could stand to stay around much longer.

It wasn't until Wednesday afternoon that he saw D.Q. alone. He was returning from the area beyond the corral, where he had been working on the trench for the sidewalk to the grove. Juan had gone to his apartment to fix himself lunch and then nap for a while. Helen and Johnny Corazon had driven into the city to buy some medicinal supplies. Pancho looked at D.Q. sitting by the pool, and for the first time that week, D.Q. did not look away. Pancho took a deep breath, braced himself, and walked over and sat in the patio chair closest to the wheelchair. D.Q. was holding the small green perico in his hand.

"Can I ask you a question?"

D.Q. nodded.

"How come you haven't been writing on that Death Warrior Manifesto of yours anymore?"

D.Q. turned his eyes fiercely toward Pancho. Despite the shakes and teas that Johnny Corazon prepared for him, he still looked as if a light inside of him was slowly dimming. "The Death Warrior Manifesto is so much bullshit," D.Q. said, and then he turned to look at the mountains again.

After a few moments of silence, Pancho asked, "Were you really writing that for me?"

"At one point."

"I wouldn't mind having it," Pancho said.

"I don't know." D.Q. looked down at the perico in his right hand. He seemed to be thinking about what to say next. Then he spoke without looking at Pancho. "The truth is that I was secretly writing it for Marisol, hoping she would read it and fall in love with me, with how brave and brilliant I was. You were right back then when you accused me of writing it for her."

"It doesn't make what you say in there any less true."

D.Q. rubbed the perico against his heart. "It's very noble of you to be so understanding and all. On the other hand, it's not hard for you to be noble, is it?"

Pancho didn't know how to answer the question. Yes, he could afford to be noble and kind. He wasn't hurting like D.Q. On the other hand, being noble and kind wasn't in his nature. He was still making an effort he didn't have to make and it was not being appreciated. He moved to get up.

"You want to know what was on my mind just before you sat down?" D.Q.'s speech was slurred.

"Yes," Pancho said. He sat back in the patio chair.

"I was thinking that when you think about it, one place is just as good as another. I've been making a big deal about going back to Las Cruces and now I don't know why I was doing it. What's wrong with this place?"

"There's nothing wrong with it, if this is where you want to be."

"This place isn't so bad."

D.Q. lifted his face as if to receive the rays of the midday sun and closed his eyes. Pancho gazed at Caramelo. The horse tossed his head and trotted round and round his corral. He looked as if he wanted to explode from his confinement.

Pancho stood up suddenly, remembering. "There's something you need to see," he said to D.Q.

"What?" D.Q. said, startled.

"If you want to stay here, there's something you should see."
He crouched in front of D.Q.'s wheelchair. "It'll be easier if I take
you. Hop onto my back."

Pancho climbed the three flights of stairs silently with D.Q.
on his back. D.Q. seemed weightless, as if his body was slowly
vanishing. Pancho opened the door to the studio. The light from
the windows was dazzling and he blinked first and then squinted.
D.Q. tugged at his shoulder to let him know that he wanted to get
down. They stepped into the room side by side, Pancho holding
D.Q. up by the waist. They walked toward the painting on the
wall nearest to the door.

"Father," D.Q. said.

D.Q. looked at the painting of his father in silence for a while
and when he nodded that he was done, Pancho led him slowly
toward the easel in the middle of the room — the painting of
D.Q. without cancer.

D.Q. gasped when he stepped in front of the painting. He
began to slip from Pancho's grasp, but Pancho held him up.
He looked away to give D.Q. as much privacy as possible. He
wanted him to see what kind of place this was, how Helen saw
him. The painting of him was a good painting, but it was a fake.
It was what Helen wanted to see and not the truth. He could feel
D.Q.'s breath quicken and his body shake slightly.

"Are you okay?" Pancho asked.

D.Q. lifted his finger to his lips but held on to Pancho's waist.
There was a look of determined concentration on his face, as
if he were seeing something painful that must still be understood. And so they stood there in silence, and after a long

while, Pancho saw D.Q. wipe his eyes with the back of his almost translucent hand.

"I'm ready to go now," D.Q. said.

Pancho stepped in front of him, and D.Q. wrapped his arms around Pancho's neck from behind.

"Thank you," he said.

CHAPTER 31

Pancho took D.Q. to their room, where he spent the rest of the day either looking out the window or lying down with his eyes open. When Pancho came in that night, D.Q. stirred and said good night to him before falling back asleep. The next day D.Q. and Johnny Corazon sat by the pool cabana, engaged in what looked to Pancho like a serious conversation. Then that afternoon he saw D.Q. writing in his journal for the first time that week.

On Friday morning Helen, Johnny Corazon, and D.Q. were sitting by the pool cabana. Pancho was walking toward the corral when he heard D.Q. call his name. As he approached, D.Q. asked him: "Pancho, do you want to go on a healing ceremony with me?"

"When?" That was a stupid question to ask since he didn't even know what he was being asked to do.

"I told Daniel that if he's truly committed to getting well, it would be good to have a healing ceremony — a ritual showing his desire for spiritual healing," Johnny Corazon explained.

"And physical," Helen added.

"And physical," Johnny acknowledged.

"You should participate. You need the healing even more than I do," D.Q. teased Pancho. It seemed like ages since the last time D.Q. had cracked a joke at his expense.

"Sure, Pancho can participate as well," Johnny Corazon said.

"Are you sure it's a good idea?" Helen asked. "I mean, spending the night outside."

"It's very important to express in some outward form your desire to be healed," Johnny Corazon declared. His voice had suddenly acquired a solemn tone.

Pancho looked hard at D.Q. to see if that was what he really wanted. D.Q. winked at Pancho. His body seemed frailer than ever, but there was a spark of life in his eyes.

"Where?" Pancho said.

"You will spend the night alone by the piñon grove. It's not that far from the house, but it is far enough for you to be under the stars, open to the sacred energy that surrounds us. I will go with you, get you started, and guide you a bit. I'll need my sacred rocks," Johnny Corazon told Pancho.

His sacred rocks, as in the rocks inside the suitcase Pancho had lugged to the third floor.

"Can we do it tonight? Let's go tonight," D.Q. asked.

Johnny Corazon seemed surprised at D.Q.'s eagerness. For that matter, so was Pancho. "Yes, I think you are ready. The sooner the better," Johnny Corazon said.

Helen started to object, but D.Q. cut her off. "That's great. You hear that, Pancho? We'll get to spend the night out in the open and fight off the mountain lions."

"What mountain lions?" Pancho asked.

In the early evening, as the sun began to go down over the mountains, Johnny Corazon led the way to the piñon grove. The all-terrain vehicle was not working, so Pancho carried D.Q. on his back. Juan and Johnny Corazon walked ten yards ahead with the rest of the gear.

"Johnny's getting his crocodile boots all dirty," D.Q. said. Pancho was glad he wasn't the only one who had noticed the unusual shine of Johnny Corazon's boots.

"Crocodile?"

"Some kind of lizard."

"What's got into you? A couple of days ago, you were miserable and sliding toward zero on that scale, and now you want to spend the night out in the cold."

"Don't talk so loud. You don't want to hurt Johnny's feelings," D.Q. whispered. Then he answered Pancho's question, his voice serious. "I don't want to waste any more time. It will be good to spend the night outside."

"Why?"

"I don't know why. It feels like I should. I'm tired of moping around, feeling sorry for myself and being angry at people for no reason." D.Q. hit Pancho lightly on the side of the head. "And . . ."

"And what?"

"I feel like I'm slipping. I can sense it. Maybe this will help. Who knows?"

"You gotta believe."

"'I believe. Help my unbelief.'"

"What's that?"

"Nothing. Something I remembered."

They walked in silence. Pancho could feel D.Q.'s body on his back, hot, as if he were carrying a sack of slow-burning coal. He said, "What if it works?"

"Johnny Corazon's healing?"

"Yeah. Not just tonight, but all of it."

"I wouldn't be opposed to it. Actually, the things he says make a lot of sense. I like talking to him. He's been helpful already."

They saw Johnny Corazon bend down to pick up a stick of wood. He brought the piece up to his nose and smelled it. "Mesquite," he said. He kept on walking, the piece of wood dangling by his side.

Pancho looked at the pale sun. Soon it would disappear behind the mountains.

"Pancho," he heard D.Q. say. "Did we bring my perico?"

"Yeah. It's in the backpack that Juan is carrying."

"Marisol is coming tomorrow," D.Q. said. Pancho couldn't see his face, but there was sadness in his voice.

"Yeah."

"Thank you for calling her."

"You want her to come, right?"

"Yes. . . . Yes, I do."

"She was looking forward to seeing you."

"Seeing us."

"I . . . I told Juan I'd go with him to see his friend Rafael. I won't be here."

"Oh. Tomorrow? Oh. You have to be here when she gets here."

"Juan leaves around five for his friend's."

"She said she was coming around four, right?"

"Yeah."

"At least that'll give us an hour together. Do you have to go with Juan tomorrow?"

"Yes," Pancho said, taking a deep breath. *It is time to carry out what I have to do*, he thought.

They reached a grove consisting of eleven or twelve piñon trees. In the middle, Pancho could see what Juan called the *kiosko*, a round structure screened in on all sides with a roof that resembled a very pointed umbrella. He let D.Q. down on the steps of the *kiosko*. Johnny Corazon had chosen an open spot a few yards away and was drawing a circle in the dirt with the mesquite stick he had found. "We'll build the fire here," he said, standing in the middle. Then he went over to where D.Q. was sitting and asked Pancho to sit on the steps of the *kiosko* as well. He sat in front of them cross-legged. His shiny crocodile boots were covered with dust.

"Let's go over what's going to happen tonight," he said. He paused as if waiting for D.Q. and Pancho to stop talking, but they were already quiet. "First thing we'll do is collect some dry wood and then we'll build a fire. Then, when the fire dies down a little, we'll put the sacred rocks in there. You will listen for the signs that come to you tonight. They'll have messages for you . . . about your healing and about the direction and meaning of your life. I'll be back in the morning and, if you want, you can tell me what you dreamt or heard or saw, and that will help me direct your healing. Do you have any questions?"

Pancho was staring at the ground. He looked up and saw D.Q.

was doing the same. Johnny Corazon's voice was different, stronger. He was like the boxers who hung around Manny's gym. Outside the ring, they goofed and clowned around, but once they stepped inside the ring, they dressed themselves in an invisible robe of authority.

Johnny Corazon waited to make sure no one wanted to speak, and then he opened the red suitcase and took out ten rocks about the size of his hand. The rocks looked like beehives, like they had been chipped off the side of a volcano. Then he took out a steel pot and after that a small green collapsible shovel. "My old army shovel," he said.

"You were in the army?" Pancho asked. He didn't figure Johnny Corazon for an army man. Pancho followed him over to the circle in the dirt.

"I got the calling to be a healer while I was in the army. After I came back, I went to the University of New Mexico at Taos and got a certificate in holistic medicine. What's the matter? You look surprised." Pancho grabbed the shovel from Johnny Corazon's hand, but Johnny Corazon refused to let go of it. "I'm glad you're participating. I'd like to help Daniel, but if that's not possible, then I'd settle for one out of two."

"What does that mean?"

"Maybe this night is for your benefit as well."

Pancho wrenched the shovel from Johnny Corazon's hand. That kind of comment wasn't worth a response. "This healing you do, how long does it last?"

"How long?"

"How long does it go for? When will we know if it's working or not?"

"Working or not?"

Was something wrong with the way he was speaking? "One week, two weeks, a month? When will we know if you cured D.Q.?"

"I don't know."

"How long will you keep on with your cures? Is there a time when you say, 'Okay, it didn't work, I guess we can stop'?"

"Well, it's up to the patient. In the case of cancer, nontraditional medicine can make the person more comfortable up to the very end."

"It's up to the patient?"

"Sure."

"So let's say someone's mother wanted you to keep on going with your treatments, but the kid wanted you to stop. Who would you listen to?"

Johnny Corazon sat on the sawed-down tree trunk. Apparently the question required some deep thinking. "I'd have to consider the circumstances," he said after a while.

"That's what I thought," Pancho said.

Johnny Corazon continued, "In the case of Daniel, because of his age, intelligence, and maturity, I'd stop when he told me to stop."

Pancho nodded. That was what he was hoping to hear.

He told Pancho to dig a hole about six inches deep for the fire. Pancho dug the hole and placed the rocks next to it, and then Johnny Corazon built a fire with the wood that Juan collected.

Johnny Corazon, Pancho, and D.Q. sat quietly around the fire. When the wood had burned down, Johnny Corazon lifted each of the rocks with the shovel and placed them in the fire.

After he sat back down, he took something that looked like tobacco out of a brown pouch and packed it with his thumb into a battered pipe. Then he lit the pipe with a stick from the fire. Johnny Corazon puffed on it lightly and then passed the pipe to D.Q., who closed his eyes and inhaled deeply. Pancho took the pipe from D.Q. and drew the smoke into his lungs. He felt something like a dry fireball burn his throat and he began to cough. He gave the pipe back to Johnny Corazon, who leaned it upright against a rock on the ground.

Then he began to speak in a low voice that Pancho could barely hear. "Let tonight be your quest for healing and for a meaning that will guide your days. Ask for help from the Great Mystery that creates and sustains all life. Stay awake as long as you can, and if you must sleep, remember your dreams. Either awake or asleep, you will see or hear what you need to see. Your intention alone can transform this into a sacred night. Let it be an outward sign that you open yourselves to the Great Mystery of life, just as you open yourselves to the stars. You are seekers of meaning and healing because we all need meaning and healing, but you know that the ultimate meaning and healing does not come from you. You open yourselves to it. You wait for it. You hope for it. And you trust in its existence even if you can't see it or feel it."

Pancho felt himself being lulled into relaxation by the smoke and Johnny Corazon's voice. Johnny Corazon paused and passed the pipe around one more time. When it came back to him, he said, "This kind of ceremony is usually undertaken by the individual seeker alone, but under the circumstances" — here he looked at Pancho — "I think it is all right for you to stay together. I can feel you two are bound to each other like two strands of one rope. Try to keep quiet, but you may talk if you feel you must. If you do, let your talk be guided by the Great Mystery. How do you feel?" he asked D.Q.

"I feel good. Better than I have in a long time. The fever is gone. The nausea is gone. Can I have some more of that pipe?"

"No, no more of this pipe. But I made you a tea that you should drink as much as possible." Johnny Corazon pointed at an old-fashioned coffeepot sitting by the fire. He stood up. "Oh. There's a cell phone over in the *kiosko*. Helen insisted. In case of an emergency, you should call. I'm taking the bread and cold cuts she packed. You don't want to have food out here. There may be mountain lions or coyotes."

"They wouldn't be interested in me," D.Q. said. He grinned at Pancho.

Johnny Corazon grabbed something that looked like a backpack and slung it over his shoulder. He disappeared into the grove of trees without a flashlight.

Pancho threw a stick into the fire. The darkness of the night made the stars shine with extra brilliance. He looked for the moon but couldn't find it. A battery-operated lantern sat nearby. He stretched himself on the ground and pulled it toward him. He might as well know whether it was a mountain lion or a coyote that took a bite out of him.

They sat in silence for about an hour. Pancho poked at the fire, and D.Q. stared at it. Pancho began to list in his mind some of the people he had met since he first arrived at St. Anthony's.

Besides D.Q. and Marisol, there were others, like Father Concha, Memo, Josie, Andrés, and Juan; and toward each he felt a closeness he had never experienced before. He was reflecting on this when D.Q. spoke. "I feel like I'm in some kind of Western movie."

"Shhh. You're supposed to keep quiet. You cold?"

"No. But it's going to get cold tonight. We should bring the sleeping bags closer to the fire."

Pancho silently moved the two sleeping bags, placing them far enough away that a spark wouldn't set them alight.

"I wish he'd left that pipe behind," D.Q. said.

Pancho sat on his sleeping bag with his legs in front of him. "I'm getting hungry," he said. "You think there's something to eat somewhere?"

"I think I saw a can of pork and beans and a pan in the *kiosko*. You should fix yourself some supper."

Pancho imagined the delicious smell of pork and beans. Then he imagined a mountain lion or a coyote sniffing the air with his muzzle, detecting the distant odor of food. "That's all right," he said. "I'm not that hungry." D.Q. extended his arm and motioned for Pancho to fill his cup. Pancho took the cup and filled it with the liquid from the kettle.

"How's the tea?"

D.Q. sipped. "Good."

"What is it?"

D.Q. made tasting motions with his tongue. "I detect a base of chaparral tea with a tinge of ginger, a couple of drops of peppermint extract, and lime juice. The chaparral tea has been reported to be good for some types of cancer, the ginger is good for settling the stomach, and the peppermint is great for nausea. The lime juice makes the whole concoction taste good, plus it has vitamin C, which is good for the immune system."

"You know all that?"

D.Q. put the tin cup on the ground beside him and tightened the red blanket around his shoulders. "When I was first diagnosed with cancer, six or so months ago, I set out to become an expert in the disease as well as in all possible cures. I spent hours, days, weeks, months, learning all there is to know. I even had Brother Javier drive me over to Juarez to buy drugs we couldn't get in the U.S. You should see the stash of herbs Lupita has in her kitchen."

"You don't believe they work?"

"Sure I do. I mean, they *can* work. Why not? They definitely help. If you go on the Internet, you can read reported cases of someone who got cured taking this or that. I don't think what we call Western medicine has all the answers. I'll give anything a try so long as it doesn't kill me any faster. I probably have a better shot at keeping my senses with Johnny Corazon's stuff than I have with the chemo. Oh! Did you see that?" A star shot across the dark night. "Quick, close your eyes and make a wish."

Pancho instinctively obeyed and closed his eyes. It wasn't a wish as far as he could tell, but the image of Marisol appeared before him. D.Q. still had his eyes closed when Pancho opened his. He could still see the phosphorescent path left by the disappearing star.

D.Q. broke the silence. "All that Johnny Corazon can do here can be done just as well in Las Cruces. I thought it would be good to go along with him because, well, it might make it easier for Helen to let go and . . ."

"You would get to see Marisol again," Pancho said tentatively.

There was a long pause. "Remember what we're supposed to be looking for here tonight?"

"Meaning. Healing."

"Yeah. I always thought that sometime before I died, I would learn what life had to teach, as Thoreau said. I was expecting some kind of answer, some kind of big meaning that I could put into words. I think I was looking for the kind of faith you talked about, or I was hoping to get some kind of revelation.

"But what I found out these past couple of weeks is that I'm probably going to die without finding that kind of meaning or that kind of extraordinary revelation. Every day I want to suck the marrow, and most every day I end up thinking that the things I did that day or that happened that day didn't even come close to the marrow. The only times I felt like I was getting close were when Marisol and I were walking together and it seemed as if all of me, all of my senses and all of my awareness, was focused on her. I didn't want to miss a single thing she said. I wanted to feel everything about her, how her hair smelled, how it felt when she accidentally touched my arm, the way she raised her hands to shield the sun from her face. During those moments, I felt like I had finally touched the marrow of life. There were other times too, like when you and I talked late at night and when we joked around, but they weren't quite as intense as those moments with Marisol, you'd be happy to know."

Pancho didn't respond. He was thinking about the time in

Marisol's kitchen when they were washing the dishes together. All his senses were tuned to Marisol standing next to him. He had experienced an expansion of feeling in his chest, a sense he did not understand, until now, as he listened to D.Q.'s words. He took a stick and stirred the fire.

"I'm glad she's coming tomorrow," D.Q. continued. "And I know she'll come to Las Cruces to see us."

Pancho shook his head, telling D.Q. he was mistaken if he thought he was going to stick around, Marisol or no Marisol.

D.Q. went on, "You know how I yelled at you that night after we came back from Marisol's house."

"You didn't yell all that much."

"I was jealous."

"You didn't need to be."

"I made it sound like I was angry at you for throwing your life away, but I was really jealous of what Marisol felt for you. . . . When Marisol and I were walking to the park she . . . I realized that she loves *you*. I had this crazy hope that she and I could be together despite everything. And then I had to let go of that hope, and it hasn't been easy."

"You shouldn't talk."

"But it's slowly dawned on me that if what happened with Marisol hadn't happened, I might have gone on being a perico until the very end."

"A perico?" Pancho asked.

"Remember when she told you I was in touch with another dimension and that she had never seen anyone with such strong faith?"

"Yeah."

"She was wrong on both counts. I wasn't in touch with any other dimension then and I didn't have any faith, strong or weak. I had some beliefs and hopes maybe, but not faith." D.Q. took a deep, wheezing breath. "The other day when you took me to Helen's studio, I realized I was as fake as that portrait of me that Helen was painting. That portrait was not me, just like I wasn't a Death Warrior. I was an angry, jealous person who was grasping at what I couldn't have and resentful of what was taken away from me. I had no love for life or for anyone else. . . . So in many ways, I've been like the perico, you know? A parrot just says things without understanding them, without believing in them. The Death Warrior Manifesto is full of words about loving life at all times and in all circumstances, but they were just words. I never truly felt that way."

"It's all right if you don't."

"But the thing is, even if I wasn't living up to it, I was wrong the other day. . . . The manifesto isn't bullshit. I did feel full of love for life once. When I was nine, Helen and I were in a car accident and I was in a coma. When I came out, I was overwhelmed with this feeling of gratitude, not just for my life but for all of life. It felt as if life was this incredible, awesome gift. I remember walking out of the hospital and the whole world seemed on fire with a glowing brilliance, like I was seeing things for the very first time. Everything I saw and touched was filled with love, and I was full of joy just to be a part of it. Then after a while, this 'dimension' that I was in touch with disappeared." D.Q. coughed.

"You need to speak less fancy 'cause you pretty much lost me back there by the parrot. What dimension are you talking about?"

"When you are with Marisol, you feel different than at other times, don't you?"

"Yeah."

"You feel like I do, I know. Being a part of that other dimension is like being with Marisol. We feel as if everything matters. We don't want the moment to end. We're happy and grateful just to be with her, we don't ask for anything more than what she gives us. We love her, but we are content even if she chooses to love someone else. Can you imagine that?"

"Yes."

"That love and peace, that's what it feels like to live in that other dimension. I mean, we can't always feel this love. There are times when it all seems so hopeless, so pointless. . . . Like this last week for me. Looking at that portrait made me realize how scared and selfish I was in many ways. But I also understood that it was all right. I'm not perfect like Helen's image of me. I'm just human. Our task is to try. Being a Death Warrior is all in the trying." D.Q. paused to take a deep breath. "If we live in accordance with the Death Warrior principles, if we live with gratitude, not wasting any time not loving, we can enter that dimension. That is my faith. I've been writing about what this faith looks like and talking about it like a perico, but now I'm ready to live it. That's so good."

Pancho and D.Q. listened to the crackling of the fire for a few moments and then D.Q. continued, speaking slowly. "Helen's need to cure me would keep me in a hospital throwing up. But I don't want to miss out on whatever living I have left. I need to be where I can try my best to be a Death Warrior. I want to go back to Las Cruces with my perico as a reminder of how to live, and I'm never going to lose my faith again."

Pancho didn't understand all that D.Q. had said, but he recognized, in a way that did not require understanding, the feelings that D.Q. had expressed.

They both sat looking at the flames of the fire for a long time. Pancho watched the mesquite stick that Johnny Corazon picked up burn with difficulty. It was on fire but there was no flame. The barking of a dog or a coyote broke his trance.

"When you saw that shooting star and I said, 'Close your eyes and make a wish,' you saw Marisol, didn't you?" D.Q. asked.

Pancho stirred the fire once again. Hundreds of blue and orange sparks ascended. "Yes," he admitted. He kept his gaze on the fire.

"Johnny's right, you know. We're two strands of the same rope. Only the rope has three strands. . . . It's all right for both of us to love her. She loves me as a friend, and trust me, friendship from her is not bad. She loves you as a friend *and* as a man. She loves *us* differently so we need to try to love *her* differently. I need to appreciate what she's given me and let her go. You need to figure out how to truly love her."

"How do I do that?"

"You'll find out . . . in time. It takes time to learn to love, unless you're a Death Warrior. Then you get to go on the accelerated ride, like me. I know you're wondering why I'm so wise." D.Q. laughed.

"Whatever was in that pipe really got you going."

"That was good stuff."

Pancho moved one of the sacred rocks with a stick. They had begun to glow. When he sat back on his sleeping bag, D.Q.

spoke. "I told you what my faith was like. Now you tell me what yours is like."

"Someday I'll be with my father and my mother and with Rosa."

There was silence and then D.Q. slipped inside his sleeping bag.

"You're not waiting around for the meaning and the healing?" Pancho asked. He was not being sarcastic.

"Mr. Pancho, I believe we done found them tonight."

CHAPTER 32

Johnny Corazon arrived around eight. Pancho and D.Q. had been up since sunrise. D.Q. was sitting against a piñon tree, his legs covered with a blanket, observing what remained of the dawn, and Pancho was cleaning up the pan where he had cooked the pork and beans for breakfast. Pancho had already taken the sacred rocks out of the fire and rolled up the sleeping bags. They packed up all of Johnny Corazon's gear and left it there for Juan to get later. Pancho carried D.Q. on his back. He seemed to have gotten even lighter overnight.

When they got to the house, Pancho went to help Juan fix the all-terrain vehicle, and D.Q. sat by the cabana and wrote in his journal. At noon, Renata brought them chicken sandwiches, potato salad, and slices of watermelon, and Johnny Corazon, Helen, D.Q., and Pancho ate by the pool. Juan went to his apartment to eat his own lunch and to nap. Pancho wished he could go with him. After lunch, Pancho took D.Q. to his room, and Johnny Corazon and Helen left in Helen's car for a conference on holistic medicine that was being held in Taos. For a moment it seemed as if Helen might change her mind and stay behind just so she could meet Marisol. But D.Q. promised to ask Marisol to dinner the following Friday night.

After they left, while Juan and D.Q. were napping, Pancho went to the corral, sat on the top post, and watched Caramelo for a while. As soon as he started to replay in his mind the conversation with D.Q. the night before, he went back to working on the wall. Juan came back and they worked side by side until three o'clock. Renata brought D.Q. out to the pool again.

"Enough work already," D.Q. tried to shout at them, but his voice was even weaker than the day before. "It's Saturday. What's the matter with you two? Pancho, go take a shower. Marisol will be here any minute and you don't want her to see you like this."

"Who's Marisol?" Juan asked.

"His girlfriend," Pancho told him, wiping sweat from his brow with his forearm.

"*Our* girlfriend," D.Q. corrected him with a grin.

"I go in my place and watch Mexican *fútbol*. Some things better for an old man not to know."

Pancho took as long in the shower as he could. All day long he had said no more than twenty words, and he did not want to be around D.Q., where he would be forced to talk. If he could avoid seeing Marisol, he would. He didn't know how he would react to her.

Someone had placed a stack of brand-new clothes on the cot that Juan had set up for him. There was underwear still in its plastic package, cotton pants and polo shirts still with their tags. Helen must have gone shopping, trying to make him look more respectable. He put on dark blue pants and a black polo shirt. He threw his sweaty clothes on the floor of the closet and then stepped into the black loafers laid out for him at the foot of the bed. Amazingly, Helen had gotten all his sizes right.

He went to the window and saw D.Q. by the pool, continuing to write in the Death Warrior journal. There was urgency in the way he moved his hand across the notebook, and Pancho remembered the painfully slow way Rosa wrote in her diary. He had a moment of fear that Helen had gone through his backpack and discovered the revolver. He opened the closet and saw with relief his backpack slouched in the corner, where he had left it. He dug it out, placed it on the bed, and fished out the revolver from inside the leg of the folded blue jeans and the seven bullets from the hidden inside pocket of the backpack. He inserted the bullets in the revolver. The .22 caliber bullets were almost too small to kill a man, and the aluminum-alloy revolver was light as a toy. The box in which the revolver had been packaged said the gun was perfect for competition, plinking, and killing varmints. He didn't know what "plinking" meant. Was he capable of plinking Robert Lewis?

He lay down on the cot and went over in his mind what he would say to Robert Lewis. When he heard the sputtering muffler of Marisol's car, he sat up. The doorbell rang, then Renata's muffled steps made their way from the kitchen to the front door. Through the window he saw Marisol hug D.Q. on the terrace and the delight that filled his face. She pulled a chair close to D.Q. Pancho went back to the cot. There was still an hour before Juan went to town.

A few minutes later, Renata came to the room. He sat up again when he saw her.

"They would like you to come outside," she said, clearly embarrassed to have to deliver the message.

"*Gracias*," he said. It made her smile to hear him speak Spanish. They walked down the stairs in silence. When they got to the kitchen, he asked, "Can I leave this here?" He showed her his backpack. She opened the door to the pantry and he placed it there. Then he took a deep breath and stepped outside.

Marisol stood up, smiled, and walked slowly to hug him. He looked at D.Q.'s face briefly during the hug and he saw no jealousy there.

"It's so good to see you," she said in his ear.

D.Q. spoke up. "Pancho, I want to show Marisol something over by those boulders. Let's all take a ride in that ATV. It's working now. It'll be fun."

Marisol shrugged her shoulders as if to say that she was okay with whatever everyone decided.

"I didn't see any kind of top on that cart. The sun is strong," Pancho told D.Q.

"I'll wear a cap. Come on, don't worry so much."

The three of them sat in the front seat of the ATV. Pancho took the wheel and Marisol sat in the middle. D.Q. gave directions. They passed the grove of piñons where they had spent the night. Two or three miles later, they reached a wire fence. Pancho stopped. On the other side of the fence, black rocks rose up out of the earth, a series of foothills for the surrounding mountains. Pancho remembered the shooting star he saw the night before. These rocks looked like they might have fallen out of the dark sky. "Now what?" he asked.

"You have to climb over or under the fence, and on the other side of the rock, there are some petroglyphs. You two got to see them."

"Some what?" Pancho asked.

"Petroglyphs," D.Q. said. "Images or designs etched into the rock by Native Americans as far back as the fourteen-hundreds."

"What about you?" Marisol wondered.

"I've seen them before. I'll be okay. Go, go. They're on the other side of that rock." Pancho looked up at the sky, calculating whether D.Q. could tolerate its heat. "I'm really okay. My temperature is normal, look." He gripped Pancho's forearm. Pancho flicked his hand away, but not before noticing that the hand was cool.

Pancho lifted the middle barbed wire for Marisol to cross to the other side, and once she was through, Marisol held it for him. They waved one last time at D.Q. and then they began to climb up the rock. Soon they were on all fours, grabbing on to jutting stones and miniature trees. It was not a difficult climb, just an awkward one.

"You're very quiet today," Marisol said to him when they were halfway up.

"I'm always quiet," Pancho answered. He refused to look at her, pretending to concentrate on finding a handhold.

"There's quiet because you don't need to say anything, and

then there's quiet because you don't want to say something. Today you're quiet because you don't want to say something."

They reached a place in the rock where they could stand up straight again. Pancho saw D.Q. down below with his eyes closed and his arms crossed. "We shouldn't have left D.Q. alone," he said.

"He wanted to give us a chance to talk."

"Why?"

"Beats me," she said, trying to hold back a smile.

Pancho didn't answer. He saw a path that would take them to the top of the rock and he started up with Marisol following. At the peak, he peered down the opposite side of the ridge. There were various options for descent. "How do they make these peterlifts?"

"Petroglyphs," Marisol said, laughing. "They're chiseled, usually with another rock."

Pancho surveyed the rock. If he were an Indian, where would be the best place to chisel a . . . something? He wanted to find one quickly and get this over with. A smooth black surface about five feet tall jutted out of a ledge that was easy to reach. He stepped carefully down in that direction. Marisol followed him. It was the most difficult of the paths they could have taken. That was good. Marisol would have to concentrate on where she was stepping and probably would not be able to talk.

"Do you think his mother will let him go back to Las Cruces?" she asked.

He should have known that a girl like her would not have any problems hiking down a steep rock and talking at the same time. "No way she's going to let him go back."

"Don't go so fast. If I fall, I want to have you close enough to take you with me."

He stopped. She put her two hands on his back to keep herself from sliding. They inched their way down like that until Pancho reached the spot he would have chosen to chisel something into the rock. He looked up the smooth, black surface and there it was. Marisol stood beside him and looked up as well.

"What the heck is that?" Pancho said. He was expecting to see a buffalo or a tepee, but instead he saw a design that might have come out of his sophomore-year geometry class.

"It looks like a kite. There's the head and that line there could be the tail and that line there could be the string."

Pancho looked at Marisol like maybe she wasn't as smart as he thought she was. "I never heard of Indians flying kites," he said.

"Not now. But the Indians originally came from the East, across the Bering Strait into Alaska, and they've had kites in the East for a long, long time. The Chinese invented them."

Pancho reconsidered. Maybe she was as smart as he thought she was. No wonder she and D.Q. never ran out of things to talk about. She sat down on a rock.

"Sit for a second," she said. "You need to tell me what's bothering you."

He sat down next to her and then spoke haltingly. "When I talked to you on the phone last week, you said that you and D.Q. had talked about the difference between friendship and love."

"Yeah."

"Well, what's the difference? Is it something you think I would understand?"

She poked his shoulder with her arm. "Stop it. You're not as dumb as you make yourself out to be." She reflected for a few moments. "Friendship is when you share a common interest with someone, something that brings you together. Love is when you are interested in each other. You want to do things with each other."

"With each other?" He couldn't help the grin. "What kind of things?"

She laughed. "Those that you're thinking just now, but not just those. Like looking at petroglyphs. When I was walking here, I was excited that we would be looking at them together, with each other. You're part of why I wanted to look at the petroglyphs, because I wanted to see them through your eyes."

"You sound like D.Q. now," he said, teasing her. But he understood.

"What are you all going to do if his mother doesn't let him go back?"

"Nothing. What can we do?"

"He's not doing well." She looked at Pancho. He looked away from her uncomfortably. Was she telling him that it was up to him and only him to help D.Q.?

"He needs you now more than ever," she continued.

"I'm here."

"Maybe here is not where you should be."

He made a gesture with his hands. *What can I do?*

She took a deep breath and then spoke in a different, lighter tone. "Remember that guy Sal that was interviewing for a job at la Casa?"

"The *pendejo*."

"That one. Well, thanks to you, he didn't get the job. But Laurie still plans to have a college student live at la Casa. D.Q. reminded me — you should apply. Not for this year, obviously, but for next year. After you finish high school. You can go to UNM or maybe even the community college that's nearby. I know you're good with your hands. There are plenty of things you can study that I bet you'd enjoy. Laurie likes you, as you know." She smiled. "And I may put in a good word for you."

Pancho grabbed his head. College? The notion was beyond funny, beyond ridiculous, it was downright sad. He shook his head. He couldn't believe that she could even think he could ever go to college. "D.Q. asked you to mention that to me."

"Yes, he did."

"Why not get *him* for the job? Where's *he* gonna be?"

She bit her lower lip softly. "Whatever happens to him, he thinks this would be something good for you."

She raised herself from the rock she was sitting on and extended her hand to help Pancho up. He took it. She held his hand, looked for the other, and found it. She rested her eyes comfortably in his. "D.Q. wants you to have something to hope for. That's his gift to you." She reached up and kissed him on the lips. It was a small kiss. It lasted only two or three seconds, just long enough for him to taste the future.

CHAPTER 33

Juan was standing by his apartment, getting ready to leave.
Pancho lifted D.Q. onto the motorized wheelchair and went to
the kitchen to grab his backpack. He came out and walked slowly
toward D.Q. and Marisol.

He said to Marisol, "I told Juan I'd go into town with him to
see a friend of his. I'll be back in a couple of hours."

She looked at him like she didn't believe a single word, but she
only reached out and pulled him to her. He hesitated before putting his arms around her. "My aunt and my cousin Aurora, the
one who is a nurse, remember?"

He nodded.

"They live in Canutillo, on the western outskirts of El Paso.
It's very close to Las Cruces. I wouldn't mind spending some time
with them." She smiled at Pancho and let him go.

D.Q. motioned Pancho to bend down so he could whisper in
his ear. "Be a Death Warrior," he said.

When they were inside the truck, and Juan was about to turn

the ignition key, he asked, "You sure you want to go?" He tilted his head forward to peer into Pancho's reddened eyes.

"Let's go. Now." It was an order.

Juan and Pancho drove to Rafael's house in silence. Pancho opened his window and let the cool air hit his face. What he wanted to do was remember his sister, recollect the words in her diary, but his mind kept returning to that one kiss by the petroglyph.

Be a Death Warrior, D.Q. had whispered in his ear. Why would not killing Robert Lewis be something a Death Warrior would do . . . or not do? It was all so confusing. A Death Warrior who does not kill, who loves life. Two kids in love with one girl and they're okay with it. Would he be okay with D.Q. loving Marisol if D.Q. weren't dying? If he looked like the D.Q. in his mother's painting? He felt like a fighter who had been knocked out but managed to stand up before the end of the eight count, covering his face with his gloves to avoid the punches from an opponent who smells blood.

Rafael's house was a one-room adobe shack on the edge of a neighborhood of one-room adobe shacks. A man who looked older and frailer than Juan was sitting on a wooden chair in front. He had a beer can in his hand and a red cooler next to his chair. Behind the chair, on a window ledge, a transistor radio played Mexican music. Rafael opened the cooler and took out a beer as soon as he saw Juan. Then he saw Pancho and he took out another beer. "Come say hello to Rafael," Juan told Pancho.

"I gotta get going."

"I see you, then." Juan deposited the keys in Pancho's hand and held Pancho's hand as he did so. Pancho interpreted the gesture as a request to be careful.

324

He spread the map of Albuquerque out next to him and he drove off, following the route he had marked in red. He drove slowly and cautiously, staying to the right wherever there was more than one lane. The truck had more power than his father's truck. After his father died, he drove the truck only for errands, to the grocery store or to work or to take Rosa to the Green Café. He couldn't afford to be caught driving without a license. When he drove the truck then, he felt responsible. He felt like a man carrying the burdens placed on him early on by life and doing a good job of it. Except that when Rosa died, all of that proved to be just a show, him fooling himself.

It would have been hard to drive and look at the map at the same time had he not taken the time to memorize the route. He parked the truck as soon as he turned onto Handel Road. If he were to rank the houses he had been to in Albuquerque from the fanciest to the crappiest, Helen's house would be way up there, then these houses on Handel Road, then there would be a kind of long jump down to Marisol's house, another jump to Johnny Corazon's, and a leap straight down to Rafael's. Casa Esperanza he would put in a category by itself. It was a beautiful place, almost as beautiful as his trailer back home.

He walked with his backpack over his shoulder on the side of the street opposite where he expected Robert Lewis's house to be. The first thing he saw was the truck that Julieta had described, bright red with the words JENSEN AND SONS painted on it in sharp white letters. It was parked in a driveway in front of a two-car garage. Robert Lewis's house was a white brick house with white pebbles in the front yard. Rosebushes lined the walk leading to the oak front door. Across the street from the house, there was a baseball field where a softball game was taking place. Pancho went to the aluminum bleachers and sat on the lowest rung. The kids who were playing were eight or nine. One team was wearing black-and-gold uniforms and was called the Pirates; the other team, in blue and white, was called the Cubs. The parents on the bleachers were women, mostly talking amongst themselves. The fathers, or the men that Pancho took to be the fathers, leaned on the chain-link fence that ran between home and third, shouting instructions to the players.

He watched the game. Every once in a while he would look sideways at Robert Lewis's house. A stone wall about five feet high ran down the side of the yard and around the backyard. On the far side of the house, there was an empty lot where a house was being constructed. In a couple of hours, when it got dark, he would enter the lot and climb the stone wall in the back.

He was thinking about how to proceed when he saw one of the garage doors open. A small green car backed out to the middle of the driveway and stopped. Pancho unconsciously stood up. The car was driven by a woman with curly white hair. The trunk of the car popped open. Then out of the garage came a girl about twelve years old. She was dressed in some kind of uniform, blue shorts and a shirt with a number in front. She was holding a net bag full of soccer balls. She lifted the lid of the trunk and threw the balls inside, then slammed the trunk shut and got in the passenger side of the car. The car backed up a few yards and stopped. The driver honked a few times. Pancho's heart sped up when he saw a shirtless, baldish-looking man in shorts and sandals emerge from the garage. The man's stomach jiggled as he walked to the driver's window. He stood there scratching his arms as if the air were full of fleas, then he blew kisses to the driver and to the girl and watched the car back into the street and drive away. As he stood in the driveway, he turned his head slowly in the direction of the bleachers. It was too far for him to see the fixed and fearless stare in Pancho's eyes, but maybe he could feel it. Robert Lewis hurried back inside, and a few seconds later the garage door clanged shut.

All along, although he had no reason to do so, Pancho had imagined Robert Lewis's kids, if he had any, to be older. It never occurred to him that the man could have a daughter that age living with him. Maybe she was his granddaughter. The fathers along the fence shouted. One of the baseball players was taking off from second to third. What did it matter to him how old she was? He picked up his backpack and started to walk toward the empty lot. He didn't need to wait for darkness to come.

He entered the construction lot and walked to the back. He peered over the stone wall toward Robert Lewis's house. There was no one in the backyard. He saw a trampoline and a blue aboveground tin pool covered with a green tarp. There was an open porch with patio furniture and sliding glass doors. Two windows stared out from the back of the house, a small one that he took to be the kitchen window and a larger one that he figured belonged to a bedroom. He could see curtains across the sliding glass doors. There was no sign of a dog. He dropped the backpack into the yard and then lifted himself over the stone wall. Once inside the yard, he crouched by his backpack and took out the black revolver. He stood up and tucked it in the back of his pants.

He approached the house slowly, walking as close as he could to the side wall. Everywhere there was evidence that the girl lived there. Diet Coke cans were strewn about a circle of chairs by the pool; a rusty girl's bike leaned against an aluminum toolshed; an abandoned pretend stove collected bird droppings. When he reached the end of the stone wall, he walked over to the larger of the two windows. The curtains were parted far enough for him to see inside the girl's room. There were posters on the wall of a blond singer he had never heard of before, a bottle of black or purple nail polish on the dresser next to the bed. On a shelf built into the wall stood the same dolls that Rosa collected. He noticed the Mexican doll, the Dutch doll with the wooden shoes, and the Danish doll with the long blond braid.

He sat down on the grass, his back against the wall of the house, his feet almost touching the aboveground pool. From inside the house he could hear the faint noise of the television. It sounded like a soccer game, an excited male voice followed by cheering. Here he was, a minute or two from killing Robert Lewis. He had planned for this. It was the hope and strength that fed him since Rosa died. It was his anger, only the anger had gone. He remembered standing at the entrance to St. Anthony's and feeling someone looking at him, the pecan falling on his head out by the hammock.

There was no need to hurry. Soccer games lasted a couple of hours. If he could, he would drag the body out to the yard. It bothered him that the girl might walk into the house and see something she would never forget. He held out his hand to see if he was losing his nerve, but his hand was calm. There was no fear and there was no doubt. There was no anger. What was in there, then? Was it a cowardly softness? No, that wasn't it. Whatever was in there was tender all right, but it wasn't cowardly.

The memory of cutting the braid of Rosa's Danish doll came to him. He couldn't remember what had prompted him to cut the doll's hair, nor why he had chosen the Danish doll; there were other dolls with long hair. He had used the scissors from the bathroom drawer. Rosa entered her room just as he snipped through the braid. Her face turned dark red as if she were about to explode. She yanked the doll from him and raised it in the air as if to hit him, but then she stopped. "Get out, Pancho!" she yelled.

He went into his room, remorseful. He thought for sure that Rosa would not forgive this prank as she had all the others. But an hour later, she came into his room with the Danish doll. "Pancho, look what I done." She held up the doll for him to see. She had taken the scissors and fashioned a new hairstyle for the doll — short and neatly trimmed. "Don't she look beautiful," she said.

He stood and walked to the edge of the sliding glass doors. Slowly, he stepped into the opening between the curtains. He put his forehead against the glass and covered his eyes against the glare. Robert Lewis was lying in a recliner, his back to him. His head had tilted to one side, as if he had fallen asleep watching the television in front of him. On the floor next to him was an empty bowl and a can of beer. Pancho reached out for the handle of the sliding door and pulled the door toward him very gently. It slid with only the smallest of screeches. Robert Lewis oiled his sliding doors well. He pulled the door a little more and now there was an opening large enough for him to step through. Robert Lewis did not move.

Pancho backed away from the sliding door and returned to his place under the girl's window. He sat down again and pulled

Rosa's diary out of the backpack. Then he took a ballpoint pen from the front pocket of the backpack, skipped to the end of the diary, and wrote. He wrote slowly, licking the point of the pen now and then as if it were a pencil. He filled three pages of the diary with a handwriting he recognized as similar to his sister's. When he finished writing, he put the diary back in the backpack, stood up, and went into the house through the opening in the sliding doors.

Robert Lewis let out an animal-like snort when he woke up. "What the . . ." he said when he saw Pancho sitting in front of him with a revolver three feet from his face.

"This is what I want to know. Did you give Rosa Sanchez alcohol the night she died?"

Robert Lewis's Adam's apple bobbled up and down in his throat. "You're her brother."

"Good," Pancho said. "If you asked who Rosa Sanchez was or if you said you didn't know her, I was going to pull the trigger."

"You don't wanna do that," Robert Lewis said slowly.

"If I think you're telling me the truth, maybe I won't. If you tell me a lie, you die. Did you give my sister alcohol or beer the night she died?"

Robert Lewis dropped his head on his chest. He spoke with his head still down. "Yes."

"Did she tell you she was allergic?"

There was a grin on Robert Lewis's face when he spoke again. "Only about a hundred times."

Pancho waited. Robert Lewis's right eye began to twitch. He pressed down on the twitching nerve with his finger.

"I don't know. I guess I didn't believe her," he said. "I didn't do it on purpose, honest." He sounded like a child. His mouth moved as if he were going to start crying.

"Why?"

"We were having a party. What's a party without drinking?"

Pancho pulled the trigger. There was an explosion and the glass of the sliding door shattered. Robert Lewis covered his ears with his hands. He opened his eyes, looking surprised he was still alive.

"Okay. I . . . your sister was not . . . She was very conservative despite her . . . She was innocent, you know. I thought the alcohol would make her more receptive to what I had in mind." He was gripping the arms of the recliner. "That's the sorry truth, I swear. I didn't think she'd die. If I had meant to kill her, I would have hidden the body or something. When I couldn't wake her up, I got out of there. I'm sorry. I didn't mean to kill her."

"You left her there."

"Oh, shit. Don't you think I know it? Don't ruin your life by killing me, son."

"Get up."

Robert Lewis rocked the recliner to a sitting position and used both of his hands to lift himself up. "Where we going?"

"Is there a bathroom in your bedroom?"

"Yes . . ."

"Does it have a bathtub?"

"Yes . . ."

"Let's go in there."

"Oh, no. Please don't. I loved your sister. I know you don't believe me, but I did. I'm a little weird, but I cared for her. So help me Jesus my Lord."

They walked out of the room with the TV and down a hall with pictures of the Lewis family. Somewhere along the wall, an older boy who had been part of the family pictures began to appear by himself in an army uniform. They took a left at the end of the hall and walked into the master bedroom.

"I told you the truth. You said maybe you wouldn't kill me if I told the truth. You're gonna kill me anyhow, aren't you? Why the bathtub? You don't want to make a mess?"

"I don't want your daughter to see you right off when she comes in."

"How do you know about her?"

"I saw her from across the street."

"You're not gonna hurt them, are you?"

"No."

"You have to find it in your heart to forgive me. God knows I don't deserve to live, but you don't have to kill me. I'll do anything. Give you anything. You need money? I got money."

Pancho stopped. "Maybe there's something."

"What? Name it." Sweat rolled down Robert Lewis's cheeks.

"You have anything that shows you loved my sister?"

"Yeah, yeah! Hold on. I'll show you." Robert Lewis moved around the bed excitedly. He opened the bottom drawer of a white dresser. Pancho moved closer with the pistol. Robert Lewis lifted an orange sweater and took out a leather notebook. Inside the notebook was a picture, which Pancho accepted. It was a picture of Robert Lewis and Rosa, taken in a motel room, maybe the same room she died in. Robert Lewis had taken the picture by holding the camera at arm's length. In the background Pancho saw a flowered headboard and a desk with glasses, a bottle of gin and a Dr Pepper can. Rosa was looking up at Robert Lewis and laughing with that loud, childish, uncontrollable laugh that so often embarrassed him.

"She was happy with me until I done went and messed it up. Please don't kill me," Robert Lewis pleaded. Pancho stuck the picture in his back pocket.

"What would you do to me if I knew your daughter was allergic, so allergic she could die of it, and I gave her something to drink so I could do more sex things to her?"

Robert Lewis covered his face with both hands and sobbed.

Pancho made him lie facedown in the bathtub. He pressed the two-inch snub of the revolver to the back of his head and spoke. "You need to count to one hundred before you get up. If I see you before one hundred seconds are up, I will kill you. Start counting." He walked out of the bathroom, closed the door behind him, went to the girl's room, and looked at the dolls on the shelf. Then, out of curiosity, he picked up the fingernail polish and examined it in the light. It wasn't black. It was purple.

CHAPTER 34

Juan was sitting on a wooden chair next to Rafael when Pancho drove up. He pretended not to be happy to see Pancho. On the way back to Helen's house, he asked Pancho, "You get done what you wanted to do?"

"No," Pancho answered, "but that's all right."

They pulled up into the driveway. Helen's SUV was there and so was the sports car she drove the time she took him to see Johnny Corazon. "Everyone's here," Juan said. He didn't sound pleased.

"Everyone?"

"*La Misses* is back. *El Señor* Stu. And he don't like Johnny Corazon much."

Pancho didn't ask why. He had an idea.

Juan excused himself to go to his apartment. He patted Pancho on the back, either congratulating him or wishing him luck, Pancho wasn't sure which. Pancho went in through the kitchen door. He felt exhausted. Climbing over the stone wall, writing in Rosa's diary, holding a gun had drained all the strength from him, but he felt the lack especially in his arms, the way a boxer can barely lift his arms in the last round of a fight. He heard voices in one of the rooms downstairs and walked toward the sound.

They were all seated in a room he had never entered before. D.Q. was in his wheelchair. Surrounding him, as if to prevent any possible escape, were Helen, a man he didn't know, and Johnny Corazon. The man he didn't know saw him first. He was thin and short and had an intense look beneath his gray eyebrows. He remained seated but extended a hand to Pancho. "Hello, I'm Stu." He squeezed Pancho's hand hard and Pancho squeezed back harder. There was still enough strength there, he discovered.

"Pancho," D.Q. said. His voice was faint but happy.

"How was your evening out with Juan?" Helen asked.

Pancho ignored her and went up to D.Q. "Do you still want to go back to Las Cruces?"

"Yes," D.Q. said. A thin, knowing smile crossed his face.

"Do you want to wait another week or do you want to go now?"

"Now."

"We're heading back to Las Cruces," Pancho told the group.

Everyone around the room looked at one another.

"I'm afraid that's not possible, legally or otherwise," Stu said. He looked amused by Pancho's actions.

"He's better off here, Pancho," Johnny Corazon added. "We're making progress."

"It's his decision," Pancho said firmly.

"He was feeling better last night and this morning with Johnny's remedies, and then that girl came, and when we got here he was worse," Helen said. "He can get better. He *will* get better!"

"What do you wanna do?" Pancho took a few steps closer to where D.Q. was sitting. He noticed that he was sitting in the St. Anthony's wheelchair and not the motorized chair.

"Will you come to Las Cruces now and then?" D.Q. asked Johnny Corazon.

"Yes," Johnny Corazon answered immediately without looking at Helen.

"Then I want to go back to St. Tony's now," D.Q. said.

"Honey . . ." Helen extended her hands toward D.Q. even though she was too far away to touch him.

"Let's go," Pancho said.

"Do something!" Helen yelled to Stu. Stu quickly stood up and put his hand on Pancho's chest.

One punch, Pancho thought. *One simple straight jab and I could crack his face.* He had already committed a crime that evening. Robert Lewis could go to the police and file charges for attempted murder. The cops might be out looking for him even then.

"You really think you can stop me?" Pancho asked.

Stu dropped his arm and lowered his eyes. "I'll have the state troopers stop you before you reach the interstate. I'll have you arrested. It's no use."

"I'll take him for a short ride, then." Pancho made his way to the wheelchair.

Helen was shouting, "Johnny, do something! I don't believe this." She stepped in front of the wheelchair.

"Mom, don't make things worse," D.Q. said. "Be smart. In Las Cruces you can come see me or rent a house near St. Anthony's — God knows you have the money — and we can spend more time together. Johnny already said he would come see me. You can help me by paying his way. You need to trust that Las Cruces is where I am meant to be."

"And the clinical trial? I'm willing to take a chance that you don't like me. You think I'm doing this for my sake? I want you to live as long as possible!"

"I know you do," D.Q. said to her. "I want to live as long as possible too. I saw that picture you painted of me. I know how strong your hope is. I'll get tested again in Las Cruces. If the clinical trial makes sense — if it makes sense all things considered, we'll talk about it. But I'll decide if it makes sense or not."

D.Q. and Helen stared at each other, neither one of them moving. Finally, D.Q. nodded to Pancho. "Let's go," he said.

Pancho looked at Stu one last time. If he was going to use force to stop him, now was his chance. But he stood frozen in place. Pancho pushed the wheelchair toward the door. Helen stepped out of the way, a look of grief on her face.

"I'll file a court order in the morning *and* a warrant for your arrest," Stu said behind him.

"I don't expect anything different." Pancho smiled. He always knew he was going to end up in prison.

"Wait," Johnny Corazon ordered. Helen looked hopefully at him. "There's a thermos of tea in the refrigerator you should take with you. I'll come see you soon." He squeezed D.Q.'s hand as he went by.

Juan came out into the driveway when he heard the noise of the wheelchair on the ramp. "I need to ask you for the keys," Pancho said to him.

"I going with you," Juan said. Before Pancho could answer, he had climbed in the driver's side and started the truck. Pancho helped D.Q. into the truck and threw the wheelchair in the back.

"They're gonna fire you," Pancho told Juan as they peeled out of the driveway.

"Is time to retire," Juan said.

"It's a good thing I had the perico in my pocket," D.Q. said, holding it out for all to see.

"Don't puke on us," Pancho warned him. "We'll set you in the middle of the desert and leave you there. You can have some of the stuff from Johnny Corazon's thermos if you like."

When they were on the edge of Albuquerque, Juan told Pancho his plan. They would all spend the night at Rafael's. Then early the next morning, Rafael would drive them to Las Cruces in his truck and Juan would return to *La Misses*. D.Q. agreed that it was a good plan and so did Pancho. If they took the truck or a bus to Las Cruces tonight, they could be stopped by the police and taken back to Helen's (or off to jail, Pancho thought). But if they reached St. Anthony's the next day, D.Q. at least could stay there a while.

"If we make it to St. Tony's," D.Q. told Pancho, "I'll make sure Helen doesn't press any charges against you."

"Oh yeah? How you gonna do that?"

"I have my ways," D.Q. said. "I wouldn't worry about it."

"I'm not worried."

"Thank you, Mr. Pancho," D.Q. said. "Damn, I'm tired." He closed his eyes and then he opened them. "I never asked you. How'd it go with Marisol by the petroglyph?"

"None of your business," Pancho said.

"That good, huh? That's good, Mr. Pancho. That's very good."

It was around noon the following day when Rafael's truck rattled into St. Anthony's. There were four or five students over by the basketball court. Memo was one of them. He shouted and jumped up and down as soon as he saw Pancho lift the wheelchair from the back of the truck. Soon everyone at St. Anthony's had gathered around them. Father Concha was the last person to emerge from the building. The students made room for him to reach D.Q. "I'm back," D.Q. said.

"Welcome home," Father Concha said, smiling a smile bigger and happier than Pancho had ever seen before.

Pancho put two hundred dollars into Rafael's hand as he said good-bye. Rafael waved to D.Q. and left. Father Concha shook Pancho's hand. "The police may be looking for me," Pancho told him.

"Helen called this morning," Father Concha said. "You'll be okay for a while. Unless you've done something I don't know about."

Pancho shrugged his shoulders mysteriously. "Is she going to try to get D.Q. back?"

"She and her husband are considering it. I told her we had

engaged a lawyer and we would file the emancipation petition for Daniel tomorrow morning. She would have a fight on her hands. She needs to think about it. If she gets him back, she'll lose him for good. If she lets him go, he will let her into his heart." Pancho felt someone punch him in the arm. It was Memo. "Come, I want to show you something," Father Concha said.

The group with D.Q. in the middle moved all together toward the basketball court. When they got there, everyone stopped and turned to study Pancho's reaction. Behind the basketball court stood the boxing apparatus from the trailer. The swing set was newly painted bright red; the heavy bag and two speed bags hung from the top pole. There were ropes and boxing gloves and headgear all lined up on top of plastic containers.

"We're gonna get back the boxing club again, like old times," Memo told him.

Pancho turned around and saw that the boxing area was visible from the window of D.Q.'s new room. Father Concha followed Pancho's gaze. "Let's go inside," he said.

D.Q. went in first, with Coop pushing him. Pancho followed. Coop opened the door to D.Q.'s room. "Oh, man," Pancho heard D.Q. say. The room was painted light green, with the reading chair and the tall bed in exactly the spots that D.Q. had described. Light streamed into the room and landed on the white bedspread. D.Q. reached into his pocket, took out the perico, and gave it to Pancho to place on the small table between the bed and the chair.

"Look at this," Memo called out from across the room.

He had opened a door that Pancho did not remember being there.

"We cut through the wall and joined the rooms," Father Concha told him. Pancho saw a small room painted pale blue. There was a normal-height bed, a wooden desk and chair, a lamp. The room reminded him of the room in Juan's apartment. They made way for D.Q. to roll in.

"This is your room, Mr. Pancho," D.Q. said.

"What's that door?" Pancho asked.

"You guys will have to share a bathroom," Father Concha informed them.

"Why does he get a telephone and I don't?" D.Q. pretended to be upset.

"So I can call Memo when you need your diapers changed," Pancho said.

They moved back into D.Q.'s room, and Father Concha told them, "I figured you guys didn't bring any clothes, so we put some regular things in the dressers. We'll leave you alone. There are some sandwiches in the dining room if you're hungry, Pancho. Daniel, Lupita can make you something."

"Tell her to come see me later," D.Q. said. "There are some teas and herbs I need her to get for me."

"Let's go, guys." Father Concha pushed the group out.

"Pancho, you wanna go a few rounds later?" Coop asked.

"Sure," Pancho said. He lied. He was going to sleep in the shade of a pecan tree for a week.

D.Q. was fiddling with a control pinned with a safety pin to his bed. He made the bed go down as far as it would go. Then he stood up from his wheelchair, lay down on the bed, and pushed the UP button until the bed was even with the window. Pancho took off D.Q.'s shoes. He moved to close the curtain to keep the sun out of D.Q.'s eyes, but D.Q. stopped him. "It feels good," he said. He turned his face toward the window. Outside, two boys were playing a game of one-on-one.

EPILOGUE

Dear Rosa, I hope you don't mind me writing in your diary. A while back I read the last pages of your diary and found out about Bobby. I searched for him and it turns out his name is Bobby Lewis. He lives in Albuquerque and is married and has a daughter. Anyway when I found out about him I wanted to go after him and kill him because I thought he killed you. I thought he might have given you alcohol on purpose at that motel and that's how you died. Anyway after I read your diary I promised I wouldn't let your life and death be in vein but I want you to know that when I finaly saw him I didn't kill him eventhough I could have. Part of me still wants to but I won't. I just want to hear the truth from his mouth about why he made you drink. Maybe after I see him I can get the police to investigate him but I haven't made up my mind about that. I know you probably wouldn't want his daughter to find out how bad he is or have him go to jail and leave her without a father. I can tell from your diary that you cared for him. You probably forgive him knowing how you were. So I wanted to let you know that I didn't kill him because of you. The other thing is that I been hanging around with a boy named D.Q. and he invented this thing called the Death Warriors. Its too long to explain and I don't understand all of it but basicly the Death Warrior always fights for life wherever. After you died I didn't care much for life. Now I think we need to take care of it. I'll put your diary away now and keep it in a safe place. I just wanted to write this to you. Your brother.

MENTS

I want to thank my agent Faye Bender, who encouraged me to write "my book." I want to recognize with special gratitude my editor Cheryl Klein for pushing the novel (and the author) to greater light. Finally, I would like to thank Jill Syverson-Stork, my wife, for her daily example of faith.